Also by Jed Mercurio

BODIES

ASCENT

JED MERCURIO

Simon & Schuster

New York   London
Toronto   Sydney

SIMON & SCHUSTER
Rockefeller Center
1230 Avenue of the Americas
New York, NY 10020

SIMON & SCHUSTER and colophon are registered trademarks of Simon & Schuster, Inc.

For information regarding special discounts for bulk purchases, please contact Simon & Schuster Special Sales at 1-800-456-6798 or business@simonandschuster.com.

Book design by Ellen R. Sasahara

Manufactured in the United States of America

10   9   8   7   6   5   4   3   2   1

Library of Congress Cataloging-in-Publication Data

Mercurio, Jed.
   Ascent / Jed Mercurio.
      p.   cm.
   Includes bibliographical references.
      1. Astronauts—Soviet Union—Fiction. 2. Fighter pilots—Soviet Union—Fiction. 3. Soviet Union—Fiction. 4. Psychological fiction. I. Title.

   PR6113.E73A83 2007
   823'.914—dc22   2006051230

ISBN-13: 978-0-7432-9822-3
ISBN-10:   0-7432-9822-5

CONTENTS

vii

ASCENT

STALINGRAD

1946

)

TWENTY MILLION COUNTRYMEN died in the Great Patriotic War and his whole family was among them.

His bare feet left footprints in the dirt as the men led him from the farm. Then they set the ruined buildings alight. What had been his life to this point vanished into smoke.

Rain began to fall. The boy watched it puddle the dirt. It obliterated his footprints and, while he waited, the wheels of passing carts and trucks cut swaths in the muddy road, but in time the rain also wiped these away.

He traveled to the ruined city in a farm lorry with his only possessions in a sack. From factories came the pounding of metal. The noise passed up from the earth like a groan.

By the time they reached the orphanage, night had fallen. The other boys watched him being led into the mess hall. He was big for his age, so therefore a target. There was only time for a bowl of broth, then it was lights-out.

Frost glistened on the window panes, but the oil ration went to the factories so the stoves at each end of the dormitory remained unlit. He was accustomed to the silence of the countryside, but in the city the pounding of machines continued through the night. There was so much to repair, so much to rebuild.

As soon as he fell asleep, two of them held down his arms while a third jumped on his chest and beat him about the face. The other boys expected him to cry himself to sleep, but he was done with crying.

In the morning blood stained his pillow, one of his teeth lay on the floor, and his sack was empty.

At inspection the warden paused at his bunk. "New boy?"

He nodded.

"Name?"

"Yefgenii Mikhailovich Yeremin."

"What's all this, then?"

The other boys stared straight ahead. None would ever admit having seen or heard a thing. Yefgenii remained silent so he was deprived of breakfast and instead made to scrub his own sheets. That night they left him alone but that was part of their game. They dragged another boy out of his bunk and buggered him over the stove that was unlit for lack of oil and Yefgenii curled up and tried to sleep. Being sent here was like being flung down a well. No one cared that it was cold and dark and no one cared if he ever climbed out.

Often the boys were made to work as unpaid laborers. A bank of mist and drizzle rolled off the Volga, making some of the boys stiffen in the cold, but Yefgenii kept on. He was strong. He was used to hard labor. There was soot in the air that made his spit turn black.

The rest of the time they were given schoolwork. In the main they were taught the history of the October Revolution and the facts proving that no nation had sacrificed more than theirs in the defeat of fascism, but they also practiced arithmetic, some trigonometry, sometimes a little algebra. They chanted multiplication tables. Babak chanted the loudest. He was the one who'd given Yefgenii his beating on the first night. When the teacher asked a question, no one's hand went up but his. This seemed to be the protocol and, though he often knew the answer, Yefgenii was wise enough to conform.

Afterward there'd be a fight in the yard. Babak's two comrades were Pavlushkin and Boytsov. They'd stand by while Babak picked an argument with one boy or another and, whether the boy answered back or not, it always led to a battering. Sometimes it was concluded in the yard. Sometimes Babak finished it in the dormitory after lights-out.

One day the schoolmaster called out Yefgenii's name. Yefgenii stood to attention. "Yeremin, your mathematics is exemplary." He'd scored full marks in arithmetic and had advanced to the top of the class in trigonometry and algebra. Babak glared at him. The other boys stared straight ahead as they did at dormitory inspection.

The master set the boys a quadratic equation. Almost at once Babak claimed to have the answer but he'd made a mistake. The master called on Yefgenii and he answered with the correct solution. In the yard the other boys knew what was coming so they stood away. Boytsov and Pavlushkin held Yefgenii's arms and Babak hit him in the stomach till he vomited.

"Lick it up, farm boy. You eat cow sick, you eat chicken sick." They pushed his face in it and fish-hooked his mouth open but he wouldn't lick it.

That night they yanked him out of his bunk. He glimpsed eyes closing, all the other boys pretending to be asleep, as they dragged him over the floorboards to the stove. Pavlushkin stretched him over it by the wrists while Boytsov pushed his head down. He felt cold metal pressing into his cheek. He could smell rust and last winter's oil, he could taste them.

"Here's your lesson, Yeremin." Babak ripped down Yefgenii's trousers and long johns then with a noise that was half snort and half laugh he dropped his own. Yefgenii heard his breath quicken, heard the slapping sound of Babak making himself hard. With his palms Babak parted Yefgenii's buttocks and made the first stab. He used his thumb then tried feeding his dick in with his fingers. Yefgenii couldn't help crying out. Babak couldn't get it in. Boytsov grasped a fistful of Yefgenii's hair and battered his head on the top of the stove. It made a clanging sound that reverberated through the dorm. No one opened their eyes. No one stirred. Boytsov pressed Yefgenii's head down with all his weight and with his other hand he clamped his jaw shut. Then Babak tried again and this time he was in. To Yefgenii it felt like a balloon was being inflated inside him. He felt an urgent excruciating need to defecate and, if he didn't, then his insides would burst. Each thrust felt like a rod piercing his pelvis from back to front while his breastbone bashed against the stove. The pain was in his viscera and in his bones. He wailed but Boytsov held his jaw shut so the sound came out as gasps with spit spraying out between his teeth and tears and snot streaking his cheeks. Babak finished with a long sigh. They pushed him onto the floor and took turns kicking him in the ass and then they returned to their bunks. A little later Yefgenii crawled back into his. As his eyes closed, he remembered his family's farm. He remembered the fields and the open sky. He tasted again his aunt's cooking, glimpsed his father and brothers sit round the table in their uniforms. His past was a dream, the present was wakefulness. Here came the day, the work to be done, the obstacles to be overcome.

Blood and semen stained his sheets. The warden asked him for an explanation but Yefgenii wouldn't break his silence. He was denied breakfast and, though he had difficulty walking, he was made first to scrub his sheets and then to join a detail working in a bombed building. The boys were recovering bricks from the ruins and carrying them by hand to laborers who were laying fresh foundations nearby. Snow was falling in flurries. It was black. Flakes peppered Yefgenii's blond hair and his lashes. He did a full day's work.

The next day the warden led him to the director's office. The director of the orphanage wore a crumpled gray suit. He coughed all the time and a wheeze punctuated the end of every breath. He missed many days through illness. "Your schoolwork is excellent, Yeremin. You're aware of the scholarship, of course."

Yefgenii shook his head.

The director coughed so hard it bent him double. "One boy . . .

a suitable boy . . . each year, one boy out of all the orphanages goes to the Air School at Chkalov."

Yefgenii shook his head again. He didn't understand.

"The Commandant . . . an important man . . . he was . . ." He coughed again and again and he had to pull a handkerchief from his pocket and fill it with phlegm. "He was an orphan."

They continued to labor each day in the ruins of the city. Mud and slush seeped through the holes in his shoes. Rubble was scattered all around him and in the rubble boys carried bricks and men laid them. The men who weren't out here, the women too, worked in the factories whose machines pounded all day and all night and whose chimneys created a black roof that sunlight never pierced.

Yefgenii's bruises became less sore but he'd got a tear that made opening his bowels an agony. He couldn't conceal his suffering because the boys did so into an open sewer.

In class the slower ones were learning their arithmetic by rote. Those who hadn't already gone were bound for the yards and factories. Yefgenii peered down at the algebra problems the master had set. He pictured himself in an officer's uniform with officer's pay and officer's status. He pictured airplanes. He imagined himself soaring. If he felt like he was living at the bottom of a well, then this was a chance to claw his way out. His chalk began to scratch out solutions. These were the rules that governed rest and motion and, though he didn't know it, they even governed the stars and planets.

Babak followed him out of the schoolroom. "Let's see how well you do when you can't write." It took all three of them—Babak, Pavlushkin and Boytsov—to pry open his fist so they could break a finger. They'd've broken all of them if he hadn't screamed out. He didn't intend to. It just hurt so much. Babak pulled him in close by the ear. He was older and heavier but they stood eye to eye. Yefgenii felt the lobe ripping. "It's my place at Chkalov, it's mine, I'm the one getting out of this shit-hole."

Blood trickled from Yefgenii's ear. He had to pull his finger straight. Tears streamed down his face while he did it. He could feel the fracture under the skin where the finger was livid and swollen. He tugged it from the knuckle. Pain jolted up to his elbow and shoulder. Later he tore a strip of cloth from his shirt and used it to strap the finger to its neighbor.

That night he lay awake but they didn't come for him. They didn't need to. If he resisted they'd injure him till he was unfit for training. It was Babak he pictured in an officer's uniform, Babak smiling, Babak soaring. From today in the schoolyard he could still hear Babak's breathing, he could feel it on his face, could smell his spit. They were eye to eye.

In the morning the warden saw his hand. "What's all this, then, Yeremin?"

Yefgenii remained silent. All the other boys were staring straight ahead. Babak glanced at him for a moment then looked straight ahead again.

The warden lifted Yefgenii's hand. Yefgenii winced. The warden unwound the strapping and inspected the fat black finger. "Well . . . ?"

Yefgenii gazed down and away. A smirk curled the corner of Babak's mouth.

The warden dropped the wounded hand. "Have it your own way—"

"Sir, it was Boytsov and Pavlushkin, they did it."

They protested their innocence of course, but the warden still led them away. They shrugged and followed. They knew no one would dare corroborate Yefgenii's story and, after a lecture from the director—interspersed with bouts of respiratory distress—they'd be back to carry out a reprisal.

Among the ruins, Yefgenii worked with one hand. He kept the other bound tight enough to press the fingers together but not so tight that he couldn't make a fist. Boytsov and Pavlushkin would be returning soon. He had only a little time. His heart drummed inside his chest. Everywhere the poundings split the air—metal on metal, metal on stone, stone on stone. The people toiled under a pall of cloud. Stalingrad's chimneys were black towers; they were mausoleums.

Babak crossed the rubble to piss into the sewer. Yefgenii had chosen a stone an hour earlier and had laid it close by and now he scooped it into his injured hand. His fingers closed. He shut out the pain. Next he was running. Babak turned at the sound of footsteps skittering over the rubble and Yefgenii struck him in the temple. Babak went down crying out with the shit and reek of the sewer all round and already the other boys were turning to look. Yefgenii crashed down onto Babak's chest. Ribs snapped like sticks of celery. He got his good hand round Babak's throat. He was choking him but the purpose was to hold the head still. Babak's knee smashed into his back and his arms battered his side but Yefgenii held on fast and dug the thumb of his bad hand into Babak's eye socket. He pressed into the eyeball and now Babak was screaming and boys were gathering round. The boys kept glancing back. Men were coming over from the other side of the site. The boys shuffled together, closing up the gaps through which the men might glimpse the fight. Babak was bucking and writhing but Yefgenii held him down and with his thumb he pressed harder and harder till at last the eye burst into blood and humor.

Yefgenii was up and among the other boys when the men got there. They found them all gazing down at the one in the sewer with his eye mashed.

The foreman looked along the row of boys. "What's going on here? What happened?" He stared at each boy in turn but none of them would speak. His gaze came to rest on one boy who was big for his age with blond hair and blazing blue eyes who looked like he might be the leader. "What happened to your mate?"

But the boy only straightened up. He shook his head and looked away.

A couple of the men were now carrying Babak by his shoulders and ankles, up into the rubble where they laid him out, the boy who'd now never go to the Air School at Chkalov. Yefgenii felt himself soaring; he imagined sunlight breaking through onto his face.

The foreman asked them again but none of the boys would say anything. So he put them back to work. There was a country to rebuild.

KOREA

1952–1953

)

A T FOUR-THIRTY, the falcons of the 221st IAP crowded into the Operations hut. All wore the same olive drab flying suit without name or rank but bearing the insignia of the Korean People's Liberation Army Air Force. Yefgenii Yeremin stood at the back with the other rookies, while the seasoned fighter pilots took seats in front and chattered about killing Americans.

Polkovnik Kiriya entered first, followed by Podpolkovnik Pilipenko. The room came to attention. As Kiriya took his chair in the front row, the banks of men behind slumped back down. Pilipenko orbited between the map and the chalkboard, twirling a pointer between his fingers like a drum majorette. "Weather for Antung, twelfth of May, 1952, 0400 Zulu, valid to 0600. Surface wind 070 at 5. Visibility greater than 10 kilometers. One-okta scattered alto-cu, base between 3 and 5,000 meters. . . ."

Yefgenii's eyes drifted to the giant chart at the front of the room. The Korean Peninsula dangled off the northeastern tip of China like a stubby finger pointing at the tail of Japan. A thick red line followed the turns of the Yalu River, which divided Korea from Manchuria. Antung was a black circle edging its mouth. A second red line ran north of the 38th Parallel, the former border between North and

South Korea, over which North Korean troops had poured two years earlier to overwhelm the South.

Pilipenko's pointer struck the map and Yefgenii snapped back to attention. "United Nations aircraft are forbidden to operate north of the Yalu. You are at liberty to operate south of the Yalu. You are permitted to engage and destroy any United Nations aircraft operating south of the Yalu. You will not overfly the sea. You will not enter South Korean airspace—that is, not operate farther south than this line." His pointer indicated the red line joining P'yŏngyang in the west with Wŏnsan in the east. "You will not transmit in Russian unless absolutely necessary. You are pilots of the Korean People's Liberation Army Air Force. The VVS is not here. Its pilots are not here. Duties will be notified at 0500." Then he ended as he always ended. "Thank you for not being here."

Outside, an arch of light mounted the horizon. Soon the dawn re-created gray mountains to the west and gray paddies east to the Yalu. A blanket of heat was settling on the airfield, raising a scent of oil and kerosene, while ground crews rolled MiG-15s out of the hangars and onto the dispersal. Their shouts and the whir of tow trucks carried into the crew hut, where the rookies gathered at the window.

The MiGs' nose sections were painted red under three light gray numerals. Between the wing root and the tailplane a red star sat in a white circle that was ringed by red and blue. The rest of the fuselage was silver. These were PLAAF markings—North Korean and Chinese, not Soviet—and the pilots' names didn't appear on a single cockpit.

Soon the first wave of pilots were walking out to their ships. On some aircraft small red stars ran in a row under the canopy. Each star represented a kill, an enemy plane shot down. Five stars or more indicated an ace. The pilots who strutted toward these were more lustrous than their aircraft.

"Welcome to Antung," said Podpolkovnik Pilipenko. The rookies came to attention. "You're each to fly a check ride with me. The business of the 221st is killing enemy jets. That comes first. You'll get your rides as and when slots become available. In the meantime, study these." He handed a manual to each. They were dictionaries of Korean flying terms.

Starshii-Leitenant Glinka took an eager step forward. "Pod-polkovnik, what are our operations today?"

"Our operations, Glinka?"

"Yes, sir. Are we escorting our bombers? Are we intercepting theirs?"

Pilipenko smiled. "No, son, we're just going up."

"Sir?"

"Just shaking our tails, looking for a fight. They shoot at us. We shoot at them. Then we count how many of theirs we got, how many of ours we lost."

"That's all, sir?"

"Yes, boys, that's all."

Jet engines were igniting on the dispersal. The first whine built. The rookies pressed their noses against the glass. Soon all six engines were running up and their turbines spun to a blur. The sound rattled the windows. Yefgenii tracked the aircraft as they skimmed out to the runway and then slid up into the sky. Condensation trails formed at around 5,000 meters and soon began rarefying in the vault of air above. From their eastern slope they arched out over North Korea. As they broadened and faded they might've been the fossils of great flying snakes.

In the Ops hut, Pilipenko reported to Polkovnik Kiriya. "I've briefed the new men, boss." He offered him the new recruits' files.

"Glinka is the one whose father is a general-leitenant?"

"Yes, sir."

Kiriya waved away the files. "Give his check ride priority. I want him getting kills as soon as possible."

He peered at the scoreboard on the wall. Pilipenko had six and a half stars next to his name, but he was not the leading ace: that was Skomorokhov, with eight. Kiriya had been first to four. Then, somehow, on the brink of becoming an ace, his luck had turned. Skomorokhov and Pilipenko had overtaken. He'd been stuck on four for months.

The rookies were deep in their phrase books when the first wave returned. Word passed down from the tower that they'd met United Nations forces southeast of the Yalu. Already the second wave was lifting off to get into the scrap.

Pilipenko peered through binoculars as the six MiGs of the first wave trundled up the taxiway. "Their guns are black."

Black powder sooting the tips of their cannons showed they'd opened fire, pockmarks on their fuselages that they'd been fired upon. Still in their bonedomes, the pilots perched on top of the ladders, answering the ground crews' excited queries. Soon one of them was calling out to Pilipenko. "We got one, sir!"

"A Sabre?"

"Yes, sir."

"Who got it?"

"Major Skomorokhov did, sir."

Pilipenko made a wry smile. Skomorokhov had now advanced to nine kills—two and a half ahead of him.

Kiriya joined Pilipenko on the dispersal and peered past him at the blackened guns and the pockmarked fuselages. They lured him like sirens. "Change the duty board, Pip. I'm leading the third wave."

"I was leading the third, boss."

"I know, Pip, but I also talked to you about making Starshii-Leitenant Glinka a priority."

Pilipenko blinked. "Yes, sir."

The other rookies' check rides were put on standby for tomorrow while Glinka—whose father, the General, had many friends in the Party—would get his ride today.

Yefgenii watched him march onto the dispersal alongside

Pilipenko. Glinka nodded as he received instructions to taxi, take off and form up as a *para*. The two pilots ascended to their cockpits. The engines ramped up, the MiGs rolled out to the runway and within minutes they melted into the blue.

Kiriya's *zveno* returned ninety minutes later. No soot blackened their guns. By the time they'd crossed the Yalu, the Sabres had vanished. Kiriya marched past the ground crew without meeting their eyes or answering their salutes, then locked himself away in his office for the rest of the day.

Yefgenii gazed up at the contrails. In the humid atmosphere they were taking hours to evaporate. White ribbons commemorated the climbs and dives of the earlier battles; they coiled and crossed in signatures. Some ended in the knot of an impossible turn and some pointed home. Some streaked the blue like the tails of comets but they were not left by comets but by men and he longed to rank among the rarefied brotherhood of fliers who'd left such marks in the sky. The previous war had made Yefgenii Yeremin a worthless orphan but this one, he promised, this one would make him somebody.

THE NEXT DAY BEGAN with the sun steaming the haze off the treetops. Yefgenii slumped in the crew hut reading and rereading the pilot's manual and struggling to absorb the contents of the Korean phrase book. He wore his flying suit unzipped, with the sleeves tied round his waist. Flies buzzed against the windows. Every now and then one would orbit in figures-of-eight round Yefgenii and he'd flap it away. The wind sock drooped. The air was still, clogged with humidity.

By midmorning the first two waves had flown and returned. They'd seen no one, fought no one.

Kiriya shut himself in his office again. He'd been over the Yalu on the second wave. No targets had appeared, so he'd led the *zveno* south through Korea and still no one had appeared. They'd fallen to minimum fuel and had had to turn back, but Kiriya had been close to ordering them to carry on. Now he was determined to keep launching MiGs into the combat zone.

No jets were available to the rookies for check rides.

"I've been assigned to the third wave," Glinka told Yefgenii. He'd be wingman to the third *para* of a six-ship *zveno*, the back man, the greenest. He was strutting as he went to his aircraft, he was pulling down his helmet as he crossed the dispersal, he was pulling on his gloves as he went up the ladder. Glinka's performance cast him as the duelist and Yefgenii as the holder of cloaks.

Two hours later the third wave returned. The ground crews could see all the aircraft were still bearing their wing tanks so, without even examining the state of their guns or fuselages, they knew the MiGs hadn't seen action. Yefgenii watched the pilots come down from their cockpits and stroll back toward the Ops hut. No one was clamoring round them for war stories.

"Gnido." Pilipenko had stepped into the crew hut. "They've given us a jet. Check ride."

Yefgenii watched Gnido and Pilipenko walk to their aircraft. Pocket maps bulked out their legs. Pilipenko swung his helmet on its strap, balancing it over his wrist. Little Gnido's steps were short and birdlike. Yefgenii watched his helmeted head bob in the cockpit as he carried out his pre-start checks and then lit the engine. The MiGs became blurs as they accelerated along the runway. The leader— Pilipenko's plane—tilted back on its mainwheels and then leapt into the sky. Something showered around Gnido's cockpit. At once the aircraft began to slow. It turned off the end of the runway and came to a stop. For a moment there was confusion, then a siren sounded. A fire truck was rolling out.

Gnido had suffered a bird strike. His canopy had shattered. His helmet, visor and mask had protected most of his face, but shards of glass and bone had made nicks like shaving nicks over his cheeks and throat.

Pilipenko met him back in Ops. "Report to the M.O."

"I'm fine, sir. But you should see what I did to that bird!"

Pilipenko smiled. "See the doc, son."

"Yes, sir." But Gnido lingered. "If the doc says I'm OK, maybe we could try again . . . ?"

Pilipenko glanced down and wrote in the mission log: "DNCO"—duty not carried out.

Yefgenii stood in the doorway. He'd donned full flying kit and slung his helmet by its strap. "Sir."

"What is it, Yeremin?"

"If there's a slot now, sir, I'm ready to fly."

Gnido bit his lip. Somehow he felt betrayed by Yefgenii trying to profit from his misfortune. But he shuffled away to see the medical officer.

Pilipenko flicked his pen out of his fingers. It looped through the air into his left hand and then he began to twirl it just as fast on that side. "I'm busy."

"Yes, sir." Yefgenii had spent yet another day listening to the thunder of jets and gazing at their trails snaking out into the blue. "Sir, I'm no use to the 221st sitting on my arse all day learning Korean. I came here to kill jets."

"Hmm." Then in Korean Pilipenko demanded, "Position?"

"Antung," said Yefgenii.

Pilipenko grinned.

"Thank you, sir." Yefgenii folded his maps and stuffed them in the leg pockets of his flying suit.

"You'll be taking *529.*"

"Yes, sir."

Pilipenko checked his watch and entered the time in the log. "You know, you're kind of big for a pilot."

"Yes, sir."

"Do you climb into the aircraft, or just strap it on?"

Yefgenii smiled.

"Come on, son, we'll do a circuit, then we'll fly."

Pilipenko called any pilot below the rank of *kapetan* "son." He was thirty-three.

From the runway they rose off the plain. A long streak of dust cloud tried to rise with them but fell back to earth. The wooden shacks of the airfield shrank to matchboxes. The forest became a felt mat. Pilipenko made a climbing turn through 180 degrees onto the downwind leg of the circuit. Yefgenii followed. Straight ahead a triangular copse stood on top of a hill. As they turned onto finals his wingtip pointed at a drying bog where ducks skimmed the brown water. From this high angle Pilipenko's plane seemed to swoop onto the runway. It was flat beneath Yefgenii, its wings swept back in an arrow, with sunlight glinting off the glass of the canopy. Pilipenko's mainwheels struck the large white numbers and then he began to accelerate again. Yefgenii hit the numbers dead center and accelerated after him. The two MiGs rose once again but this time climbed straight out.

Pilipenko transmitted, "Get in close, son, and follow me up."

Yefgenii aimed the nose at Pilipenko's drop tank and snuggled into formation just off his tail. Women and children were working in the paddies below. Some gazed up and waved. Pilipenko waggled his wings back at them. They ascended through 1,000 meters, 2,000. At long last the heat thinned out. Cool air filled the cockpit. Yefgenii tugged out the collar of his vest to let it onto his skin.

Shreds of cloud were slicing past the canopy. The forests and fields had shrunk to green and brown oblongs. In sunlight wheat fields shone in yellow dabs. Villages dotted the country, but the people had become too small to see. At 5,000 meters Yefgenii gazed down and could've been one of the last two men on earth.

"There's the river."

Ahead of them the Yalu ran like a blade between low gray foothills. Boats were gliding over waters the color of steel. Yefgenii was learning the landmarks. He studied the shapes of the hills, which way their slopes pointed, the turns of the river itself, its bridges.

"This side is Manchuria, the other is Korea," Pilipenko said. "We're safe on this side—they're forbidden to cross. The other is the theater of war. There they're fair game—but, the moment you cross, so are you."

They flew upstream, keeping the river off their starboard wings. In the far north a mountain range was pushing up at them. Its peaks wore caps of white snow. The horizon was sharp. Sparse white cumuli were heaped below, looking like coral. A little cirrus drifted above, not thick enough to be white, only blue-white.

"The Suiho Dam."

Pilipenko orbited to give him a good look and then they turned back downriver. Roads and railway lines hatched the land. Yefgenii noted bridges and villages. A sector map lay in his thigh pocket visible through a cover of clear plastic. When he picked out a feature he related it to the map. Soon the river was opening into an enormous bay.

"The Yellow Sea. Korea Bay. Do not overfly."

Pilipenko pulled round, hard and tight. Yefgenii's g-needle flicked as he followed. Pilipenko didn't roll out. He kept in the turn past 360 degrees. The games had begun.

Pilipenko opened the throttle all the way to the stop. He pitched up the nose and rolled hard over to select the attitude for a max-rate turn in the opposite direction. Yefgenii matched the maneuver. The two MiGs circled in an MRT, pulling 6 g. Pilipenko was guessing that, because Yefgenii was big, he'd have problems at high acceleration. It was the easy way to break him before the sortie even got interesting. Yefgenii sucked in short sharp breaths and strained during expirations like shitting a brick. The planes cut up the air. Vortices hung and swirled. When the planes struck them on the next orbit, it came as a kick in the seat of their pants. Yefgenii was still holding tight on Pilipenko's tail. The formation was no looser now than when they'd been in a gentle climb.

Pilipenko grinned; it was going to get interesting after all; he rolled out and pulled up. They tilted almost to the vertical. Their wingtips cut the horizon. The altimeter wound up to 12,000. Speed bled away. Soon the stubby white needle was barely moving, the longer thinner one making only a slow creep round the clock. The aircraft trembled. They were on the buffet. A stall threatened. Yefgenii saw Pilipenko's plane tip over and vanish under his nose. He pushed hard over, minusing 2 g.

Pilipenko reappeared. They were plunging straight down. The wide green earth was swallowing them. The altimeter spun down, the airspeed built. With Pilipenko still on his nose, a hurricane of air rushed over Yefgenii's canopy. Soon he was bouncing in Pilipenko's slipstream. The planes burst through layers of cloud. In split seconds sunlight flashed off then back on. Yefgenii saw Pilipenko's wings rotate through 90 degrees and the elevators on his tailplane waggle up. He reacted at once. Pilipenko glanced over his shoulder expecting to see clear sky. The nozzle of Yefgenii's intake loomed in his five o'clock position.

"Fuck."

Pilipenko leveled out at 5,000 meters and stirred the control stick out and back. As his nose tilted it began to describe a circle. His wings slashed the horizon and he rolled through the inverted. Again Yefgenii had reacted at once and matched the speed and angle of the maneuver. Pilipenko was corkscrewing round in a barrel roll hoping to loop onto his tail. Yefgenii made his roll wide enough and slow enough to hold formation. Pilipenko's head twisted round again and again the nose of Yefgenii's MiG was right behind.

"Fuck."

Pilipenko snapped into a hard turn to the left, then to the right. He climbed and fell, rolled and looped. He couldn't shake loose. Under his vest sweat was gushing over his skin. It was trickling out of his helmet and down the back of his neck. He could taste a gob of it mixed with snot on his top lip. He pushed up his visor to get air flowing round his eyes.

"OK, son, take us home."

Yefgenii throttled into the lead. Pilipenko sat out on Yefgenii's wing wondering if he'd radio the tower for a steer. He could see him studying the ground and studying the map. After a few seconds, Yefgenii turned onto the correct heading.

The MiGs sailed over Manchuria. The Sun had crossed its zenith and was beginning the long slide toward the mountains in the west. Pilipenko smiled. He loved days like this, days with clear air from horizon to horizon and hardly any chatter on the radio, when the flying was easy and with good men.

Yefgenii followed the pattern of landmarks he'd learned and it led his eyes to the airfield. In the heat it was shimmering. It appeared not to be part of the world, but to be hovering a few meters above it. No fighter pilot would wish to be anywhere else or to live in any other age.

O N THE CHART in Ops, the name YEREMIN stood against the last wave. The moment he saw it Yefgenii's heart started drumming. He'd be flying in Kiriya's *zveno*.

Gnido's name was up there too and he couldn't sit still for a minute. He gave Yefgenii a playful punch on the arm. Gnido had passed a second check ride with Pilipenko but scabs still mottled his face. They made him look diseased.

They peered at the big map of the Korean Peninsula. Airfields were black circles, danger areas were red—marks crammed the airspace between the Yalu and the P'yŏngyang-Wŏnsan parallel. The infantry lines crawled in months the distance the pilots covered in a matter of minutes, while all the time the borders stayed the same and each side's war aims got no clearer.

Yefgenii checked the updates every hour, worried his flight would be lost to an operational revision or an unserviceable aircraft. At noon he slipped behind the Ops hut. In the west, the mountains fell back low and vast, driven out of the earth by an eon of tectonic creep. Above them a heap of cloud inched across the sky like a giant snail. He breathed the hot air. Another day was burning away.

At last the fifth wave got airborne. The MiGs became silver beetles crawling across the dome of the sky and as they crawled they shed long white tracks.

The sixth and last wave waited on the dispersal, waiting for visual sightings of enemy or reports of blips on radar screens to be fed through the radio into their ears that were pressed hard, tight and bruised inside their helmets.

Then the report came through that the fifth wave was recovering to base so the tower cleared the sixth to light their engines. By now it was late afternoon.

They crossed the river and climbed into the war. At 15,000 meters they were nuzzling the roof of the world. This place between earth and sky was a great lens with cloud banks embedded in it like cataracts. Outside the canopy the water vapor of the jet exhausts froze into ice crystals. The condensation trails streaked the sky until the crystals drifted apart and melted and then the trails would vanish. They weren't concerned about leaving contrails. They wanted the enemy to see them, to come looking for a fight.

The MiGs traveled south, and then east. The sky was empty. Minute by minute, their fuel burned to vapor.

A voice came over the radio: "Red Leader, Red Three."

Yefgenii didn't recognize the other pilots' voices yet, only Kiriya's, which answered: "Pass your message." The empty sky made him feel safe speaking Russian.

"Min fuel."

Yefgenii's fuel gauge indicated he was still holding another twenty liters over minimum. He sighed. Kiriya was going to order them home. Instead he heard, "Five more minutes."

The MiGs sailed on. The day was ending and no enemy was appearing.

"Red Leader, Red Four, min fuel."

"Same, Red Two."

"Red Five, same."

The needle on Yefgenii's gauge was nudging the mark. Another minute and he'd have to make the call too. They awaited the click and hiss over the radio and Kiriya's voice ordering them home. Instead they heard only the rumble of their jets and the rush of air.

Yefgenii sighted a dot on the horizon. It was laying a trail like a fine cotton thread, so small that when he blinked the image skipped with the tidal flow of his tears. He waited a moment, but over the radio no one called it out. Only he had acquired the target. He could let it sail on and the others would never know.

He transmitted. "Contact, Red Six."

"Where?"

"Three o'clock, on the horizon, moving right to left."

"I'm not visual. Anyone else visual?"

"Negative."

"Negative."

"Neg—"

"Red Six, none of us are visual. Are you sure?"

"Yes, boss. In our three, on the hor—"

"I can't see shit."

"Me neither."

"Red Six, is it closing?"

"Negative. Looks like it's moving in parallel, maybe even receding."

"Well, that's no fucking use. I'm under min. If there's anyone out there, he's 50 kilometers away or more."

"I'm ten liters under."

"Five."

"No way could we chase him down and still make it back over the Yalu."

"Shit." That was Kiriya again.

The seconds stretched. Yefgenii tracked the tiny gray point as it crept along the horizon. It was getting smaller.

Still Kiriya didn't give the order. He was contemplating burning what fuel he had left to hunt down a target he couldn't even see. He knew Yeremin had sharp eyes. If only he had sharp eyes. If only he'd seen it half an hour ago. He'd been stuck on four so long now. "Fuck it. We've got to go home." He clicked off. *"Shit."*

The MiGs turned north. Yefgenii glanced out past his wingtip at the contact. It was shrinking to nothing, a Sabre of the 16th Fighter Intercept Squadron flown by a Second Lieutenant named Buzz Aldrin. A few moments later the aircraft had gone, leaving only a bare patch of sky. Even the cotton filament of its contrail had vanished. The air was clear, empty and silent. Yefgenii felt the hunger for the first time. It reached down into his gut. It filled the gap between earth and sky.

THEN, AS IF BY CASTING A SPELL, things changed. The Sun rose like glory. Intelligence had reported a wave of B-29 raids on North Korean hydroelectric plants. PLAAF pilots had engaged the B-29s' fighter escort over Panghyon. Both sides had suffered losses. Sightings were coming in thick and fast. As fighters clamored to join the action, dust erupted from the runways north of the Yalu.

Pilipenko scribbled duties onto the board with flourishes of a black marker. The pilots crowded round. Yefgenii read he'd fly with Kiriya once again. It was because of his eyes—Kiriya wanted them picking out targets for him and not for anyone else.

They sat in their cockpits for an hour. Kiriya called the tower every five minutes. His voice turned shrill. He wanted to know why their orders hadn't come through yet. He had to get into the fight even if it was only to scavenge for scraps. Just as he was beginning to lose hope, the fighter controller's voice broke through from the tower: "Clear to taxi."

Kiriya had them test-firing their guns almost the second they left the circuit, but when they crossed the Yalu the battle appeared over. The blue was empty. Kiriya could've wept. For some men there'd been a sky filled with glorious sport, but for him now there was nothing.

Yefgenii clicked the button on his stick to transmit a word of Korean: "Contact."

"Good boy!" In Russian, Kiriya was almost squeaking.

No one else replied. Apart from Kiriya they were Kubarev, Baturin, Dolgikh and Glinka. None of them could see it yet. On the ground civilized men could get by without sharp eyes. They had evolved beyond natural selection and were free of it. The men who fought in the sky were not.

"No contact," said Kubarev in Korean.

Yefgenii said, "One o'clock."

Each pilot alone in his cockpit peered southward, through banks of cloud scattered like coral, in search of a fleeting glint of metal. They scanned up to the horizon for creeping black specks and then above for contrails. Yefgenii's eyes were that much sharper that seconds passed without the others acquiring the sighting.

"Repeat, contact, one o'clock," Yefgenii said.

"Red Six, lead."

The words didn't mean anything to Yefgenii. Kiriya's pronunciation of Korean was idiosyncratic. "Say again."

"Red Six. Lead."

"Say again."

Kiriya snapped in Russian, "Take us to him!"

Yefgenii slid the throttle to its forward end-stop. The engine roared behind him. It kicked his backside. He held the stick hard forward to keep the nose level and stood on the rudders to hold the aircraft straight. Yefgenii's airplane accelerated out of formation to assume the lead. The contact was below the contrail level, just a black dot only he could see. As they closed it began to crystallize into its components.

At last the others could see them. Kirya ordered, "Drop tanks."

Again Yefgenii couldn't decipher Kiriya's pronunciation but he saw the others dropping their wing tanks so he reached under his seat and swung the small lever that released them. The fuel tanks broke from the MiGs' wings and seemed to hold in the air for a moment before tipping over and gathering speed and plunging down toward the green land below. He felt weight fall from the airframe but he held his controls against the rise and pitch the plane wanted to make and then he trimmed out the pressure in the stick.

The MiGs crossed the sky and in crossing to their prey they descended through thousands of meters. The air grew thicker and warmer. Their exhausts remained steam. No trails formed.

Yefgenii's mouth dried with the taste of rubber on his lips. Noise pounded his helmet. He tightened his straps. He toggled down his mask. The mask began to hurt the bridge of his nose.

They recognized the four aircraft ahead and below as F-86 Sabres of the 334th FIS. The Sabres had snub noses and swept wings. Yellow slashes decorated their tailplanes and midsections. The American squadrons were proud of their identity; each had its own markings, and some pilots even wore individual designs on their aircraft. The MiGs were anonymous.

The Americans broke formation into two elements. They had seen them. They pulled apart and next released their wing tanks which tumbled like meteorites end over end toward land.

"Break!"

Glinka and Dolgikh chased one Sabre element. Under the leader's canopy a scarlet bonedome glinted in the sunlight. Six stars blurred on the cockpit. The other pair of Sabres streaked between them and Kubarev and Baturin while Kiriya led Yefgenii high above the battle.

Dolgikh was stumbling over his Korean, unable to get his words out. "Fuck it!" he said in Russian. "Red Six, you've got a Sabre element under you, should be popping into your two o'clock anytime now." Then all at once all the voices were speaking Russian.

Yefgenii's hands were shaking. His knees were knocking against the stick. He swung hard to follow the pair that were crossing beneath him. As his plane rolled, the Sabres reappeared below him and arcing round behind. Their wings glinted in the sun as they tilted into the turn. Yefgenii swung the stick over the other way and pulled back to the edge of a stall. The airframe shuddered. The controls felt spongy but he held the turn. Outside the canopy the sky wheeled round. He hung on his straps with one wing pricking the heavens and the other boring into the earth. He pulled harder on the stick, harder, at full throttle, the turn tightening and g-forces driving his ass hard into the seat and weighting his head forward and leadening his arms. The shoulder straps cut into his flesh. Yefgenii tensed the muscles of his neck to keep his head straight as he craned round to follow the Sabres turning behind him. He was turning too. The nose swung along the horizon at the precise angle to give a max-rate turn. The needles were motionless. Every drop of the plane's energy was driving the turn; nothing was bleeding into a climb or a descent or a roll or a yaw. The MiG shook. The airflow over the wings was on the verge of breaking up. The boundary layer was tearing away. He held the turn, held her on the buffet, pulling round, harder, tighter, pulling, clenching against the acceleration. Grayness crept into his peripheral vision. It turned hard and black and began to close like an iris on the wheeling lens of blue sky and glinting smoky warfare. He strained hard against a closed glottis, the Valsalva maneuver forcing blood into his head and back to his retinas, not letting it drain into his belly and arse and boots. He strained and it pushed open the black iris.

From under the nose the Sabres reappeared. The nearer of the pair was 100 meters away. Yefgenii lined it up in his gun-sight and clicked the trigger. The 23 mm cannon spat out shells. He felt the recoil in his boots and in his butt. He closed in then fired a second round. Tracers leapt out ahead of his cockpit. They glowed as they crossed the void between him and the Sabre, drifted past it and vanished into the earth.

The Sabre turned and now Yefgenii followed. He fired again. The shells jumped across space and struck the Sabre's fuselage. Smoke burst from its tail and flashed past Yefgenii's canopy. The American aircraft shuddered but did not fall. Trailing wisps of white smoke, it turned in an arc to the south and then straightened up. Now Yefgenii was closing in. He made out a charred gouge of metal at the Sabre's tail where the shell had struck. Damaged, the American was slow; he was heading for base.

Yefgenii followed for the kill. He knew it now. He was a killer. He'd join the brotherhood and he'd wear the small red star on the side of his cockpit that was the star of victory and the star of murder.

The American plunged south. In normal conditions the Sabre might outperform the MiG at lower altitude. The American knew, however, he had no hope of outmaneuvering the MiG and his dive was to gain speed. The twisted shrapnel on his aircraft's fuselage made him less aerodynamic. An aileron was damaged. His controls were sluggish. His aircraft had become too clumsy for a fight. He was racing for the line between Wŏnsan and P'yŏngyang where Yefgenii would be forced to turn back and the American would live to fly another day.

Yefgenii shoved the throttle to make certain it shunted its endstop. He fingered the trim tabs on the control column and to the side of the cockpit. Over and over again he trimmed out the controls to make his MiG as sleek and fast as possible. He watched the needle of the Mach meter nudge 0.9. The MiG snaked at this speed but with each minute and each adjustment the American appeared closer and more vulnerable.

The two fighters raced southward, rupturing the air with a

blasting of jets and slashing of wings, while the clouds that lay in clumps crept along the horizon like slugs and a patchwork of green fields and brown hills lay still and quiet below. The Nan River drifted toward them. The welcoming land of the South beckoned to the American. In only a few minutes he'd be safe; even if he couldn't land, he could eject.

Yefgenii hunched into the gun-sight. He glimpsed the Sabre duck and bounce through the crosshairs but never for even a second settle in them. The American swung left and right. His plane was fat and weak and he must've known the end was coming.

Diving through thousands of meters, to them the earth grew big again. Soon it cradled their expanding shadows that skimmed over steepening hills and slithered through widening valleys.

A third shadow appeared. A fighter bobbed into Yefgenii's slipstream. Yefgenii glanced up into his rearview mirror ready to roll hard away but instead of a Sabre he glimpsed a blunter snout with an air intake divided by a vertical septum—a MiG. "Retreat," Kiriya ordered.

Now the flat dark buildings of P'yŏngyang were beginning to fall under the leading edge of his right wingtip. In a few more seconds, when the Nan River slipped under his belly, the American would be safe across the border.

Kiriya had not made a turn as tight and accurate as Yefgenii's and had missed the chance to strike the Sabre. Now he struggled to hold position behind. The Sabre's jet-wash buffeted Yefgenii's aircraft but Yefgenii held true to the American's tail. Over and over again Kiriya bobbed in and out of line and at times he overcorrected. He tried to believe that his position was the more difficult one but the truth was plain: this nineteen-year-old virgin was the greater master of his craft.

Yefgenii had closed to point-blank range. He drew back the

throttle. On the instrument panel gauge needles swung over as the rush of the engine diminished. The plane steadied and Yefgenii's finger crooked round the trigger.

"Retreat." Kiriya's voice rose. "Retreat!"

The American slid into the crosshairs and Yefgenii held him there. Only a second passed but this was an age, this was a pilot's lifetime and his death. Yefgenii could claim his radio had failed. He could kill this American and then he would be at base with the red star upon his fuselage.

Kiriya cut through in Russian. "Get the fuck out of there, Yeremin. He's mine."

Yefgenii let out a long profane scream but didn't click on the radio for Kiriya to hear it. With his mouth gaping in a shriek that no one heard he tilted the wings and throttled back and so Yefgenii drifted aside into the quiet of a calming engine and a slowing rush of air. A moment later Kiriya's tracers were burning into the Sabre's tail and a short moment after that a shell tore open the American's fuselage.

A wing crumpled. The Sabre slid sideways then spun and toppled. Metal sheared away in chunks. As if in tranquil recovery an amputated section of wing straightened all of a sudden and took flight again. It rose and glinted in the sun but then it flipped and then it twisted and then it began the long sink to earth.

With the battle over, the survivors were dispersing. Streaks of ice pointed north into Manchuria and south to the 38th Parallel. The Americans would report their contacts as North Koreans or Chinese. Most they met were ill-trained and, to the U.S. pilots, the war in the main was a duck shoot. If they thought different they saved it for later and the dark quiet corners of the officers' club. Some had picked up enemy R/T that didn't sound like Korean or Chinese, but they called the best of their opponents Honcho or Casey Jones, never anything else. The Soviets weren't in the War. That was official. They weren't here nor were their seasoned jet pilots.

Yefgenii watched the Sun slide down to the Yellow Sea. It threw back a glow as if a great red fireball had toppled off the edge of the world, causing a golden crust to simmer at the clouds' edges and coloring their undersides pink like the bellies of salmon. The aircrafts' condensation trails were evaporating into the thin dry air. Soon the ice crystals would condense again and someday they'd fall as rain.

I N DUSK the last pair of MiGs reappeared over Antung. White landing lights and blinking red and green navigation lights glowed, while in gloom the planes themselves had turned to ghosts. The lights floated down to the runway. They were spirits returning to earth; they were demons creeping back into the underworld.

Yefgenii landed with despair cladding the cockpit. His mask reeked of it. It was in his gloves. It was in his boots. His wheels flung up a plume of dust and, behind the aircraft, the jet engine whipped it into a vortex that scattered and drifted and, by the time Yefgenii turned off the runway onto the taxiway, the dust had sown itself once more into the ground.

He snap-turned his QRB to release his harnesses. Because the ground crews were massing round Kiriya's plane, only one of them stayed back to help Yefgenii. She was a pear-shaped girl perhaps five years older than him with dirty blonde hair and oily skin. The men said she was a widow. None of the senior pilots wanted her in their ground crews. A woman was bad luck; a widow, twice so. The junior pilots tolerated her till they got a kill or bribed the Starshina with a bottle of vodka, then she'd be moved on to someone else's crew farther down the pecking order.

The widow said nothing to Yefgenii as she placed the ladder for him to step down. He paid her no attention. He didn't much believe in luck or in superstition.

Pilipenko was leading the celebration for Kiriya's kill. He had his arm round Kiriya and was kissing his cheek. Kiriya raised his arm in triumph while the ground crews applauded. The Starshina was already stenciling a small red star under the cockpit of Kiriya's jet. Five now lay in line, proclaiming him the newest ace of the world's first jet war.

Yefgenii turned away. Hunched under his aircraft, Yefegenii fought hard not to sob.

The widow peered at him. She wondered if he might've taken ill. "Leitenant, are you all right . . . ?"

Yefgenii swallowed his tears. Without a word to her he marched across the dispersal toward Kiriya's celebration with the hose of his PEC slapping sharp against his thigh.

Pilipenko and Skomorokhov and Kiriya were numbered among the brotherhood. They were sunning themselves in their glory. They laughed as only gods can laugh.

Yefgenii stood on the periphery. At one point Kiriya caught his gaze and something passed between them. In that tiny moment Kiriya's expression softened. Yefgenii's hands came together and he joined in the applause for his commanding officer's triumph.

Later, in the crew hut, Glinka claimed he'd been close to downing one of the Sabres. "You know, Yeremin, the more I think about it . . . I might even have damaged him. The pilot who wore red—"

"Red . . . ?"

"A red bonedome. That was Jabara."

Major James Jabara had become the first ace of the war, the first jet ace in history. He'd appeared in a newsreel standing at his Sabre's wing wearing his Mae West and his parachute pack buckled over it, with his hands clasped across his groin holding that famous scarlet helmet. His jet kills had made him as famous as a movie star or a

world champion, the most famous American aviator since Lind-
bergh.

Yefgenii shrugged. He felt numb and all he wanted was to be
alone. To desert the crew hut before duty's end would invite disap-
proval, so he wrote up the mission in his logbook and hung around
till the ground chief's report was ready to sign.

At night he returned to barracks. In the polished scrap of alu-
minum they used for a mirror he registered for the first time the
burst capillaries mottling his face, neck, and chest. They had ruptured under high g. He peeled off his undershirt. The straps of his
harness had grazed red bands into his shoulders. They were sticky
and beginning to scab. He dabbed them with iodine. It scalded so
much he wanted to scream.

As the men strolled through the humid night air to the mess, Yef-
genii could hear Glinka trying it on with Dolgikh. "You know,
Kapetan, the more I think about it . . . I'm pretty sure I damaged
Jabara's Sabre."

"The only way you could've done that was if he'd shot off your
tail and accidentally flown into it."

Those who heard laughed.

"No, I'm serious, there's so much going on in the heat of battle,
I wasn't sure at the time, but now I can remember seeing my tracers
hit him—"

"Well, I was sure at the time, and I'm sure now. Jabara's eating a
Texas steak and your tracers are floating on the Yellow Sea."

"Are you saying you won't back me up when I claim it?"

No one was laughing now. Glinka had friends in high places.
Dolgikh shrugged and shook his head. After all, it was only damage.
You could damage every plane in the U.S. Air Force and it still
wouldn't amount to a kill.

In the bar Yefgenii watched Kiriya get drunk on bad vodka.
Kiriya's mood appeared joyous. Though a formality on becoming an
ace, he looked forward to being awarded the Order of Lenin and the

Gold Star of Hero of the Soviet Union; but in his stomach stung an ulcer of truth that, despite the Gold Star and the Order of Lenin and the five stars on the Ops scoreboard and the five stenciled on the side of his plane, he had only four and a half kills because one half belonged to Yefgenii Yeremin.

He became so drunk he could no longer stand and had to slump in a chair pushed under him by little Gnido. Kiriya made loud talk of going to find the ugly young widow in her barrack-room bed. Pilipenko leaned over him and whispered, "She'll bring bad luck."

Yefgenii stood outside under the black sky. The cold air carried the noises of banter and drinking coming from the mess. Treetops rocked in the breeze. Patches of cloud drifted over stars. Planets turned. A man was nothing. Yefgenii's head sank and his shoulders heaved.

O VER ŬIJU the sky flickered with tracer fire. The radio spat out ranges and vectors that collided with the shrieks of combat. Across Korea the chosen pilots were going up twice, even three times in a day. Sabre and MiG jockeys alike were claiming multiple kills while on the ground a hundred thousand Chinese reinforcements trudged to the battlefront. Men were fighting and dying over patches of land that to the pilots were no more than dots on a map.

At Antung the air rumbled. It reeked of oil, fuel, and hot metal. Enemy shells had dimpled the fuselages of nearly all the returning ships and every cannon was charcoaled. Skomorokhov had got one, of course. Kiriya had got one too. Pilipenko claimed a kill—now he had seven and a half. Kapetan Dolgikh had been shot down with no reports of a parachute being seen.

The fourth wave was already airborne over the Yalu and reporting more contacts with the 51st FIW. Skomorokhov demanded another mission. Pilipenko was pushing to go up again too. Yefgenii's name had been on the board but it got scrubbed to make room for the aces.

Glinka's jet rolled in off the third wave. He threw back the canopy and stood on the seat, punching the air. He ripped off his helmet and in that moment Yefgenii saw the sharp red print of his mask crease

41

into a smile. As Glinka came down the ladder the Starshina questioned him and then they were shaking hands.

Pilipenko descended his ladder. He glanced at Glinka with a quizzical expression. But the look was lost as he fielded questions from the ground crew.

Yefgenii turned away. He'd come to Korea to write his name in the sky but his tour was becoming an unbearable creep into oblivion. Life was falling behind him like a runway. The takeoff strip was shortening.

Kiriya was standing outside the Ops hut with binoculars, waiting for the latest wave to rejoin the circuit. Pilipenko joined him, drinking from a flask. He took a gulp of water, gargled and spat it onto the ground. It bubbled in the dirt. Pilipenko said, "We engaged eight Sabres and six flew home. That makes two kills, one for me and one for Kubarev. Glinka didn't shoot shit."

Kiriya lowered the binoculars. "It's chaos up there."

"I can count to eight, boss."

"So can the Americans, but they'll admit one lost to engine failure and claim a couple of ours into the bargain."

Kiriya raised the binoculars back to his eyes. The air looked tranquil. Its hundred churning vortices were invisible. He said, "They claim, we claim—you know, Pip, when this war's over, someone's going to add it all up."

"Who's going to?"

"Whoever wins."

The CO was content with his kill for the day. That ulcer was healing. Whether he had six kills or only five and a half, he was still an ace and deserved to be called one and was worthy of his decorations. Kiriya didn't need to fly again today, so he ordered Pilipenko to see that Yeremin's name was restored to the board.

Pilipenko led them across the border. The MiGs patrolled as far south as the Chŏng-ch'on River. There they climbed back toward

Chŏsan. Pilipenko kept them airborne, but the realization developed that they'd get nothing today, not even scraps. Soon the needle of his fuel gauge was slipping toward minimum. "Recover to base."

They crossed the Yalu into China and turned southwest. Yefgenii retracted the throttle and lifted the nose to hold altitude. Power drained. Airspeed plummeted. He transmitted, "Blue Six."

"Blue Leader."

"I've got a rough-running engine."

"You can make it back?"

"Affirmative."

"How's your fuel, son?"

"I've got enough, sir."

Gnido transmitted, "Blue Leader from Blue Five, I'll escort him home."

"OK, boys. See you on the ground."

Yefgenii watched the MiGs stretch ahead. Gnido tucked in beside him. The two of them made slow progress down the Yalu. The Suiho Dam drifted under their port wings. Yefgenii waited till the other four planes had shrunk to gray points, then he opened up his throttle again.

Gnido saw the MiG lurch ahead of him. "What's happened to your engine?"

"It got better." Yefgenii was turning back into Korea.

Gnido watched Yefgenii's wings tilt. The Yalu swung beneath him. Streamers threaded off his wingtips.

"Fuck it." Gnido opened his throttle and together they dropped down to 5,000 meters. Down in the thick air, the American Sabres were the predators, but Yefgenii trusted his sharp eyes to preserve him.

A bank of white floated beneath them. The shadows of their planes slithered over the undulations of the cloud top. Their wings sank and a moment later they worked within a white shroud with their heads immobile and their eyes flicking from gauge to gauge.

First the white thinned and then the Sun's light burst into their canopies and then the earth opened below them like the leaves of an atlas.

Yefgenii turned a wide circle from which he scanned the sky over and over and over again. His eyes darted to the fuel gauge. He was approaching minimum.

A speck crossed under the nose. Yefgenii pulled round 30 degrees and the speck popped out low in his eleven o'clock. Dark over dark terrain, it could've been seen by few, perhaps by him alone. His heart drummed. He pulled his harnesses tight and toggled down.

"Contact."

Gnido couldn't see anything, but Yefgenii was dropping a wing and pitching hard over. He followed him down. The VSI dropped and the long thin white needle of the altimeter spun through the hundreds to a blur while the short stubby white needle wound down through the thousands. Air streamed over the canopy. It thickened as the planes plunged and it made their wings shudder. The Mach meter needle trembled on 0.9.

Yefgenii drew back the throttle. The airframe snaked. The airstream blasted like a hurricane. At 1,000 meters he began to ease up and at 500 the plane was flying straight and level onto his target's tail.

Here was his scrap. A dark blue F4U-4 Corsair was chugging southwest for the coast, keeping low to creep under radar. The Corsair didn't represent a bomber returning from a raid or even part of an escort. It didn't represent anything apart perhaps from a lost aviator and for sure an unlucky one.

Gnido was a few seconds behind. He saw Yefgenii's wing tanks drop. The MiG lofted as its load lightened. The tanks floated down toward woodland. One landed in a clearing and Gnido saw it shatter. Birds took wing with a flapping that was infinitesimal compared to the metal machines above. Yefgenii pressed in behind the Corsair as it plunged across hinterland and out into Korea Bay.

"Yeremin!"

The blue waters blackened as the seabed dropped away from the shelf of land. White gulls scattered. A shoal of fish glided under the waves as if one beast. Yefgenii pressed on.

Gnido refused to contravene regulations by overflying the sea and so he swung back toward land.

Yefgenii closed in on the Corsair and after only the opening burst from his 23 mm cannons it stuttered in midair. Its nose tipped forward, and propeller first the aircraft plunged into the sea. Under a plume of spray the Corsair stood for a fleeting moment on its nose then toppled onto its back.

The aircraft rocked on the waves. One wing broke loose and floated free. Fronds of spray mixed into the gray rolls of water. A gull perched on an up-pointing wreck of undercarriage. The Corsair's inlets funneled in water till at last it slipped under and the gull took flight. The sea frothed for a time before it flattened, then it rolled over like a great gray slab.

Yefgenii pulled up and inland. Pain bit the bridge of his nose so he untoggled his mask. His shoulders stung. The harness straps had lifted the scabs on his shoulders. He felt blood leaking from the wounds.

The two MiGs regrouped and headed home. No crowd gathered for them on the dispersal, but the widow noticed black powdering around Yefgenii's cannons, so she signaled to the Starshina, excited on behalf of the boyish blond Leitenant.

She gazed up at him as he perched on the ladder. He was vast and drab and seemed to blot out half the sky. He appeared colorless except for the blue blaze of his eyes. "Is it congratulations, sir?"

Gnido perched on the neighboring ladder. He and Yefgenii exchanged a look.

The widow held a smile on Yefgenii. Her face was round, her nose a bobble. "Any luck, Leitenant?"

"No," he said. "No luck."

On the walk back to Ops, Gnido diverted him. "Claim it,

Yeremin." A jet was starting up. No one could hear them. They could barely hear each other. "Say it was on the Yalu. I'll back you up."

"It wasn't on the Yalu."

Pilipenko awaited them in the crew hut. He gave them a short sharp nod as they came through the door. Glinka, Skomorokhov, Kubarev and some others lounged on seats. Pilipenko watched Yefgenii pour himself a cup of water from the near-empty jug with the plate over it to keep out the flies. He studied the quick accurate movements of the boy's big hands. He wanted to warn him but it was too late.

Kiriya entered. "Yeremin. Gnido."

Yefgenii glanced round but already Kiriya had retreated into his office with the door half closed behind him. Yefgenii gulped down the cup of water and followed. Gnido picked up his beret from the hooks. Pilipenko tossed Yefgenii his—it bore no rank insignia.

Kiriya's office was bare except for a wooden desk, chair and cabinet. Flies buzzed at the open window. Yefgenii and Gnido saluted then removed their berets and held them in their hands as they remained at attention. Yefgenii felt a trickle of blood inside his flying suit.

The Starshina's report had come straight to Kiriya. Aircraft *529* and *648* had returned low on fuel and *529* had blackened guns. "You're aware of the regulations regarding minimum fuel."

"Yes, boss."

"Yes, boss."

"How do you account for your aircraft's fuel levels?"

"Sir, I had a rough-running engine. It must've overconsumed."

"Sir, I was flying at low speed to escort Leitenant Yeremin home. My aircraft's performance was suboptimal."

"Yeremin, how do you account for the condition of your aircraft's guns?"

"Sir, I engaged an enemy aircraft."

"You had a rough-running engine."

46

"Sir, it corrected itself."

"It corrected itself?"

"Yes, boss."

"Gnido?"

"Yes, boss, it corrected itself."

"I've been flying these lumps of metal for three years. Not one 'corrected itself.'"

Through the window they heard tow trucks revving up. They were starting to return MiGs to the hangars.

"You engaged what?"

"Sir, an F-4U Corsair of the United States Marine Corps, I believe."

"You believe?"

"It was distant."

"Gnido?"

"We were returning to base, sir, when we made visual contact."

"Then what happened, Yeremin?"

"It passed out to sea. I shot from a distance. I was hoping for a lucky strike."

"You didn't follow it over the sea?"

"No, sir."

"Gnido?"

"Yes, sir, that's how it happened."

"If there were an accident, if the Americans recovered one of us from the water, it wouldn't be the pilot alone who'd suffer."

"Yes, boss."

"Yes, boss."

"It'd be his family. There would be reprisals."

"Yes, boss."

"Yes, boss."

"Did you get it?"

"Sir?"

"The Corsair—did you get it?"

"I, er, I'm not sure, sir."

"You're not sure? Gnido?"

"I, er, I'm not sure either, sir."

Kiriya studied them for what seemed like minutes. "Gnido, you will never again fail to observe fuel minima. Dismissed."

"Yes, sir. Thank you, sir."

Gnido put his beret back on, saluted and exited.

Kiriya turned his gaze on Yefgenii. "Of course, if there's more . . . If you want to claim it . . . but if the gun camera suggested a violation . . . that's not something I'd be minded to overlook. I have to consider how it would reflect on the Polk."

Inside he was distraught but Yefgenii didn't break eye contact. "Yes, sir."

"And? So?"

"I'm not making a claim, sir."

Kiriya nodded and looked away. Agony flashed in Yefgenii's face. "You want glory. Of course. There's nothing else for us in this shitty war. We're not defending our cities. We're not winning new lands. The war's nothing but the chance of glory." Through the window the two men watched the tow trucks hauling MiGs into the hangars. "I want glory as much as any man does." He shot Yefgenii a sideways glance. He was awkward. An apology was beyond him, an apology for stealing Yefgenii's kill all those weeks ago. "I believe, Yeremin, on one occasion I wanted it too much."

Yefgenii hesitated. He didn't know how to answer.

Kiriya nodded. "Dismissed, Yeremin."

Yefgenii replaced Pilipenko's beret, saluted and left. There was blood on his chest and through his T-shirt it bloomed like a rose.

In the crew hut, Glinka was recounting his kill to anyone who'd listen. He must've been telling it for the twentieth time.

Yefgenii expected to feel changed in some way, but he didn't at all. The victory in itself wasn't enough. What was required was that other men treat him as different, as changed. He slumped in the corner, wearing the same drab overalls as the other men, without name, rank or insignia. They were meant to look the same, yet the celestial ones like Skomorokhov and Pilipenko owned a quality that dazzled. But they weren't stars or comets; they were like the Moon: they glowed with reflected light. The painted red stars on their cockpits weren't the source, nor the gold stars of their decorations. The light was cast by the adoration of their peers.

He wanted to beat his chest. He wanted to scream that he was a killer. He wanted the eyes of other men to turn toward him and recognize his achievement, so that he could blaze in their adulation like the Moon blazes with the light of the Sun.

Later the Starshina found him and asked him about the film from the gun camera. The widow stood beside him, holding the reel in its small metal capsule.

Yefgenii hesitated. "The film?"

"Yes, Leitenant." The Starshina studied him.

The widow showed him the reel. She smiled at him almost like mother to child. "Do you want it developed, Leitenant?"

Yefgenii shook his head. He was a dark body. He gave off no light. "Destroy it," he said.

I T WAS THE HEIGHT OF SUMMER, the summer of 1952. Sunlight blazed from the early hours till evening, the sky was blue and open, and the pilots of the 221st were seeing action almost every day. Yefgenii flew as Kiriya's wingman. He sighted four Sabres operating beneath the contrail level. They were specks, not even cotton threads. While Kiriya and Skomorokhov scored kills he held back to guard their tails with no chance of getting any for himself. Kapetan Baturin got one, his fourth. One more kill and he was an ace.

On another excursion they made contact with the 4th Fighter-Interceptor Wing of the U.S. Air Force. Yefgenii recognized them by the yellow slashes on their midsections and tailplanes. Four Sabres of the 334th FIS swung below them, luring the MiGs down into the thicker air. Kiriya ordered the MiGs down. Yefgenii tipped his nose over, opened the throttle and Glinka rolled in behind his wing. The Sabres saw them all the way and splintered into elements. Another flight burst out of the Sun and then it too split up.

At once the noise struck Yefgenii. Men were screaming into their radios in Russian without even a thought of stumbling through words of Korean. A hurricane of air rushed over the cockpit. Shells banged hot stipples into the fuselage like the rivet guns in the factories where the MiGs were built. He strained round to find Glinka. Glinka had left his wing. A Sabre filled the gap. Yefgenii rolled hard over to the left with the Sabre matching the turn. He continued the roll, passing through the inverted and then he was derry-turning right. Over his right shoulder he could see the Sabre tipped over on its side trying to pull round but slipping wider and wider till it disappeared. Yefgenii was straining to hold the turn and gasping with fear. Again he glanced over his left shoulder but saw nothing; he could only hold the turn tight and strain to keep the black iris from closing over his eyes. Then the Sabre came into view. He was off Yefgenii's left wing and wide and loose in the turn. The Sabre had lost a few seconds in misreading the maneuver and now Yefgenii was turning inside him. Acceleration hung weight on Yefgenii's arms and clawed his oxygen mask down his face. If he could hold the turn he'd soon come onto the American's tail and he'd have a shot at him.

Two streaks of metal meteored past Yefgenii's wing. A Sabre was chasing a MiG down to its death. It was Baturin.

A pair of MiGs had isolated a Sabre. Cannon shells jabbed at its tail. The tips of the MiGs' guns bloomed in yellowy-white flickers. Tracers were flashing. Bangs cracked the air but became lost in the roar of engines and rush of wind.

Yefgenii held his turn but another Sabre was sliding in behind him. Its air intake was a dark cave. *"Glinka!"*

Kiriya's MiG soared above him. He was dogging a Sabre that trailed gray smoke. That was five MiGs accounted for, but Yefgenii couldn't locate the other. *"Glinka!"*

Gunfire crackled below. A snake of black smoke wiggled downward, becoming thinner and darker until the plane at its head struck the ground. Baturin had gone in.

Yefgenii was closing on the Sabre ahead but behind him the other was lining up for a shot. *"Glinka, get him off me!"*

Two Sabres swept in behind Kiriya. He glanced back over his shoulder and saw them closing. *"I'm in a world of shit!"*

In despair Yefgenii opened fire on the Sabre ahead of him, flown by a wingman only a year out of flight school, named Gus Grissom. Yefgenii's shells reached out but Grissom was too remote and the shells entered a long arc to earth. Yefgenii rolled into an opposite turn. The borderlands of China and Korea wheeled beneath his nose. Grissom's Sabre swept across the horizon to safety while the one behind was too wide to stay on him. The Yalu River swung into Yefgenii's ten o'clock position and settled there. Its waters looked like cold steel and beyond them lay safety.

The Sabres above weren't letting Kiriya go. *"There's bastards all over me!"*

Yefgenii turned tail to the river and climbed toward them. The second Sabre—the wingman, the shield—broke off to attack him. Yefgenii watched him arc round and calculated he had a few seconds to remove the one Sabre that remained on Kiriya.

He swept in beneath the Sabre and pitched up. As his speed bled away he opened fire. 23-mm shells ripped into the Sabre's belly. The Sabre pulled up and out of the battle and Kiriya was free. "Red Leader, you're clear!"

Now Yefgenii's MiG was slow and sinking, and the American's wingman was swooping toward him for the kill. Yefgenii rolled to the inverted and pulled the stick hard back into a dive. The Sabre chased him down through thickening shelves of air. Yefgenii held two hands on the stick and planted his elbows on his hips. Straining, he drew back the stick and the g-meter began to climb. Shells clattered his fuselage. In his peripheral vision he glimpsed tiny lumps of metal being gouged out of his wing. He held the g-forces till the world righted itself and the Yalu slid down onto his nose. This time he held course for it. At full throttle he'd be there in two minutes.

The MiGs hurtled toward the river with the Sabres in pursuit. At this altitude they were equal for speed. Shells peppered his wing but did no serious damage. Far beyond the wingtip he saw Kiriya's plane flying in parallel.

Optimistic gunfire spattered from the Sabres' guns but they couldn't hope to close in time. As the MiGs neared the Yalu, the Americans, forbidden to trespass into Chinese airspace, broke off and rolled south.

The MiGs regrouped north of the Yalu. Glinka was circling there. "I got separated. A Sabre was on me. I had to cross the river."

Yefgenii waited for Kiriya to challenge Glinka. A few seconds passed. "Recover to base" was all he said.

The MiGs aimed for home and Yefgenii's fury rose. His hand began to strangle the stick. He had to force himself to relax.

In Manchuria the evening was growing cool. A wind was gathering. Yefgenii angled into his space on the dispersal. The widow put up the ladder for him to climb down. "Leitenant Yeremin, welcome home!"

He unhooked the chain from his helmet and slapped the mask from his face.

"Is everything all right, sir?"

He took a moment, then nodded.

"Is there anything I can do?"

"No," he said at once. Then he paused as he left her. "Thank you."

She smiled.

Kiriya marched to his office and shut the door. Instead of becoming the Polk's fourth ace, Kapetan Baturin had gone in. Kiriya began writing the letter that'd be dispatched to some small town where Baturin's family knew nothing of the air war in Korea. They'd be told their son and brother and husband and father had died in a training exercise. He'd get a gravestone in a backwater cemetery somewhere. It was the irony that haunted all these men. A good pilot like Baturin could die out here and his story never be known.

Air surged in great rising breaths that could have been the breaths of the mountains themselves. Yefgenii got up and went out into the night. The terminator crept farther west bringing darkness behind it like black oil slicking over half the earth. The stars rose. They sparkled in patterns he didn't recognize that to him were nameless.

Wind whistled through the trees and whipped his ears. It squeezed between the buildings and rattled their slats. The first spots of rain dotted his face.

Voices distracted him. From the mess the women trudged toward their barracks, having dined separate from the men. The widow paused and held out her palm to catch the rain. She leaned back to feel the drops on her face. In that moment Yefgenii didn't know if she was ugly or if she was beautiful. Perhaps it was true she'd only bring bad luck.

THAT NIGHT brought the first monsoon rain. Streams of mud dribbled between the buildings. Rainwater swelled the trench under the latrines, making them overflow. Turds floated across the mud field till they bumped to a stop or slipped into gutters.

In the barracks they fired the oil stoves that had lain idle all summer. Now they burned with a sooty smell that reminded Yefgenii of Stalingrad's ruins and of its industry.

It poured for a week. With every dawn he woke longing for the clouds to lift so he could fly. Instead a pale gray unmoving mass squatted on the hills and at times even appeared to clog the treetops. Rain pounded the barracks and hangars. Mud, rain, sewage and oil mixed in puddles sliced by spectral lines. These puddles spread out of every depression of the runway, taxiways and dispersal.

He passed his time in the crew hut studying maps and manuals and in the hangars, with his flight reference cards on his lap, memorizing his flight checks. Already he missed the rush of engines. Of the aircraft all that remained was the smell on his clothes of oil and kerosene and hot metal. The smell would be there again at dawn and his body would ache for it like a lost lover.

At night he went to his barrack bed with the feeling that the clouds were suffocating him as much as they were the land. They were denying him his identity. He was a falcon and in the actions of a fighter pilot he expressed his true nature. He wasn't one to dwell on his past because he considered doing so a sign of weakness, but, as he lay in the dark surrounded by the snores and fidgets of the other men, thoughts of his past scratched at him like mice under the floorboards. Before, he'd been worthless; he'd possessed no skills of value to the surrounding society. He'd existed as the statue conceived in stone but inchoate till the first cuts of the sculptor's chisel. What he was now had always lain within; flying had only chipped away the pieces.

The next day the ground crews dug trenches to direct the water off the airfield. Without a word to the pilots who were sitting around the stove repeating old stories, Yefgenii donned his flying jacket and trudged out through the mud to join them. The ground crews paused for a moment to appreciate the spectacle of an officer shoveling mud in the rain, but then they returned to work.

Gnido went to the clothes store to claim a foul-weather jacket and then he went out too.

In the crew hut the men were watching and laughing. Kiriya watched Yefgenii bending his back into each swing of the shovel and little Gnido giving his best to keep up.

Skomorokhov turned to the room. "Let's arrange a transfer—they obviously want to be sappers."

Some of the men laughed but Kiriya's eyes narrowed. "Get out there. Get dressed and get out there."

The men fell into silent resentment but no one argued. Even Kiriya went. When they saw him, the ground crews stood to attention, holding their shovels like rifles. He grinned at how comical they looked but thanked them for their work and invited them to continue.

Skomorokhov approached Yefgenii. The shoulders of his flying jacket were already darkened by rain and mud caked his ankles. "Why the fuck are you doing this?"

Yefgenii said, "The sooner the airfield's drained, Major, the sooner we can fly again."

Skomorokhov snorted and shuffled along the line of men to start digging.

Kiriya took up work alongside Yefgenii. "We've got to get flying again."

"Yes, sir."

Kiriya breathed a long sigh. A film of rainwater dribbled down his face. His wet hair looked thin. Yefgenii could see patches of scalp through it. All at once Kiriya looked old. His next words failed in the splatter of the downpour. "One day this war'll be over." He was racing to clear the water, to open the airfield; he was racing against the inevitability of armistice, and against age itself.

A cumulonimbus loomed. The men watched the great black anvil of cloud slide into the overhead. Wires of lightning cut the sky. Thunder clapped. At once Pilipenko waved the men indoors. They staked their shovels in the ground and began scrambling toward the huts.

Yefgenii stood alone among the rows of shovels pointed into the heavens like lines of crosses over makeshift graves.

Lightning flashed. For a fleeting moment it cracked the sky like eggshell and, as Yefgenii gazed into the cracks, it seemed to him that in that instant he was receiving a glimpse of a great light beyond.

THE RAIN STOPPED after four more days. At last the MiGs soared again out of the damp Antung plain. Below them streams had broken their banks. Fields were flooded. Bogs had swelled into small lakes with ducks skimming their tops.

Yefgenii's mask molded to his face. His harness felt snug. The aircraft fitted him and he fitted it. The picture outside the cockpit represented a universe in its most comfortable and understandable aspect: a patchwork land below, a sky above, and in between a sport of death and survival for men to play.

The rains had given him a glimpse of life without flying, of his life as it would be without his becoming any more than he already was. In an ordinary life, opportunities never come, or they come and aren't taken, or they're taken and squandered. Whatever the reason, the obituary is blank.

Out of the clouds he reappeared into the tall sky. His true self was reborn in this place where his uncommon abilities had both a purpose and a value and he could express that self in the splitting of air and the tearing of metal.

Flying on Kiriya's wing, he spotted the enemy when they were still only black points inching along the horizon. Kiriya gave him the lead till the other pilots could see them too. By then the six of them—Yefgenii and Kiriya, Kubarev, Gnido, Skomorokhov and Glinka—were swooping into combat. As hoped for they were Americans. They were close and Yefgenii was expected to relinquish the lead but he held on to it. Kiriya transmitted, "Red Six, drop back—" but his voice was lost as the aircraft joined in chaos.

Soon a Sabre's tail rose into Yefgenii's crosshairs. He opened fire. He felt the jolts of the guns and then he was passing through clouds of black smoke. When he emerged the Sabre had toppled nose down and was plunging to earth. Seconds later the canopy blasted free and the pilot rocketed clear on his ejector seat.

Yefgenii pulled left with Kiriya now above him and Glinka tracking round on his right wingtip. The g-meter's white needle flicked to the right. He looked all around with his head as heavy as a medicine ball. A Sabre crossed left to right from his ten o'clock position into his two and Yefgenii rolled hard right, holding the nose level with the stick and controlling yaw with right rudder. The stick juddered on the buffet. His shells ripped open the Sabre's wing. The tailplane was bobbing in his crosshairs. Debris broke free and fell behind in a stream of confetti. The American knew his aircraft carried a mortal wound and he was in the long desperate struggle to make it home or else abandon ship. Yefgenii closed for the kill, but silver wings glinted as they swooped in behind him, so with a shriek of anguish he had to let him go. Yet again he twisted his head round. A black rim spread into his visual field. It crept in like liquid. He strained to push the virtual iris back open. He was searching for his shield but Glinka was gone.

Glinka had broken from his wing to pursue the damaged American. The Sabre was making a sluggish turn to get away but Glinka was on him with cannon fire and the American plummeted.

Bursts of R/T were colliding.

"*Got him! Got him! Got him!*"

"*Fuck, fuck, Yeremin, four o'clock, fuck!*" It was Gnido, doing Glinka's job for him.

Now Yefgenii swung left into a max-rate turn with a pair of Sabres in pursuit. Yefgenii twisted round to acquire the Americans and then glanced front to judge attitude and instruments. Hunched into a turn, pulling 6 g, his head flicked left and forward, left and forward. Then Gnido scissored between his tail and the Americans. The Sabres broke off to avoid a collision and Yefgenii was saved, but in a slick move the Sabres switched to Gnido. Gunfire hatched dotted lines along Gnido's fuselage from nose to tail and gouged a lump of flesh and rubber out of his boot. Soon his plane was struggling for height.

Yefgenii shrieked, *"Fucking eject, fucking get out of there!"*

The MiG fell in a long arc. Gnido wept with pain and with foreknowledge of the end. They were a good way south of the Yalu, operating over UN-controlled territory. He could still eject but to be captured would betray the presence of the VVS. If captured and then returned, no doubt he'd be persecuted as a traitor. He stayed in his straps and rode the jet all the way down. When it hit the ground it shattered. The splinters were so small and they were wrought so fast that the aircraft appeared to vanish.

Yefgenii glimpsed Kiriya and Skomorokhov turning in parallel with a pair of Sabres. Glinka had relocated to Kubarev's wing but was operating too high to protect him from attack. A moment later a Sabre punched in behind Glinka. Yefgenii thought of Gnido and of his body smashed because of Glinka's dereliction of duty. Had they been on the ground he could've abandoned Glinka. On the ground his acts meant nothing. But how he conducted himself in the air expressed his values, and in the air a countryman remained a countryman even if he was a coward.

Wisps of smoke trailed past his cockpit as Yefgenii soared back into battle. Some of the wisps curled. Some stretched. Jet-wash had churned this piece of sky into a hundred vortices that kicked his nose and belly and tried to spin his wings. He was still rocking when his guns opened on the Sabre. Fumes puffed out of its engine like a giant string of beads. Yefgenii kept on him. Shells kicked out from his nose into the American's wings and tail. They were ripping up his ailerons and elevators. The Sabre began to buck out of control. Seconds later the pilot ejected. Yefgenii and Glinka were clear.

"Glinka, follow me down!"

With Glinka covering his tail, Yefgenii sank behind the Sabre pair that was scissoring in and out of engagement with Kiriya and Skomorokhov. He opened fire and the wing of the rear Sabre sheared clean off. It spun off to the side and on the second or third spin its fuel tank ruptured. A point of light expanded into a sphere of flame that burned itself out in less than a second. The surviving Sabre swung south for the P'yŏngyang-Wŏnsan line.

Someone was transmitting. "Min fuel."

Kiriya clicked. "Shit, me too, we'll have to let the fucker go."

The MiGs disengaged. Soon the Sabres and the MiGs were pointing home, leaving behind them a sky beaded by puffs of gray and black smoke and beneath the smoke a shower of metal and far beneath that two parachutes blooming like new white flowers on the green and brown oblongs of earth.

In the tower they took Kiriya's transmission that, of the six aircraft that set out, only five were returning to base. The widow looked into the east. She wondered if the young blond leitenant was among the ones coming home. She recognized his plane, felt something this time, for the first time.

Ground crews watched them angle onto the dispersal. All the guns were blackened. All the fuselages were pockmarked. The ground crews dragged chocks on short thick ropes, then, when the pilots cut their engines, wedged the chocks under their wheels.

The widow held the ladder as Yefgenii stepped down the rungs. "Any luck, Leitenant?"

He gazed down at her. He was the biggest of the pilots and he was two rungs off the ground. "Two and a half." He grinned.

She'd never seen him smile. He had a big boyish smile. "Half?" She laughed. "What happened to the other half?"

He realized she had an image in her mind of half an airplane flying home, maybe cut off at the wing roots with the pilot's bare ass hanging out behind the cockpit. "No!" he laughed. She started laughing too. He said, "When the actions of two pilots lead to a kill, each gets half."

Now she blushed for not having known. "Yes, of course, how silly of me." She ducked away and pretended to examine the tires for cuts and creep.

Yefgenii wondered if perhaps he'd sounded too arrogant, too flippant. He'd enjoyed her laughter. He wanted to hear it again soon.

He dropped to the ground and began to stride across the dispersal. The other pilots converged on him from all angles. He glanced over his shoulder. The widow's bottom was large and round. Her back hunched. Her hair was tied back and dirty. She rose from her haunches and as she did so she glimpsed him looking at her.

Glinka was crossing toward him fastest. He was pulling off his glove, holding out his hand. "Yeremin, that Sabre was all over me, you saved my fucking life!"

"That's the fog of war for you, Glinka."

Glinka half-laughed, half-hissed, not sure how to respond, but now the other pilots were around them and Yefgenii turned away.

Skomorokhov waved a glove overhead. "We got three! Yeremin got two!"

Yefgenii smiled. He couldn't stop himself even though little Gnido was dead. "Two and a half."

"Two and half! He's just a boy and he's halfway to an ace already!" Skomorokhov slapped Yefgenii on the back then rubbed his hand as if it had hurt. The men were enjoying the horseplay. Even Yefgenii kept grinning a big wide grin. He was sunning himself in the recognition. The light was shining on him at last. He felt its warmth.

Kiriya scanned the group. His face was set hard. He wasn't yet giving away what he thought about Yefgenii disregarding his order to relinquish the lead. "Who else got anything?"

Glinka stepped up. "Me, boss—a half."

Kiriya said, "What happened to Gnido?" He saw Yefgenii glaring at Glinka. "Yeremin?"

"We were south of the Yalu, boss, when he got hit. He went in rather than eject."

"He put out a mayday?"

"No, but I'm pretty sure that's how it happened."

"He was dead already," said Skomorokhov. "Dead, or wounded, or else he'd've put out a mayday."

Kiriya shrugged. "Sounds like he just went in." He turned and left the dispersal for Ops.

Yefgenii chewed his lower lip. "Gnido took the long fall."

Skomorokhov smoothed hair over his bald patch. "Forget it, Yeremin, it never happened."

Yefgenii returned to the crew hut. He accepted his comrades' congratulations and ignored the dark jealous looks that were barely hidden. Glinka carried on without the least sign of guilt. He urged Pilipenko to mark half a star on the scoreboard. Later he was ordering the ground crew to do the same on his MiG. Yefgenii gazed out of the window as they stenciled a half star on the cockpit while Glinka milked their admiration.

The clock on the wall ticked. The cloud closed into a white ceiling. The temperature fell. The cloud sank lower. Light leaked out of the world. The tower reported the last wave inbound for the airfield.

Yefgenii waited by the latrines. A door opened and Glinka stepped out. "Boss wants to see you." Glinka gulped. He nodded and began to walk toward the buildings. "No, he's this way."

They marched away from the wooden shacks. The lights of the

runway and the tower became remote. Over their heads passed the whine of jets rejoining the circuit. The landing lights of the last wave lit patches of cloud into gleaming white orbs that sailed through the cloud like ghost ships. In the no-man's-land between the dispersal and the runway itself, Glinka could barely see Yefgenii, let alone Kiriya. "Where is he?"

"Here he is." Yefgenii struck him hard on the angle of the jaw. Glinka didn't go down, so Yefgenii hit him again and this time he crumpled to the ground with a sound that was almost a sob.

"My father—"

Yefgenii kicked him in the stomach. "You talk to anyone and I'll find you in your bunk, before morning you'll be dead." The breath hissed out of Glinka and for a few seconds he was openmouthed and gasping. From the ground he gazed up. Yefgenii was becoming a blur.

A jet thundered overhead making the earth tremble. Its landing lights ghosted through the cloud. For a moment they crowned Yefgenii like a halo.

Yefgenii began shrieking at Glinka but the roar of the jet was drowning him out. In a blur Glinka saw him framed beneath a great gleaming white nimbus with his mouth snapping open in brutal shrieks. He rained down blows in between which Glinka caught only snatches of his rant:

"... *war* ..."

"... *work* ..."

"... *team* ..."

"... *country* ..."

"... *glory* ..."

"... *victory* ..."

"... *kill* ..."

Yefgenii's face appeared to be floating within the great white glow and then Glinka saw the light sail on. The jet roar rumbled away. It was the last aircraft of the last wave. He spat blood and tried to get up again but Yefgenii kicked him back down. He kicked him till he became breathless himself and he was spitting too when he shrieked, "Don't you want to kill Americans?"

Glinka coughed in the dirt on all fours. "What's the point of this shitty war?"

Yefgenii struck Glinka again and again. Glinka attempted to slap away the punches and kicks but soon gave in and rolled over. Yefgenii peered down at the crumpled figure. He could beat him to death out here in the darkness. Instead he hoisted Glinka onto his shoulder and carried him the half kilometer back to the transport trucks. The other men saw Glinka's wounds and the bruises on Yefgenii's knuckles and said nothing. Kiriya saw them too but he didn't say anything either.

Night deepened as the men rode back to their barracks. They were in good cheer. Tonight there'd be celebrations in the bar. In the barracks Yefgenii rested on his bunk. His neck ached from the sortie. Pain ran in cords from the back of his head down to his shoulder blades.

The bunk beside him was empty. The sheets had been stripped down to the tatty, yellowing mattress. Someone had already packed Gnido's effects into boxes.

"Come on, Yeremin!" The others were changing out of their flying kit. "Come on, half-ace!"

Yefgenii swung off his bunk and began to change into the uniform that resembled a demobilization suit. It marked him out as a rookie, since his seniors had accumulated enough flying pay to replace theirs with smart civilian dress.

Skomorokhov offered him one of his shirts. Yefgenii took it, sweeping some of Skomorokhov's hairs out of the collar. At that, both men turned away lest their mutual embarrassment about Skomorokhov's hair loss ruin the moment.

In the bar they flew the sortie all over again. Hands performed dogfights, then broke off for more cheap vodka.

Wearing Skomorokhov's shirt, Yefgenii at last looked like a pilot of the 221st IAP, though the buttons appeared ready to pop. Skomorokhov told him he could keep it and bought him a drink for the third or fourth time that night. He dug him in the ribs and winked at him. Yefgenii turned to Pilipenko. "One more vodka and he'll be kissing me."

Over and over again, in an obsessive tic, Skomorokhov smoothed hair over his bald patch. He'd grown the front long and combed it back. On occasions such as these he considered himself more on show than any other man. He was the Polk's leading ace. His status, like that of royalty, surpassed rank.

Kiriya observed the men's high spirits. Morale was up. Toward the end of the night he decided it was time to beckon Yefgenii. He did so with a twitch of his fingers.

"All day I've been thinking what I'm going to do about you, Yeremin. You're supposed to be my wingman. You're not supposed to lead me into battle and nick all the kills for yourself."

"It happened very fast, boss. I wasn't even thinking."

"Bullshit, you were trying to prove what you're capable of."

Yefgenii shifted. He was drunk. He didn't trust himself to say the right thing.

"To cap it all, you beat up Stalin's nephew."

"Glinka is *Stalin's nephew?*"

"So you admit beating him up."

Yefgenii gulped.

Kiriya roared with laughter. "Of course he isn't Stalin's nephew!"

Yefgenii wanted to laugh, but remained too tense.

"Fuck him. I'm moving you up from wing to lead; I'm promoting you to *starshii-leitenant.*"

Yefgenii looked stunned.

"How about 'Thanks, boss'?"

"Thanks, boss."

Kiriya clinked glasses with him. "Enjoy it while you can." He studied this gauche boy standing before him more than a head taller with hair so blond it looked white and eyes that burned blue, and round his chin and neck acne that stippled his creamy skin. He wondered if he might be one of those few whose names the brotherhood would one day incant as if casting a spell.

He said, "This is a war between great nations. Not the same as a great war. But enjoy it—it's the best one we've got."

"Just like this vodka!"

Kiriya grinned. "What do you care? You're a *starshii-leitenant* with two and a half kills!"

"I am, boss!"

The men stayed late. There were more hours of drinking before they drifted back to the barracks.

Out in the darkness, Yefgenii paused. The Moon hung in the east. He breathed. The air carried a smell of pinecones from the forest that divided the base from the airfield.

If he'd been killed yesterday, there'd've been only a blank space where his life had run. Now something of substance was forming in the space that some of us fill and others leave empty. He hated men like Glinka who aimed only to survive this tour so they could return to their lives. Glinka's type didn't long for battle and that which comes with it: the chance to measure themselves against other men. Perhaps only in sport does a man measure himself against another man in any sense that's true. The air battles were sport, but they were also more.

Yefgenii's dream had been born in a sewer and now he could dream of vying with the likes of Jabara for the title of Ace of Aces. He wouldn't dare announce his ambition to the others. They would only laugh.

As it happened, Jabara wasn't even in Korea anymore—he'd been sent back to the U.S. on a publicity tour. At this time the leading ace of the war was Major George A. Davis Jr., with fourteen victories, though Davis wasn't in Korea anymore either. He'd been shot down and killed in February by Kapetan Mikhail Averin of the 148th GvIAP.

"Congratulations, Leitenant."

He spun around. The widow stood a short distance away but he couldn't see much of her except that she was smoking a cigarette. A light breeze wafted the smoke toward him. "On what?"

"Your victories."

"Thank you."

"Do you smoke? I have only this one, but we can share it."

He hesitated.

She smiled. He was still only a boy. She walked toward him and offered him the cigarette.

He took a drag, then handed it back. She stood beside him in silence. They breathed the cold night air that smelled of pinecones. He looked at her. Gnido was dead, but he was alive.

THE AIR WAS SPLIT. Metal clashed like the clash of cymbals. An F-86 floated into his crosshairs and he pulled the trigger. Tracers flickered. Smoke ballooned till it enveloped him and then, when he broke out of it, the Sabre was far below and trailing a plume of soot.

Another day burned and from the brown foothills, 5,000 meters down, came a burst of light. Maybe it came from water or from glass. A few seconds later he glimpsed it again a half kilometer farther south and now he knew it to be the glint of metal that was moving at hundreds of kilometers per hour. He tipped his wings over and dropped the nose. The other five pilots in the *zveno* knew not to question. They followed him down knowing soon enough they'd see what he'd seen. It was a Gloster Meteor. As he closed he identified red-white-and-blue roundels on its wingtips and on its fuselage aft of the wing roots. The British pilot didn't even see the MiGs. He'd never known it was a fight and now it was his death. Yefgenii's shells struck his fuselage and the Meteor swung into the hillside.

At 10,000 meters four B-29s were sailing toward targets in North Korea. Eight Sabres flew escort. In the first pass the fighters scattered. MiGs and Sabres divided into elements and then it became a free-for-all. He isolated a Sabre and his cannons ripped into its tailplane.

The hits went on until smoke burst from its engine, then it stuttered and fell.

He was an ace.

As he thought of medals, a Sabre locked onto his tail. Gunfire peppered his wing. As he pulled round hard he glimpsed splinters leaping off and vanishing into his slipstream. The turn tightened to the buffet. The stick was quaking but the needles held still on their marks as he sucked in short breaths and strained out long ones. Grayness encroached on the rim of his vision and he had to quicken his respiration. He was going at thirty a minute and beginning to feel light-headed. Then the Sabre swam into his gun-sight. He'd outturned it. His finger hammered the trigger and in seconds the American was smoking. Three MiGs were lost but the Sabres had been cut apart and now Yefgenii was climbing up to a B-29. His guns nailed its starboard engines. It was trying to turn but it was big and clumsy and the pilot must've been calling for fighter support but those who were left were down among the MiGs fighting for their own lives. Yefgenii's cannons began to rip the bomber's port engines. The big gun stuttered out of ammunition so he continued with the 23 mm guns. The B-29's cowling splintered. Blades and the shaft of the propeller spiraled apart. The bomber plunged and one by one the men began bailing out.

The widow stenciled the new red stars on his cockpit. She'd started without even asking his permission. She felt a share in his success.

From the Ops hut Kiriya watched her paint on the stars: he had eight. Skomorokhov watched: he had twelve. Pilipenko watched: he had nine. The hunger drove all three. Each man nurtured a dream of becoming Ace of Aces. Behind the camaraderie, dark thoughts poisoned the brotherhood.

Glinka didn't look. He couldn't bear even to meet Yefgenii's eyes. Resentment ate away at him.

The following week Yefgenii claimed two more and overtook Kiriya. Kiriya offered his congratulations but inside it was agony. The boy stood a realistic chance of making the kind of reputation in this war that would crown him a king among kings. The line of stars after his name on the scoreboard in Ops got a little longer. Now only Pilipenko and Skomorokhov had more. They were going up at least twice a day to get kills, to stay ahead. In secret Skomorokhov had started aligning a pair of mirrors to help him comb over his bald patch.

The land was turning brown. Only the pines remained green. In the mornings frost glistened on the bare trees. The snow line was creeping down from the mountains; a soup of cold air seeped onto the plain. Even at lower altitude, the MiGs laid white trails that lasted half the day, and, below them, the Yalu River appeared no longer steel but darker, like the gray of slate.

Stars sparkled overhead as Yefgenii stood under the black sky. He was the youngest ace in the VVS, the youngest jet ace in history, yet in his chest remained a space to be filled. He'd set himself on the long journey to the heavens, to become celestial himself, but he feared no number of kills would be enough. His eyes drifted over the patterns of the stars. Already it felt too late to learn their names. The race against death would be too swift.

He heard footsteps crunch over the hard ground. They approached from the barrack shacks and stopped at the perimeter where he stood.

"I knew it would be you," she said.

"How?"

"You want to be alone. I get that from you, when you come back from flying."

"Now I'm not alone."

"No." Her breath formed a thin vapor. It gave her evanescent tusks. "D'you want me to go?"

"I'm not inclined to tell you what to do."

"What would you say, if you were?"

He appeared not to understand. She smiled at him. She felt so much more experienced than him, and, of course, she was. She had to

71

take his hand to draw him near, and then he understood he had permission.

Soon his palms were gripping the widow's ribs. Her breasts slapped against the backs of his hands as he thrust in and out of her from behind. The smell of her cunt rose into his nostrils. Her wide buttocks shone like ivory in the moonlight. They were globes.

Yefgenii felt his semen rising and he knew in the next few seconds he'd come. He pulled out of her and with two or three jerks of his hand he spurted into the shrubs around their feet. His come clung to the leaves, where it glistened like some strange kind of resin.

She turned. She blinked at him as she straightened up. Only his eyes had color. Though they were his only notable feature she didn't like them. She would have preferred them large and brown but his were animal eyes. He gazed back at her with a look that could have presaged love or murder but in truth was a look that meant he would do nothing and that he felt nothing.

He wondered why he'd acted like this with her. The answer was because it was on the ground. By his actions on the ground he would not be known and therefore they weren't worth troubling over.

The next morning he and Kiriya scrapped over a kill. A damaged Sabre was struggling south trailing black smoke. The MiGs were scissoring over each other's wings to launch the fatal shots. Yefgenii got the American in his crosshairs and blew off his tail.

"You jammy bastard, Yeremin, I had him." They were flying home, crossing the Yalu. Kiriya's laugh sounded hollow as he clicked off.

"Boss, you know you've owed me one for a long time."

"I suppose I have."

In the bar they toasted each other but the muscles in Kiriya's face were twitching. Skomorokhov and Pilipenko raised their glasses too. Every day at the scoreboard the boy's line of stars lengthened. It was creeping toward theirs like a snake, like a monster. Pilipenko stopped calling him "son." Skomorokhov would sometimes slip out of a room when he strutted in.

His eyes were always first to the target. A Sabre kill over Sŏnch'ŏn made him a double ace. There were four more F-86s and then a U.S. Navy F9F-2 Panther that swung out into the Sea of Japan but lost power from the damage his guns had done to its engine. It toppled forward toward the sea. The canopy burst open and a moment later the pilot was launched out over the gray waters. A white parachute bloomed. The sea broke the plane's back and flung up a plume of spray.

He led six MiGs after a pair of Sabres. The Americans fought with courage but they were outnumbered. The first struck trees. He damaged the second but before he could finish him off the pilot made it over the Nan and then ejected. So now he'd overtaken Pilipenko. In the 221st IAP, only Major Skomorokhov had scored more kills. The moment Skomorokhov heard the news he marched into Kiriya's office and demanded to go up on the next wave. They both went up, Kiriya and Skomorokhov, but for them the sky had emptied. Kiriya contained his emotions but it felt like dying inside. Skomorokhov hit the runway so hard he burst a tire.

On Yefgenii's twentieth birthday there were drinks in the bar. Kiriya led the toasts. Despite his own pain, he could admire Yefgenii's triumphs: it was white envy. He kissed him on both cheeks. "Congratulations, *Kapetan* Yeremin." Pilipenko threw an arm round his shoulders. Yefgenii Yeremin had become the youngest *kapetan* in the VVS.

Glinka was still a *starshii-leitenant*. His eyes drifted to Skomorokhov's. Both men had the same look of a gap in them that'd never be filled.

The next day, once airborne, they tested their guns as usual and then Yefgenii led them over the Yalu. From 15,000 meters they swooped into a squadron of Sabres. In the first pass he got one but his wingman was killed. *"Glinka, get on my wing!"* Yefgenii's head swept round the cockpit. *"Glinka!"*

Glinka was climbing out of the battle. Yefgenii saw him crossing above. Two more MiGs were battling a Sabre pair. Glinka looked down and saw Sabres converging on his leader. It was a simple move to tilt in their direction and open fire but instead he turned away and kept on climbing.

Yefgenii was alone and vulnerable. A pair of Sabres had seen him and were swooping in behind. He jerked his aircraft into a sharp evasive turn and in doing so he spotted Skomorokhov turning in from the edge of the battle. *"Sko! Get the fuckers off me! Sko!"*

Skomorokhov watched Yefgenii's MiG curve along the horizon. Two Sabres were banking round behind him. Cloud matted the sky and the land. Against white, the aircraft stood out in isolation. Their dance was the only living thing in creation. They were cut off from the world.

The leading Sabre opened fire on Yefgenii. *"Sko!"*

Skomorokhov tilted away. He watched over his shoulder. His heart was pounding. Sweat chilled on his skin. To desert a comrade was unthinkable but so was losing his place at the top of the mountain.

Yefgenii pulled round. Tracers were flashing past his cockpit. He saw a Sabre climbing onto Glinka's tail. *"Glinka, check six!"*

Glinka snapped his MiG into a turn. The move was so sudden and violent that the airflow ripped away. Yefgenii glimpsed Glinka's wings glinting in the sun. They were tilting up to the vertical. For a split second the MiG hung in perfect stillness on its side. Then the wings shuddered and it stalled. Glinka plunged straight down and struck one of the Sabre pair that was closing on Yefgenii. The Sabre's wing sheared clean off. It spun away and on the second or third rotation its fuel tank ruptured. Glinka's MiG divided into a thousand nuggets and Yefgenii could even imagine them tinkling as they sprinkled into the air.

Someone shouted *"Taran!"* It might've been Skomorokhov but Yefgenii couldn't be sure. *Taran,* the ramming maneuver—on any other day he'd've laughed at the suggestion. The *zveno* was scattered and disorganized and Yefgenii ordered them to run for home.

"Taran!" Skomorokhov repeated in the crew hut. He wore a strange expression as if he found the whole thing hilarious. His heart was still drumming from his betrayal. He hated himself for it but wasn't glad that Yefgenii had survived. He felt he'd learned that his competitive drive knew no moral limit and that this was a thing to be proud of.

Kiriya turned to Yefgenii. "Yeremin?"

"It wasn't a ramming maneuver, sir. It was a fuck-up. I'd call it a midair collision."

In his office Kiriya considered his report to Moscow. The officials there would know nothing of the sortie apart from his dispatch. His account would enter the records. It would become history; it would become the truth.

With one act, Glinka's life would be defined, and it was up to Kiriya to choose the definition. He began to write. Cornered by the Americans, Glinka committed the supreme self-sacrifice, the ramming maneuver. He took one with him rather than surrender. This was the stuff of comic books. Kiriya was recommending Glinka for a posthumous Order of Lenin. He'd be remembered as a great hero and a great pilot.

As winter approached, the flying days became shorter, but it wasn't long before Yefgenii overtook Skomorokhov. The news came down from the tower. Skomorokhov nodded. He felt the other men's eyes on him. He was deposed from his royal status and now he knew they'd all see him the same way he saw himself—as tubby and balding.

As Yefgenii returned to base, frost glistened on the edges of his canopy. Sweat chilled under his suit. When he took off his mask, his breath condensed into a small cloud. He had more kills than any pilot in the 221st. He was a Hero of the Soviet Union, had won the Order of Lenin and only Pepelyaev and Sutyagin had more jet kills in the entire VVS.

Kiriya would often seek him out in public places so that the ground crews could see them talking together, the boss and the spectacular young hero, in a mutual reflection of celestial glory. He'd taken to calling him "Yo-Yo". Kiriya chose to believe that he was the Sun to Yefgenii's Moon; the boy shone with a brightness he supplied.

Anyone who got a kill wanted to report it first to Yefgenii. His approval had begun to count more than Kiriya's. He couldn't go anywhere on the base without someone calling out a greeting. At dinner, the rookies would keep a place for him at their table, and be crestfallen if he gravitated to a rival clique. If he approached, their hearts would race, like teenagers with a crush.

Pilipenko had accepted him as his equal in the air despite his junior rank, but, now that Yefgenii had surpassed them all, Pilipenko was at a loss to relate to his status. The best approach was not to consider him a man at all but a myth. His gifts were inscrutable, his achievements imaginary and his name could only be whispered, never said aloud.

When with swooping hands they'd recount their stories in the bar, it was Yefgenii's everyone wanted to hear. Skomorokhov would follow with one of his own—the day he became an ace, how he became a double—but it was never enough. At one time he'd been a prince; unburdened by Kiriya's responsibilities to command, he'd been in a position to dispense grand favors. A word of praise to a young pilot would be greeted with fawning appreciation. A stinging put-down to a runt would win laughter.

To a group of rookies Skomorokhov recounted how he was bounced by a pair of Sabres and ended up with smoke in the cockpit but still made it home. He received no looks of wonder. Instead the rookies turned to Yefgenii for his reaction. Skomorokhov flushed with resentment. "Yeremin, ever flown with worse viz inside the cockpit than out?" No one laughed at the joke.

Yefgenii hadn't called him "sir" or "Major" for weeks. "You know, Sko, I think the superior pilot uses his superior judgment to stay out of situations that test his superior ability."

Skomorokhov flung his vodka glass into the fire.

Now, as Yefgenii climbed into the east, a dusting of snow lay across the fields below. The peaks of the Changbai Range were shrouded in fog, but the Yalu remained clear, the dividing line between the offices of mortals and the arena of those who wore wings. His sharp eyes hunted two more kills and a share in another and when he landed back at Antung the runway was hard as stone with bands of frost fringing its shoulders.

The widow had instructed the other women not to return to their barracks until at least an hour after dinner. They knew it was so he could visit her but no one dared object. He was the glory of the 221st encapsulated in one man. To deny him would bring misfortune.

They had sex in her bunk and as usual he withdrew before the end. Her fingers inched down his body, teasing him; she laughed; then she took him in hand and in mouth and in a few seconds he came.

Afterwards she smoked a cigarette. "You've never told me how long you're here for."

"I don't know. It could all end tomorrow."

She passed him the cigarette. He drew in a breath. The tobacco was stale.

"I know. I meant how long's your tour?"

"I'm here as long as I'm needed."

"But don't you get homesick?"

"This is my home."

The next day he claimed his twentieth victory. As the MiGs returned Skomorokhov's hand strangled the control stick. He'd gone from being ace of the 221st to picking up Yefgenii Yeremin's scraps. He let the boy's MiG float into his crosshairs. He crooked his finger round the trigger. MiG *529*'s exhaust hung behind the cross. *"Dugh-*

dugh-dugh-dugh-DUGH!" Skomorokhov shouted as he released the trigger. His mouth was laughing but his eyes weren't.

By the time the jets were being towed to the hangars, snow was falling in flurries, yet the whole base must've been on the dispersal to greet him. They carried him on their shoulders. At twenty years of age Yefgenii Yeremin was a quadruple ace. He was the pride of the 221st and the spirit of a nation.

AS THE NEW YEAR OPENED, the war—the half war, the shitty war—languished in stalemate. The status quo on the Korean Peninsula had been reestablished at the cost of more than four million lives and the public in America, Great Britain, Australia and Canada were turning against their countries' involvement, but the competition to become Ace of Aces continued to beguile them. It was front-page news. Major James Jabara had returned to the war and begun adding to his victories. Captain Manuel "Pete" Fernandez and Captain Joseph McConnell were closing in on the score of fourteen kills claimed before his death by George Davis. These men were household names like Marciano, Fangio, and Hogan were household names.

Soon winter receded. The pine and larch shed their frosting. White peeled off the runway. As a clear night opened, the Milky Way arched like a backbone. The stars wheeled round night after night and he watched them not knowing what they were other than points of light. Yefgenii was looking up to be told his place. He looked inward and wondered the same.

The Starshina saw him enter one of the hangars. He appeared

to be carrying a tin of paint. The Starshina said nothing. No one questioned him anymore.

It was still dark as tow trucks rolled out the MiGs. Soon gray light seeped down onto the plain, finding MiG *529* parked in the first slot of the dispersal, and astern of the wing root the PLAAF markings had been overpainted with the single large red star of the VVS. A hammer and sickle adorned the tail fin.

The pilots strutted out from the Ops hut. One by one they stopped in their tracks but Yefgenii kept on walking.

Kiriya and Pilipenko came out. Five pilots peered at Kiriya for an order. He gazed at the red star of his country, the hammer and sickle. He smiled. He said, "Go. Follow Yo-Yo."

Pilipenko whispered, "Boss, what if he gets shot down?"

Kiriya shook his head and waved the pilots out. "Go. Fly!"

Yefgenii led them over the river and into battle. A pair of Panthers from the U.S. Navy's VF-51 were cruising east to their carrier in the Sea of Japan. He hit the first with a burst from his 23-mm guns and must have found a fuel tank because the Panther bloated into an orange globe that for its short life became a second sun in the wide Korean sky. The second Panther he struck with his 37-mm cannon. It swung out to sea, but power bled out of its damaged engine and it stalled and toppled. The canopy burst open and the seat rocketed out; a parachute bloomed and the pilot dangled over the gray waters.

Next Yefgenii tipped his wings over and pulled north. The compass bobbed round and the DI tracked a half circle. As Yefgenii rolled out onto his heading he glanced over his shoulder out to sea and glimpsed a dark blue Sikorksy skimming the waves toward the ejected Panther pilot.

He slid the throttle forward and rolled his MiG's wings over and pulled a max-rate turn back out to sea. He let down to two hundred meters. The pilot bobbed on his life raft, waving his arms above his head to signal the chopper.

Yefgenii opened fire then pulled up hard as blood flashed behind the glass panels of the Sikorsky's cockpit and the tail rotor whirled out across the sea. The helicopter corkscrewed straight down into the water. The winchman bailed out but the pilot never appeared and when Yefgenii looked back for the last time the winchman was clambering aboard the life raft while the helicopter's broken pieces bobbed on the waves.

At Antung the first *zveno* touched back down and the second began to roll off the dispersal. A report had been passed down from the tower and Kiriya and Pilipenko strolled out to offer their congratulations. Today Yefgenii Yeremin had surpassed Pepelyaev. He'd scored more jet kills than any pilot who'd ever flown.

The Starshina had one of his men ready to stencil three more stars alongside Yefgenii's cockpit. "Polkovnik, what should I do about *529*'s markings?"

"Do?"

"Yes, sir, should I make them regulation?"

The whine of the jets was creeping up the taxiway. Pilipenko had to raise his voice. "Yes, boss, do it for Yeremin's sake—there may be reprisals."

Kiriya shook his head. "Pip, a hero can always fall into disfavor. He can be killed. He can be forgotten." The jets were swallowing his words now. Pilipenko could only read his lips. "But a legend never dies."

Out at sea a second Sikorksy picked up the men from the life raft and transported them to the carrier USS *Essex*. The Panther pilot and the winchman both reported that the MiG had borne the Soviet star on its fuselage and the hammer and sickle on its tail. VF-51 officers came in and out of the wardroom. One of them—an ensign who was the same age as Yefgenii Yeremin—ladled out a helping of soup from the pot on the stove. The men were talking about the Russian. The ensign, whose name was Neil Armstrong, didn't say anything. He'd flown fifty combat missions, but he still preferred to listen.

"Shooting up the rescue ship—that Honcho was one son of a bitch."

"Shit. Ivan's here. Ivan the Honcho."

"Ivan the Terrible."

D AY AFTER DAY Ivan the Terrible entered the arena. The red star drifted over flooded paddies. The battles that followed were chaos. MiGs and Sabres looped and scissored. From a flicker of tracers and a flash of metal, a globe of fire ballooned, then out of that fire burst the MiG with the red star on its body, the hammer and sickle on its tail and scorch marks on its wings that spun streamers of evanescent gray smoke. Below him a Sabre toppled back to Earth. Some days their trails floated in the sky for hours after the battle, some ending in the knot of an impossible maneuver, but his always pointed home.

Every pilot wanted to fly with him and even the lowliest *ryadavoi* would ask if he was going up that day. Some would even run up into the tower for an update on his mission and then convey each installment to the men on the flight line as if they were reading episodes from a comic book. "Kapetan Yeremin is engaging the Americans!" They'd applaud. "Kapetan Yeremin is returning with a kill!" They'd cheer. They'd take turns waiting on the dispersal to paint the newest star on his cockpit.

The widow gazed into the east, counting the planes as they reappeared. When one or more were missing she'd turn from the sky and devote herself to her work. She wouldn't look up again until they were rolling up the taxiway and she could read their markings. *529* with the big red star on its fuselage would always be there, would always be leading the others back in. When he cut his engine, she'd swing the chocks under the wheels and push the ladder up to the cockpit. She'd ask, "Any luck, Kapetan?" and he'd answered as if to any man, and this was how it would be apart from their times alone in her bunk or, if the night were mild, out in the wild grass on the edge of the woods.

He was leading a *zveno* south when they encountered a flight of F-84 Thunderjets from the 136th Fighter-Bomber Wing. He got one. Skomorokhov got one. A U.S. Navy exchange pilot, Lieutenant Walter Schirra, got one of theirs.

The survivors dispersed. Yefgenii watched a pair of Thunderjets turn south for the P'yŏngyang-Wŏnsan line. He glanced at his gauges. "I'm still good for fuel. Sko?"

"Me too."

"Come on, let's get 'em."

Yefgenii and Skomorokhov went to full throttle and began the chase. With every passing minute their fuel burned, but with every passing minute they closed on the Thunderjets.

Cloud cover obscured the Nan River but Skomorokhov could see bits of P'yŏngyang looking like a gob of bubblegum stamped on the land. Yefgenii was just ahead of him. He'd already opened fire. There was no chance of hitting the Americans but it might provoke them into doing something suicidal like turning back for a fight.

Skomorokhov let Yefgenii's MiG float through his crosshairs. They were far from home, surging into battle, with no witnesses. A dead man might become a legend but he wouldn't be around to claim the spoils of victory, the status, the adulation. He throttled back.

"Sko, what's happening? Keep up, will you?"

Skomorokhov didn't want to desert a comrade, but if Yeremin was reckless enough to chase two jets toward their own base then that was his own lookout. "Sorry, I'm already at min fuel." He had plenty left, of course.

"I thought you had enough."

"Must be something wrong, got to turn back."

Skomorokhov watched Yefgenii press on after the Americans. There was still a fair distance to close and two of them to tangle with. He swung north knowing Ivan the Terrible wouldn't give up the chase.

The other MiGs were orbiting just south of Sinanju, waiting for them. "Where's Yeremin, Major?"

"I told him to turn round. He wouldn't listen. We can't wait here. We're too low on fuel."

"We can't leave him."

"Sorry, no option. Recover to base."

Word came down from the tower that only four ships were coming back. They touched down and taxied up to the dispersal. As the minutes expired, more and more people gathered on the airfield. Some of the youngsters—no more than boys—were weeping. The pilot of the downed MiG had been a new *leitenant*. No one even mentioned his name.

Kiriya passed binoculars to Skomorokhov to search the column of sky above the river, but his hands were trembling so much that he couldn't focus. He'd abandoned Yeremin to his fate. It was at worst a sin of omission. If the boy believed himself indestructible, then he got what he deserved. "He's out of fuel by now, boss, he's not made it."

Shelves of stratus streaked the eastern dome of sky. A blue haze colored in the gaps. The wind sock was fluttering but pointing toward them, to the west. "There's still a chance," Kiriya said.

He took back the binoculars. He was hoping Yefgenii had broken free of the Thunderjets. He could've outclimbed them and at 10,000 or 15,000 meters been flying in the best configuration to conserve fuel. He'd be running on vapors for a time and then his jet would stutter and flame out. About now he'd be entering a glide. There was still a chance he could stretch it all the way home. With the airplane held in the precise gliding attitude, with every control force trimmed out to perfection, with airspeed gauged against altitude, with the wind in the right direction . . . with all these things, there was still a chance. He was the spirit of the 221st.

The Starshina was marshaling fire trucks onto the airfield. They were lining up at the end of each taxiway with their lights flashing, waiting.

Every man and woman of the Antung VVS Station seemed to be out on the airfield now. No one said a word. Even the pilots of the next wave who were supposed to be taxiing out had climbed down from their cockpits and were peering into the east. The widow ensured the chocks were fixed against the mainwheels and the pitot-head covers were in place. Hers was the one head not turned up to the sky.

The Starshina ran to Kiriya bearing a short-wave radio. A message was being relayed from the tower. "There's no reply to his call sign. There's been no reply for twenty minutes."

With a tilt of his head Pilipenko ordered the Starshina to give them some privacy. "Boss, I'm as sorry as anyone, but there's a whole base away from their stations and six ships waiting for the order to roll out."

Skomorokhov was pacing up and down, unable to settle. He said nothing.

Kiriya gazed into the east. Some of the men had stopped looking into the skies. Their heads were down. Some looked ready to fall to their knees.

Then the Starshina pointed. A drop of mercury was condensing out of the haze.

Kiriya trained the binoculars on the sighting. The MiG was floating down from 5,000 meters. It left no trail—he was long out of fuel, in the long glide back to earth.

"Yo-Yo."

The pilots and ground crews gasped, then a cheer went up. Skomorokhov's hands managed a clapping action. The weeping boys wiped their faces, laughing in embarrassment. The widow looked up from her work. She could see him now. He was over the paddies and, even if he didn't make it back to the runway, he could eject over friendly territory.

Pilipenko took a turn with the binoculars. "He's going to make it."

Skomorokhov mumbled, "Worse. The fucker's going to hit the runway." Maybe what he hated most about Yefgenii Yeremin was that he was tall enough to see his bald patch even from the front.

The MiG floated down the glide slope toward the airfield. For a minute or two it looked as if he might sink into the undershoot but he held his nerve and his wheels struck the dirt at the very beginning of the strip. The plane rolled about a quarter of the way along before coming to a halt.

Fire trucks sped toward the plane. Kiriya signaled to a tow truck and leapt aboard. People were hanging off the sides and waving their arms as if the war had been won.

The widow squatted in the back of a jeep. As it hurtled over the dirt, a rush of air scrambled her hair into her eyes. She blinked and brushed it aside.

That night in her bunk as she smoked a cigarette she said, "Did you ever think you wouldn't get back?"

"Yes."

"Why did you chase the Americans?"

"'Why?'"

"If you knew you might not get back?"

"If I didn't chase them, who would I be?"

Ivan the Terrible had claimed both Thunderjets he'd pursued south to the P'yŏngyang-Wŏnsan line and five more Sabres in the month that followed. He was by for the Ace of Aces. Cheering ground crews carried him on their shoulders from his cockpit; that night Kiriya toasted him in the bar and then in private he said, "Your honor is the honor of the 221st. I'm going to recommend you for a second Gold Star or a second Order of Lenin. Name it."

"If I can name it, then I name it for Gnido. He earned it. Make it his."

Kiriya gazed back at him. He would have to inform the authorities that new information had come to light. Gnido was already forgotten by just about every man in the Polk, a rookie who'd come and gone and made no mark. It was a considerble inconvenience for a matter he regarded as so unimportant. But he nodded. Who could refuse Ivan the Terrible?

Skomorokhov died the following week. He got a kill—his sixteenth—and was just turning to see what was behind when a shell ripped through his canopy and opened a 10-centimeter gash in his neck. In reflex his hand went up to the wound but he was unconscious before he'd even looked at the blood on his glove and dead before his plane hit the ground.

Spring bloomed at last. The fields lay like felt. In the trees, eggs were hatching. Chicks shivered into the world, their feathers sticky with yolk; it was impossible to believe they'd be taking wing in only a few weeks. The MiG with the great red star on its body and the hammer and sickle on its tail soared above it all. Ivan the Terrible churned the air into a vortex that no one could see but that could turn the wings of any aircraft that came his way.

NEWS CAME FROM MOSCOW. Joseph Stalin had suffered a stroke. Kiriya took the morning's briefing himself and broke the news to the men. Some wanted to grieve, some to rejoice, but they kept their sentiments to themselves. It was as if they were waiting to receive a diktat on what to feel.

That night Yefgenii lay with the widow under the stars. They made love while above them planets crept along the line of the ecliptic. As usual he withdrew at the last moment and his semen congealed in the grass.

She peered at him. "You don't want children?"

He didn't answer. The smoke of dying airplanes, the blooms of parachutes, the flames of victory—they were his children.

"We must all have children. One day. Or else there'll be nothing left behind when we're gone."

In that moment he thought that, though he didn't love the widow, perhaps he should marry her. He should marry her because she understood that men must die.

Four days later Stalin did. Within a month prisoners of war were exchanged at Panmunjom. Though hostilities continued between Communist and UN forces, it seemed an armistice was nearing. Eager to analyze Soviet technology, the Americans announced a reward of $100,000 and political asylum to any Communist pilot who delivered a MiG-15 into UN hands.

Kiriya invited Yefgenii into his office. "Any day now, this war will be over." He waited for Yefgenii's reaction. The Ace of Aces had thirty-four kills. Perhaps he still expected to claim his thirty-fifth.

"I know."

Kiriya unlocked a cabinet in the corner of the room and took out a bottle of vodka. "Not the piss they've got in the bar. I've been keeping it for a special occasion. I thought maybe when I became an ace . . . then I thought maybe when you became Ace of Aces . . . still . . . let's drink now, Yo-Yo, before it's too late."

He poured shots into two glasses. "To war." They looped their drinking arms and downed the shots.

Kiriya refilled the glasses. This time they sipped. "I never opened this bottle because I thought none of those occasions was an end in itself. But now I know for certain they'll finish, these days of sport and glory."

He poured two more shots. They looped arms and gulped. Kiriya studied his empty glass. "Sometimes, in life, we don't win or lose. We just run out of time."

Kiriya took off alone without filing a flight plan. The tower requested his intentions. "A general handling sortie. I'll be operating this side of the border." Of course the controller cleared him and Kiriya climbed into the east, over the Yalu into North Korean airspace. He turned south along the coast and opened the throttle. He surged toward P'yŏngyang and soon the city passed under his port wing. He crossed the Nan River and continued south, soaring over the 38th Parallel.

Eventually an airfield drifted onto his nose. He could make out the Kimp'o flight lines—Sabres with their silver backs, some with yellow flashes and some with black-and-white checkerboards on their tails, their wings swept back like darts. Soon a pair rolled out and climbed up toward him.

Kiriya clicked through the frequencies. He passed a squeal and dialed back to it. American voices were exchanging messages in volleys. He understood none of it, of course. Even when someone addressed him in Korean, it remained futile.

The Sabres were sitting out on each of his wings. He could see the pilots signaling to him. Each was jabbing a single finger down toward the airfield below. Kiriya understood. They wanted to escort him down. *They thought he was defecting!*

Kiriya threw back his head and laughed. He released his drop tanks and let down into the thicker air to give them an even greater advantage. The Americans dropped their tanks and swept in behind him for the kill but the first evasive turns he made were quick and tight and successful and it occurred to him then that he should at least make some sport of it all. More Sabres were scrambling off the Kimp'o tarmac. Soon four of them were chasing Kiriya north, west, south, whichever way he swung. He was running out of fuel and if he ejected there was always the chance his pistol would jam. That would be his luck.

The Sabres pushed him down to the deck and the first tracers began flickering past his canopy. He leveled the wings and raised the tail to make it an easier target. Even if they could piece his body together, with no insignia on his uniform and no papers, they'd never know who he'd been in life, or what he'd achieved, if anything.

IN APRIL OF 1953, during a raid against the Suiho Dam, Joseph McConnell had been shot down but had steered his stricken plane out over the East China Sea, where he'd ejected and been pulled out of the water. His conqueror that day had flown a MiG-15 bearing markings of the People's Liberation Army Air Force and had been officially recorded as being of Chinese or North Korean origin. The pilot had been Kapetan Semyon Fedorets of the 913th IAP.

McConnell went on to amass sixteen victories, surpassing the tallies of Jabara and Fernandez and the late George Davis to become the Korean War's assumed Ace of Aces, celebrated as the leading jet ace of all time. All three men—McConnell, Jabara and Fernandez— were posted home early to eliminate the risk of their being lost in combat, such was their propaganda value.

Unsung pilots weren't just Soviet. There were many fighting on the UN side who remained nameless. They knew McConnell's score lay beyond their powers. His wasn't the name on their lips as they launched into MiG Alley. Another was being whispered on the flight lines and in the officers' clubs late at night, whispered as if it were a curse. That name was Ivan the Terrible, and, for every pilot who dreaded ever meeting him, another hungered to vanquish a legend and in so doing become a legend himself.

On the last day of the war, the MiG-15, displaying the great red star on its body, the hammer and sickle on its tail, and thirty-four little red stars on its cockpit, accelerated down the Antung strip. Behind him the clouds of dust raised by the aircraft were settling back onto the ground. Within seconds they'd vanished, become part of the earth again.

He led a *zveno* of six MiGs east to the Yalu and then over the border. The air was saturated with damp and their trails of ice crystals weren't vaporizing, but instead were spreading into ribbons of cirrocumulus artifacta that feathered all the way back into Manchuria.

Hurtling north to intercept them were eight ships of the 25th FIS. An exchange pilot from the U.S. Marine Corps led one element. His name was Major John Glenn and he'd already bagged two kills in the last week. His wingman in the Marines had been Ted Williams. Ted Williams was a baseball star. In the season of 1941, Williams achieved the highest batting average of all time, while his rival Joe DiMaggio amassed a fifty-six-game hitting streak. The seasons light up, but then they're gone forever.

Ivan the Terrible saw the Sabres first, of course. They were sailing 5,000 meters beneath. He recognized who they were by the checkerboard patterns on their tailplanes. "Drop tanks," he said.

He pulled the lever and as he did so he felt a clunk and the airplane lurched to the right. The port tank was tumbling down to earth but the other remained slung under his wing. He'd got a hung tank. The asymmetrical weight and drag were tilting the right wing down into a turn and swinging the nose round in the same direction. He trimmed out all the forces and threw the lever again, but the tank wouldn't drop.

"Fuck it. Let's go."

They swooped down into the Sabres. He picked out the trailing plane and his guns hammered down at its tail and spine and shattered the glass of the canopy. He saw the pilot's helmet cracking open like a nutshell and the spurt of blood before the aircraft listed and began the long fall.

He sailed over the others but they were already splitting into element pairs. He called, "Break!" and the MiGs astern selected their opponents; it was the last order he gave; from now on it was every man for himself.

As he began his first turn back into the arena, he glimpsed over his right shoulder that three Sabres were following but were crossing each other's lines to get on his tail. They'd seen the red star. They were battling each other to be the one who conquered Ivan the Terrible.

He rolled hard right, as the drag of his hung tank would help the turn. Ahead of him appeared a Sabre side-on. His cannons ripped into its fuselage from wings to tail and an orange globe ballooned out of its rear. Its forward section broke off and plummeted. As it fell, it crossed a trail of black smoke being left by a MiG that was also on its way down.

A Sabre barrel-rolled in behind a MiG and its guns began ripping apart the tailplane. That was Glenn scoring his third kill. Another Sabre nailed another MiG; a MiG was chasing a damaged Sabre to its death.

Above him a Sabre floated into view. He pitched up and opened fire. Metal showered from its belly. Pieces the size of hubcaps were tumbling down, spinning fine threads of smoke as they went. The Sabre banked hard left and Yefgenii struggled to match the turn.

The first of the three Sabres behind him had closed. Tracers flickered past the canopy. Again he swung hard over to the right and tried to pull round. The Sabre reappeared behind his right wing. Gunfire hammered along his fuselage. Pain exploded in his right leg. A .22-caliber shell had pierced the cockpit armor and buried itself in his thigh. Blood dribbled over his knee and he could smell the singeing of his own flesh.

He dropped his flaps and throttled back. The Sabre flew by and he managed to fire off a burst into its tail. Black smoke billowed and the American swung south, running for home. At the same time he glimpsed two trails of soot pointing north. Two MiGs were damaged and fleeing for their lives with Sabres in pursuit.

Now he was alone with two Sabres. He throttled up again and the aircraft crabbed and banked to the right. He leveled the wings, kicked in some rudder with his good leg and trimmed it all out again. In despair he pushed and pulled the lever but the tank wouldn't drop, it was never going to drop.

The Sabre pair locked in behind him. They were leader and wingman. The leader opened fire. Pings and clangs reverberated along the fuselage as Yefgenii swung up and over in a barrel roll. He passed through the inverted and out of the top of his gaze he glimpsed the land tumbling round and the Sabres entering the same maneuver. As he rolled round and then pulled up to the horizon the Sabres appeared on his right wingtip and he jerked the stick across in that direction striking his leg and making himself shriek in pain.

He sliced between the two Sabres. Now he had the wingman on his tail and the lead ahead. He banked hard left and for a fleeting moment had the lead in his crosshairs. His shells tore off the Sabre's tailplane and the aircraft veered into a flat spin. A second later the canopy flicked up, the pilot rocketed clear and his parachute blossomed.

The remaining Sabre opened fire into Yefgenii's tail. He pitched forward and began to dive. The Sabre looped in a split-S and followed him down through thickening bands of air and cloud. He made a sudden pitch up, pulling round hard to the right. For a split second the g-meter flicked to 8. Every joint in the aircraft's body groaned. The hung tank ripped free, shed like a teardrop.

Now he was sleek and maneuverable and, though he was in the weaker position, he had a fighting chance. If he could get the turn going he could kill this Sabre and live to make it home. The MiG began to judder round, nibbling the buffet, pulling 6 g. Yefgenii was gasping and straining, gasping and straining.

The Sabre was making the same turn, describing a circle in the sky. They were at opposite ends of a diameter, canopy to canopy; the pilots could see each other. Their heads were still. Theirs could've been the heads of mannequins.

He held the turn tight. Every needle was motionless on its mark of speed or power or altitude. Any small error lost him valuable energy and gave his opponent an advantage of speed or of height or of turn. He was still pulling 6 g and straining. He was getting tired. The gray iris started to close and he had to strain harder to get his eyesight back. He had to settle for tunnel vision. When he breathed in he lost half his field. Still he wasn't gaining on the American. The turn continued, the great circle in the sky, canopy to canopy, and whoever tired first would perish.

The minutes passed. He felt sick and light-headed. Blood spilled out of his boot. His hands and feet were tingling. His fingers were turning numb inside his gloves. He peered up through a haze of sweat with his field of vision contracted to a narrow coin of light in which the Sabre's swept wings and yellow flashes were tracking round the diametrically opposite patch of sky.

Neither man was going to surrender. The American was a wing-man, probably a first lieutenant with only a few missions to his credit, an officers' club wallflower. But he could fly. Now he was on the brink of being the man who brought down Ivan the Terrible.

They went on turning at full throttle. They were burning fuel, liter after liter, and maybe the loser would just be the poor bastard who ran out first.

To Yefgenii the American appeared to be losing height. He glanced at his instruments. With a massive strain he pushed open the fringe of his vision. As it opened he read the gauges and they told him his turn was flat. The American had made a tiny error in his turning attitude and it had accumulated into a height difference.

Yefgenii let the nose sink a fraction toward the horizon. His airspeed increased by 10 kilometers per hour and he used them to tighten the turn. He was pulling 6½ g but he was getting inside the American. He sucked in breaths and pushed them out but the nickel of light in which the Sabre sparkled was getting smaller. He fought to keep the straining maneuver going. Sweat pooled in the well of the seat. He could feel the dampness seeping through his pants.

The American was drifting onto his nose past two o'clock then a minute later he was on one o'clock. They kept on turning. He was floating into Yefgenii's gunsight. His left wingtip brushed the crosshairs. The Sabre was bobbing but Yefgenii held the turn. With every breath in, the iris closed and with every strain out it opened. Every time it opened the Sabre's tail neared the crosshairs. He breathed in again. Blackness closed round him. He pushed out. The tail was there. He opened fire. His cannons ripped into the American's tail. He held the trigger even when he was blind and when he could see again he saw black smoke billowing out of the Sabre's jet exhaust.

The Sabre rolled out of the turn and tried to accelerate away. Yefgenii leveled his wings and let the stick forward. The g-force abated. He could see again. He could breathe again. Blood had congealed into a jelly that coated his seat and boot and rudder pedal. The needle of his fuel gauge pointed at the stark red line at the bottom of the scale. The Sabre was hurtling into the west where the sun had wheeled round and now glimmered through clouds heaping over Korea Bay. The aircraft had dropped to a few hundred meters and was running for the coast. Yefgenii could turn north and see how far he could get before his fuel burned out, but if he went down and the Sabre made it home then the American would be entitled to claim a victory over Ivan the Terrible.

Yefgenii followed the Sabre. Black smoke whipped past the canopy, trailing from the American jet in wisps that from time to time thickened into coughs of soot. Yefgenii closed the gap, sat behind and opened fire. The Sabre ballooned into fire and Yefgenii let out a shriek of triumph and also of anguish. He tried turning back for the coast. Ahead lay a narrow beach, then shale rising to rocky ground. The last gulp of fuel burned and he flamed out. He lifted his dead leg up to the seat and then reached under to yank the black-and-yellow handle.

The canopy blew clear and, in an instant, indistinguishable from it, he felt a kick up the ass and then he was following the canopy through a hurricane of wind and cold. The canopy floated away. His chute opened. The MiG spun to the right and struck the shallows. The red star broke apart but the hammer and sickle jutted out of the water on the tail.

Pain speared his lower back. Yefgenii was swinging over the gray waters on his way down with the beach about fifty meters in front of him. Wreckage bobbed on the waves below. His flying suit was blood-red from hip to boot with the bullet hole in his thigh edged in black. He hit the water with the chute fluttering down above him. An American helicopter would be on its way to the crash site. It might get here before the North Korean ground troops could rescue him. His leg stung in the salt water. He couldn't move it. His back muscles were locked up by a lumbar fracture. He was going under. The water was just deep enough to drown in. The chute settled on the surface and darkness engulfed him.

The air was silent but for the lapping of waves. The thunder of engines had receded. The names of Jabara, McConnell, Fernandez and Davis were already fading from the skies.

Over the western horizon channels were opening in the clouds. Slanted bands of sunlight fell through onto the sea, like an artist's strokes of yellow. A giant brush was sweeping over the palimpsest world. A new one was being painted over the old. Neil Armstrong had returned to college to complete his studies in aeronautical engineering; Gus Grissom was promoted to jet flight instructor; John Glenn was going to the Navy's Test Pilot School at Patuxent River and Wally Schirra to the Naval Ordnance Training Station at China Lake. Schirra was going to help develop an air-to-air missile system called Sidewinder; close aerial combat, gun to gun, man to man, was going to be obsolete as jousting. And, in a few years, Buzz Aldrin would formulate the mechanics by which manned spacecraft might rendezvous in orbit.

This had been the first air war between the great powers and it would be the last. They would find new ways to compete, and the men also.

Yefgenii Yeremin drove himself to the surface and lifted the chute enough to snatch a breath. He began to paddle toward the beach. The water shallowed and he struggled into a crawl. He dragged himself across the beach and curled up on the shale. The tide was coming in, washing away the blood and prints he'd left in the sand, but in the sky great white ribbons commemorated every swoop and twist of the fight. As time passed, winds drew out their edges. They became giant feathers linking one side of the sky to the other. When at last men scrambled along the beach toward him, they looked up and thought them clouds.

FRANZ JOSEF LAND

1955–1964

)

S OME THOUGHT he should've chosen Kiriya's way. It was sheer luck North Korean troops reached him before the Americans, and only his extraordinary haul of victories that kept him out of the labor camps. He was stripped of his honors, no longer a bearer of the Order of Lenin, no longer a Hero of the Soviet Union.

But the widow wept with relief. She sought permission to see him. Pilipenko asked why. She lied, "Because we're engaged to be married."

She traveled to the Korean northwest, where she found him in a stinking field hospital overrun with military and civilian casualties. He lay immobilized by the fractured lumbar vertebra with a blood-caked dressing on his leg wound that hadn't been changed in days.

The widow kissed him on the cheek. His only other visitors had been Soviet intelligence officers who'd debriefed him with brutal questions colored by threats of reprisals. No wonder his smile for her was wide, his eyes beaming.

"You wanted to live," she said.

He relived sinking under the sea, the rush of salt water into his nose and mouth, the choking, then the darkening as the parachute settled on the surface like a lid being sealed. Maybe the easiest thing would've been to give in. But all he'd achieved was not enough. He'd fallen short of perfection. There remained the hunger for one surpassing feat, for one perfect sortie. He craved another mission.

"Yes," he said, and she didn't question whether he'd been driven by love for her or by something else.

He didn't love her. Yefgenii was a young man returning from war, expected to take a wife and start a family, but he found connections difficult. The widow accepted his coldness as part of his nature, instilled by the childhood he never talked about. Instead of a courtship, a sequence of compromises and accommodations accompanied his evacuation from Korea, so that she could remain at his side. He was an officer in disgrace, but given that she was a widow with commonplace looks, status, and personality, he was as strong a marriage prospect as she could hope for.

She acted as an attentive and faithful companion, following as he moved wherever the VVS decreed. More, she was a woman willing to open herself to him in many physical ways. He had little enough experience of women to be overwhelmed by her devotion, yet he had large enough experience of them to reach the same conclusion. So these mutual assessments of their circumstances culminated in marriage, in a small ceremony in her home village.

The wound in his leg soon healed, but it took another year for him to be able to walk without a limp, two for full flexibility to return to his back. He'd been assigned to administrative duties, but, when he was fit again, the question arose of what to do with him. Pilots of his ability were uncommon, and there was no longer a theater of war in which he might cause further embarrassment. He could be posted somewhere remote and continue to serve a purpose, while the legend of Ivan the Terrible, that had passed like a curse through the flight lines of Korea, would slip into oblivion.

In the autumn of 1955 he received a posting to Franz Josef Land. The archipelago lay high in the Arctic Circle, only 1,000 kilometers from the Pole, only 2,000 from American airspace.

He traveled from Murmansk on a transport plane carrying a dozen posted personnel. Some were bound for the "weather station" at Nagurskoye on Alexander Island; they were bomber crews or air defense radar operators. The remainder were assigned to the fighter base on Graham Bell Island. The existence of these bases was a state secret.

The other men said little to one another, and Yefgenii said nothing at all. He gazed out of a porthole as they crossed the Barents Sea. Pack ice swaddled the Franz Josef archipelago. Only Northbrook Island, the southwesternmost, was free of it. The islands ranged from tiny outcrops to enormous plates of volcanic rock bearing ice fields and tundra. Cloud squatted over the eastern islands, where the fighter station lay. The aircraft descended. It was the sinking under the sea once more, the cloud smothering him as his parachute had done, like the lid being sealed all over again.

When they landed at Graham Bell Station, the thermometer read minus 20. A huge snow-covered dome of rock stood on the south of the island. Here, the north was considered the hospitable part.

Snow fell, decking the runway and coating the buildings. It gathered round his boots and crusted the fur fringe of his parka hood. But aircraft were moving, snowplows were shifting. Work details were digging up a taxiway to lay underground hot-water pipes. Jets and props howled.

A junior officer had seen his name on the assignments list and word got out at once: Yefgenii Mikhailovich Yeremin was coming to Graham Bell. The younger men hadn't even heard of him, or if they had they thought he was a myth. The first night in the mess, he ate alone. He understood he'd fallen out of favor and people didn't dare appear to be his comrade.

For the other fighter pilots, to have among them a man with thirty-seven combat victories, the greatest jet ace of all time, but to ignore him, even to treat him with contempt, was unbearable. So his achievements had to be disregarded. Ivan the Terrible had never existed; if he had, he was not this man among them. Besides, regulations still forbade discussing the Soviet participation in Korea.

Once, in the mess, in whispers, one man claimed to have served at Antung in the year before Yefgenii joined up with the 221st IAP. "Do you remember the heat? And the flies! What I'd give for them now!"

Yefgenii gave the man a small smile.

"And the food. It tasted like shit. And those terrible metal bowls we ate out of. Mine was always rusty."

"They were wooden."

"No." The man glared. *"Metal."*

Yefgenii shrugged. "It's not important."

The man leaned forward. "It *is* important. Where was the Ops hut?"

Yefgenii pictured the Ops hut lying alongside the crew hut. He pictured the dispersal and taxiways, dust lifting off the runway in the wake of MiGs, the pine-covered mountains to the west. He smiled. Every man would remember them in his own way. "As you know, comrade, neither of us was there."

The widow, traveling by icebreaker, arrived weeks later with their belongings, and pregnant. The time apart had been their first since the end of the war. In the beginning he'd missed her hardly at all, but toward the end he understood that he was a little less content, a little lonelier, than before. He met her at the quay and hugged her. He felt her gravid belly push against his crotch, felt something physical he hadn't expected to.

Soon he was accustomed to her again, and his sentiments for her lost their sharpness. She was his wife but he believed many other women could have fulfilled this place in his life, if they'd chosen to, if he'd chosen them. So this was the understanding, almost a bargain, and the widow set about transforming the small house they were provided with into a home in which to raise a family, while he got to flying.

It snowed most days that first autumn. Nearly all ops below 2,000 meters were on instruments save the bottom 100, under the cloudbase, that they needed to climb out and scoot in under VMC. The Dome's apex was 500 meters and it was easy for a man to get disoriented. They lost two pilots the first month. Some days, when the weather cleared, Yefgenii could see bits of wreckage littering the peaks and crops of all the eastern isles.

His back ached. On long sorties, he felt the muscles at the base of his spine harden to steel. He'd try rocking his hips in the seat, or turning his shoulders from side to side, but by the time he set down the pain would be excruciating. He suffered in silence. To reveal it would've been the end of his flying career. He'd take a few moments longer than the others to get to his feet and descend the ladder. As winter approached, the stiffness got worse. He invented a series of checks and maneuvers to extend the time it took him to leave the cockpit; the ground crew assumed they were superstitions.

The widow rubbed oil into his back. She warmed the flesh with massage and then she'd force her thumbs hard into the muscles that were like steel rods. Sometimes it hurt so much he'd cry out.

Temperatures plummeted further. Some mornings it was minus 30. They couldn't ignite the jets. One got airborne and, as soon as it hit the runway, the nosewheel and the mainwheels snapped clean off. From the moment he strapped in, Yefgenii felt a slow numbness spread across the base of his back and buttocks. His legs tingled. In the short hours of daylight, it was white on white, earth to sky. From October there was no day at all.

The commanding officer was a bitter little man named Kostilev who rarely flew. In fact he seemed to hate flying, given how often he preferred to sift paperwork in his office with the door shut. When Yefgenii first reported to him, he stood to attention while Polkovnik Kostilev remained seated behind his desk. "Some men come here with a reputation, Yeremin, but first they have to prove themselves to me."

"Yes, sir."

"No one receives any privileges. I treat every man the same."

"Yes, sir."

"If a man is part of the team, he'll get on. If he sets himself apart, well, he won't."

Yefgenii was a *kapetan,* so by rights he should have been made at least a flight leader. Kostilev assigned him to his *zveno* as a wingman. Yefgenii knew he'd remain a *kapetan* till the day he died or retired. No one would want to be known to favor him with promotion.

They flew the newest version of the MiG-17, armed with air-to-air-missiles. The days of dogfighting, of close combat, were gone. In the event of war, bombers would cross from one country to the other, their fighters would attempt to intercept as many as they could, but it was a game of numbers, of which country launched more bombers, of which country *had* more bombers to launch. The great powers were building nuclear arsenals heavy enough to obliterate the other, and the world. This was now how they measured themselves against each other: in weapons production, in the projected millions of civilian casualties, in the certainty of mutual assured destruction.

Snowplows kept the runways open. The MiGs climbed out on

instruments, up through dense cloudbanks. Once above them, stars sparkled over their canopies. The aurora shimmered. The planes were invisible apart from their nav lights floating through the blackness. They flew these patrols for hours on end. American bombers were on constant standby to cross the Arctic and press deep into Soviet territory to deliver their payloads. Sometimes a B-52 would skirt Soviet airspace to mobilize their interceptors. On rare occasions, American aircraft penetrated the interior of the USSR, running in and out at high altitude. It was brinkmanship. They were testing each other's defenses.

Yefgenii lived with the widow in the base's low redbrick housing that was always cold, but the widow never complained. She'd wanted children right away. He remembered she'd asked him if he wanted to be a father. Then he'd considered his progeny to be the smoke of dying airplanes, the blooms of parachutes and the flames of victory. They were gone now. She'd said, "We must all have children or else there'll be nothing left behind when we're gone."

The first, a girl, came before their first spring on Franz Josef Land. After the birth, the widow grew fat, her face got rounder, her nose more bulbous. He changed too. Though still only a young man, his hair was thinning at the front. He gained a high forehead, those blue eyes set beneath.

With the spring, the Sun opened a small hole in the endless night. The hole widened, the nights shrank. The northern isles remained locked in pack ice but the southernmost were released. Flying down over Hooker Island, Yefgenii could see the colony of seabirds in the bay. South of Northbrook Island, the sea was open; whales were schooling. As his MiG swooped low overhead, walruses flopped onto the ice, their hides slick in the sun. In summer, the temperature rose to freezing, occasionally a few degrees higher. The sea teemed with life. This was the seasonal cycle between ice and water, but always keeping more ice than water, as heavy banks of vapor massed into clouds, releasing liquid that fell as snow or hail but never as rain.

He flew patrols through cloud and wind while supply ships and the vessels of the Northern Fleet trailed frothy white wakes. He spoke little to the other men. He followed orders. He flew the MiG to the best of his ability. From time to time came alerts and the interceptors were launched. So far it was Cold War brinkmanship, not the heat of battle. To the north, banks of cloud blanketed the Pole like a ridge of white mountains, and one day soon the overlying sky would fill with slow-rising lines of silver wings.

On October 4, 1957, the Soviet Union fired *Sputnik 1* into orbit. The news came through to Graham Bell the next day. The men toasted its success in the bar that night. Yefgenii raised his glass like the other men. He swallowed his shot of vodka.

The next winter, a second child was born, a boy this time, but Yefgenii felt remote from the event. A space existed between him and other people.

One year was the normal tour of duty in the Arctic, one year or at most two, but after three and a half years, Yefgenii received orders in the spring of 1959 that he remain in Franz Josef Land for the remainder of his flying career. This was his exile, yet he clung to a fragile hope. One day the American bombers would cross the ice in earnest and Ivan the Terrible would rise again.

Having been beaten by *Sputnik,* the United States declared its intention to send the first man into space. In April they selected a group of seven test pilots to begin training for spaceflight. Among them were John Glenn, Gus Grissom and Wally Schirra; they'd been distinguished supporting players in Korea but now they were the heroic stars of the Space Race. The Americans called them "astronauts"—star voyagers. Magazines carried their life stories. They appeared on television. In interviews some of them referred to God as if he really existed.

But the Soviets had more powerful and reliable rockets. Recruitment teams were already traveling out from Moscow. In utmost secrecy they toured VVS bases across the Soviet Union in search of pilots with the talent and courage to venture into space. No one came to Graham Bell.

Yefgenii flew long, lonely patrols. Afterwards, he stowed his kit in his locker and hung his helmet on the rack. He took the base bus home. A light glowed in the little redbrick house, snow matted the roof, and icicles glistened off the gutters. In the sitting room, the widow nursed their infant son, while their daughter lay sleeping in the bedroom. This was his life. This was him now.

THE SEASONS CYCLED. Ice moved in great shifts up and down the islands. Snows fell and melted. Yefgenii changed too, the face becoming gaunter, the forehead higher, and so did the world. Both nations had missiles now, not only capable of carrying a bomb from aircraft to target, but rockets that could carry nuclear warheads over oceans and across continents. They were building enough ICBMs to destroy every major city in their enemy's homeland, enough to destroy civilization. If war came, the missiles would soar high over Franz Josef Land. The fighters were redundant; the job of air defense lay in the gloom of radar stations and SAM silos.

Two bomber squadrons were removed from Nagurskoye, a fighter squadron from Graham Bell. The crew rooms were airier, the streets and schools quieter. Empty cabins were pulled down, others were left to rot.

Yefgenii remained, of course. He feared he'd be kept here even if there was only one aircraft, only one man. He looked to the north, the cap of ice and cloud shrouding the curve of the earth like a ridge of white mountains. He longed for a sky filled with metal, but he knew the American bombers would never rise, Ivan the Terrible would never rise again.

That winter, the winter of 1960–1961, the darkness fell fast. The aurora's spectral lights shimmered on the cloud tops and on the gleaming metal of his wings and the clear plastic of his visor. His blue eyes swam behind a flickering cascade of reds, greens and blues.

Icicles glistened on the gutters of the redbrick house. Snow blanketed its roof. The house smelled of cooking. He shook snowflakes off his coat and slapped them off his hat. The widow stood at the stove. The boy slept in the bedroom. As Yefgenii pulled off his boots, the girl told him her news. Yefgenii smiled. Anything that wasn't flying struck him as unimportant, but he indulged her. The widow took the girl to bed. Yefgenii kissed her as she went and then he sat at the small wooden table in the single downstairs room while a meat stew bubbled on the stove.

When the widow returned she said, "She keeps asking about the dog."

"What dog?"

"The one in space. What's this one called?"

"Chernushka."

"We were so sad about Laika, but this one will come back, won't it? That's what I told her, anyway."

Soviet rockets were carrying dogs into space; the Americans sent chimps. Soon it would be a man. Both nations proclaimed the man would be theirs. The winner would secure the advantage of the military high ground; they would also lay claim to the superior ideology; and the man himself would be renowned for the remainder of human history, longer than there'd be countries.

The widow put out two bowls and ladled the stew into them. Steam rose from the surface. He stirred the liquid. They sent dogs into space. He felt lower than a dog. "This is good stew," he said. "Just what I needed," he said.

Yuri Gagarin flew into space aboard *Vostok 1* on April 12th. Crammed inside a capsule too small for a man of average size, he made one orbit of the earth then landed near the city of Saratov, on the Volga. Premier Nikita Khrushchev himself greeted Gagarin when he returned to Moscow. They stood along with leading Party members atop Lenin's Mausoleum while the crowd in Red Square cheered in jubilation.

At Graham Bell that day, Yefgenii Yeremin didn't fly. The whole country was celebrating the victory over the Americans. Yefgenii admired Gagarin's valor, admired the qualities he must've had in order to win selection ahead of all the other cosmonauts.

He drank toasts with the other men. They were young, they were full of vigor. Many of them wanted to apply for the space program. It was a new world, and theirs. Yefgenii felt aged beyond his years. The cold and emptiness of the Arctic had bit by bit desiccated the life out of him. He swallowed vodka and studied his reflection floating in the veneer of the bar top.

He shambled home, alone, drunk.

Snow fell in clumps and the wind drove it in his eyes. It stuck in his hair and lashes, stung his cheeks, beaded his hat and coat. He was turning white, becoming a ghost that stumbled along the empty streets at the edge of the base, bent against the wind. The wind pushed him to a standstill. Snow blinded him. He threw off his hat and coat. He opened his arms to the wind. He challenged it to drain him to a husk and blow him away. The wind here was strong enough to knock a man over. Yefgenii's boots slipped on the snow as he struggled to stay upright. A gust caught him off balance and he tumbled.

The falling snow began to cover him. The wind heaped it against him in a mounting drift. He felt ice biting through his skin. However courageous Gagarin was, however dedicated and resolute he was, however intelligent and personable and handsome he was, a VVS pilot with no combat experience who was so short he needed to sit on a pillow to see out of the cockpit of a MiG-15 had become the first man in space. In less than two hours of flying Yuri Alexeievich Gagarin had become the greatest of all Heroes of the Soviet Union.

He'd even been promoted during the flight, not one rank but two, going up a *starshii-leitenant* and coming down a *major*. Yuri Gagarin's single victory over the Americans counted for more than all of Yefgenii Yeremin's put together. Soon the Americans would be going up too, already rich and famous, some of them men who'd flown over Korea and achieved so much less there than he had.

New fields had opened for the great powers to battle over; for machines, it towered in the rarefied flight paths of missiles, high above men and airplanes; for men, it lay in space, and Yefgenii Yeremin played no part in any of it.

He let the cold take him.

When the widow came looking for him, only his head, shoulder and hip poked out of the snow. "Yefgenii!" She shook him. She could feel how stiff his body was, how cold. *"Yefgenii!"* His hands were livid, his nose, his lips. "YEFGENII!"

He moaned.

She tried to drag him to his feet. She held him up but he fell again.

"Leave me," he said.

She dragged him up again, calling for help. "Let's get you inside," she said.

"Let me die."

People came out of one of the houses, men in uniform, coming to help.

He fell again. He lay there crying, with the widow clinging to him and men barking out orders to get him inside, to get him in front of the fire.

THE WIDOW NURSED HIM over the next few days. She brought him hot food and hot drinks, she massaged his hands and feet. The tips of his fingers and toes and the tip of his nose were gray from frostbite that would either recede or turn gangrenous.

She kept a fire burning day and night in the little bedroom they shared. His face turned pink and sweat glistened on the high dome of his forehead, but he said little and his eyes were pale and empty when she looked into them.

The door to the room hung ajar. One morning it creaked as it swung open a little more. Two tiny faces peered through the gap, one's eyes at the level of the doorknob, the boy's, and the other's, the girl's, a head higher. Yefgenii turned his pale empty gaze toward them. The widow turned and shooed them; they defied her, which was just like them, but they said nothing, which wasn't.

Because the Americans had been beaten, President John Kennedy appealed to Congress for the United States to commit itself to landing a man on the Moon before the end of the decade. To many the proposal seemed ludicrous, of spending vast sums of money on an endeavor carrying so little prospect of success. But

116

then that was the reason to target the Moon: a goal so far beyond current technical capabilities that it gave the United States a fighting chance of overtaking the Soviets.

The widow kept Yefgenii warm, she kept him well fed. Some days she went without so he would have extra to eat. He watched her with blank eyes. "You could say thank you," she said.

"Thank you," he said.

He watched her go about her routine. She'd gained weight, lost what looks she'd had. She rubbed warmth into his fingers and toes. She massaged the stiffness at the base of his back. She laughed that if his willy had been affected she would be happy to massage that too.

He found himself laughing in return. He stroked her hair. She peered down at him, surprised by the gesture. He kissed her.

She gazed back at him, a spark of youth and beauty returning to her eyes. He knew now he'd been wrong all these years to suppose she was one of any number of women who would've fulfilled his expectations of a wife. No other would've been so devoted, no other would have been so faithful. If you were a romantic, you would call these criteria "love."

In the mornings, the children would sneak into their bed. They snuggled with their mother but, now that he wasn't leaving before dawn for the flight lines, they found him there too. The girl would bounce on his chest. The boy would bury his face in the pillow when he looked at him. He would tickle them and they'd laugh. He'd tickle them and they'd cry. They wouldn't want to kiss him. They'd want to smother him in kisses. He was discovering these strange creatures of little parts, of soft chubby flesh, of big eyes and unpredictable behavior.

His strength returned. He walked about the base but there was little for him to do. He had no hobbies or interests. He was not a reader of books. Because of the frostbite in his hands, he wasn't suitable for a desk job.

That summer the wall was built to divide Berlin. Cold War tensions accelerated the Arms Race. On a large wasteland to the south of Franz Josef Land, named Novaya Zemlya, the Soviet Union detonated a 100-megaton hydrogen bomb. It was named the Tsar Bomba, the King of Bombs, and for fear of its strength it was detonated at half yield.

They saw the flash on Graham Bell. Seconds later, they felt the ground tremble. The explosion was nearly four thousand times more powerful than the one that had devastated Hiroshima; it was the biggest explosion recorded on Earth barring natural cataclysms such as the meteorite impact that obliterated the dinosaurs. The dinosaurs had ruled the planet for more than a hundred million years and the nuclear arsenals of man contained energy on a par with that which had made them extinct.

Yefgenii watched the mushroom cloud ascend. If men destroyed man, this would be their closing vision, the endpaper of history.

He turned inside. Photographs stood in frames all around the little house. He'd hardly noticed them, these pictures of the widow, the children, some of him in uniform. If one day he was gone from their lives, this would be all that remained. The children would gaze at pictures of this man, they might remember a moment between them and not know for sure if it was a dream or a reality; over time even that memory might be lost.

One day the widow asked him, "Why did you do it?"

He lay on his side. He spent many hours like that, awake on the bed in the middle of the day, or slumped in an armchair, his face blank, his mind empty. After she said it, he wanted to roll away from her but she clasped his elbow and held him still.

"Why did you do it?" she said. "Why did you want to leave me a widow, leave your children without a father?"

She slapped his head, surprising herself with the suddenness of the action. He stared at her, mute, his eyes the eyes of a dumb animal. She struck him again and again about the head and back and shoulders.

"Six years we've lived here! Six years. Other families suffer for one, they can tell their children next winter won't be so cold, it won't be so dark, because daddy will be posted somewhere nice, but what can I tell our children, what can I tell myself? We'll be here for the rest of our lives!"

She hit him one last time, but sadness and despair weakened her anger. She said, "Your wife loves you. Your children love you. We're the only warmth you've got."

That night, after she'd put the children to bed, they ate supper together at the table in the communal room that served as kitchen, diner and lounge. From time to time the little house trembled under jets passing overhead on routine night patrols.

"You could take the children somewhere else," he said. "You could live somewhere warmer. I would send you money, what money you needed. Perhaps you and the children would be happier without me."

A spoonful of stew was about to pass her lips. She held it in midair.

"Who knows how long they'll keep me here? Maybe till the end."

Steam rose off the spoonful of stew. "The end?"

He hunched his shoulders. He peered down into the bowl between his elbows. "I don't expect my life to have a happy ending."

She said, "Nor do I, Yefgenii Mikhailovich," and of course that was the reason he'd married her.

He'd regressed to a man who steps into a bath and displaces no water. Yet he'd found a part of existence hitherto obscure to him. The widow cooked the next supper. The boy traveled under furniture, always pursuing a ball, or being pursued by one. The girl loved to draw. She would hunch at the table, with her fine blonde hair fringing her eyes, choosing colors from a fistful of pencils. He'd come close to leaving their lives, and now, for the first time, he feared what it would mean if they left his.

Before winter came, the frostbite began to recede. The doctor was ordered to visit him, and, as he conducted his examination, he asked if he'd intended to kill himself. "I got drunk celebrating the triumph of Comrade Gagarin," Yefgenii said. "I fell and couldn't get up." The doctor asked him if he'd lain in the snow because he'd wanted to die and Yefgenii said, "I was so drunk I didn't appreciate the danger, I just fell asleep, like a drunken idiot."

"You've been here a long time, Kapetan. Did you lose hope?"

Yefgenii shook his head, a firm movement, a fixed look. "The toughest flying conditions in the VVS, the Americans so close you can smell their fat. I belong here."

The doctor nodded and made a note.

Yefgenii Yeremin was pronounced fit to fly. He'd continue to serve out his days. In the authorities' eyes his collapse in the snow proved he considered his own life as expendable as they did, and perhaps one day this would be useful to know.

Alan Shepard was America's first man in space, and Gus Grissom the second. In 1962 John Glenn became their first astronaut to orbit the Earth. Wally Schirra followed.

The Soviet Union answered by keeping men in orbit longer. The next stage was already in development: to launch a two-man crew, then to operate outside the capsule. Now that both nations had proven to themselves that their rockets worked and their men could operate in space, they were ready to commit the necessary resources. Perhaps it would even divert attention from obliterating each other. Each nation's goal was simple: the enemy must not be allowed to fly his flag over the surface of the Moon. The Space Race had a finishing line.

Ivan the Terrible patroled the Arctic seas, invisible, unknown. He waited, always he waited, for American wings to rise across the white ridge at the top of the world. His own wings turned, the endless patrol went on.

I N THE FIRST WEEK OF APRIL, the Sun rose at midnight and set in early evening. By the end of the month, it had stopped setting at all. It was their eighth spring on Graham Bell. Gulls and kittiwakes circled the volcanic outcrops. Once again the ice cap had begun its long recession but only the southern isles were released, never this one.

Yefgenii let himself out of the little redbrick house. He eased the door shut so as not to wake the widow and the children. A few other men were emerging from their houses, leaving their wives and children asleep. The bus paused at the stop; he mounted the step and nodded an acknowledgment to the driver. Two more men entered the bus, talking to each other, laughing; they nodded at Yefgenii but sat elsewhere.

Today was May Day, the festival of the worker and of spring: May Day 1963. The whole country was starting two days of celebration. Only essential personnel were required to work. Yefgenii was one of the unlucky ones.

After met brief, Yefgenii put on his kit. His hands ached with weariness as he endured the routine of zipping into his immersion suit and g-suit. Then he slumped in a chair in the crew room. For the rest of the country there were plans for parties and parades—his children had been making banners all week—but he'd read, he'd sleep, he'd update his logbook.

Hours evaporated in the crew room. There was only one crew on duty, and they didn't fly till afternoon. The *zveno* leader, Kapetan Ges, gave the men a twenty-minute warning. He passed out cigarettes and the men strolled clear of the fuel bowsers, chatting among themselves and with the ground crew.

Yefgenii found a space nearby to bend and stretch. He worked his fingers hard into the hollows of his back, to keep it supple. Ges watched him. This was Ivan the Terrible. He'd noted already he was an outstanding flier, quick and precise in formation, a smooth stick in maneuvering, wheels banging the numbers at every touchdown. Ges stubbed out his cigarette and ordered the other pilots to stretch too.

They flew in a four-ship that skimmed out over the Barents Sea. Ges took them down so low their wings lifted froth off the flat slate-gray waters.

A call came from Nagurskoye. "White Formation, you are ordered to steer 350, climb flight level 50."

Ges responded, "Copy, Nova. 350, 50, White 1." His voice was calm and crisp. In person Ges was clean-cut and handsome and had the knack of being liked by his superiors while still getting along with his peers. He'd volunteered for patrol on a national holiday.

They turned and entered a climb. Yefgenii's eyes were trained upward, already searching for contrails. They crossed George Island, the glaciated south slipping under their noses, then the tundra of the northern tip. The vast polar ice field was opening out ahead of them, and slabs of cloud hung in scatters from horizon to horizon. The MiGs were tilted up, each with two missiles and a pair of drop tanks slung beneath them, laying twisted columns of contrail behind. At 5,000 meters Ges ordered them to level out. He reported to Nagurskoye and they were ordered to continue north.

Ges asked, "Nova, White 1. What's going on?"

"Continue north, White 1. Information will follow."

Something was happening. Yefgenii's pulse quickened. He said, "We need to know what we're looking for."

A pause hung. The air rushed, their jets roared.

Ges answered, "I concur." He dialed the Nagurskoye frequency and transmitted, "Nova from White Leader, I respectfully request further information for air recognition purposes."

There was silence. The MiGs pressed north. The volcanic islands were far behind them now, a mottling of dark patches on the pack ice behind their tails.

At last Nagurskoye cut in. The air defense radar was tracking an unidentified contact at 20,000 meters or higher, heading north from the Plesetsk region at about 600 kilometers per hour. It was too high and too fast for interceptors and antiaircraft artillery. There were fighters in the air from every station in the Volga-Ural Command, but only the MiGs from Graham Bell stood any chance of making contact. They were to rendezvous with an M-4 tanker that was already airborne 100 kilometers to the north, and to await further instructions.

Yefgenii's heart beat. He understood what must be up there. He knew the prize.

The ice cap curved toward the Pole. In the distance Yefgenii saw the top of the world with ridges of white cloud above and above them just the emptiness of the clear sky into which they pressed, with frost in crystal patterns glistening on their canopies. Waves of turbulence shook their ships.

Yefgenii was first to spot the tanker. His back was numb—the flesh stone-cold, the muscles rigid.

It was many minutes before Ges and the others could see it. They heard radar control advise that, on their present course and speed and on the contact's extrapolated course and speed, the contact would be crossing through their overhead in about forty-five minutes. That's how long they had to take on fuel and climb to ceiling.

Yefgenii peered ahead at the tanker. The converted M-4 glinted silver in the sun. Vortices corkscrewed off the tips of its huge swept-back wings.

Ges gave the order to line up for refueling. Turbulence buffeted the MiGs. A couple of times it shook the pilots in their straps. Ges, in the lead, advanced into the tanker's wake. An umbilical dropped out of the rear and began to snake toward the MiG's nose. The end of the umbilical enlarged into a receptor. Ges bounced in the airstream, trying to line up the MiG's refueling probe with the bobbing waggling receptor. He drove into the umbilical and the probe locked into its receptor. He shifted a lever to open his tanks and fuel flowed into them from the M-4. Ges disengaged with a full tank and the next MiG took his place. The pilot accelerated past the receptor and had to throttle back. He lost height and had to let the tanker move ahead again so he could climb back into position. He tried to line up the probe on the receptor but he was veering from side to side. The receptor struck his nose and canopy and he throttled back out of range again.

Over the radio Ges was getting impatient. Soon their target was going to be coming overhead. He gave the MiG pilot one last go and, when he failed to engage the umbilical, he ordered the next MiG to take his place.

The turbulence was roughening. The third MiG bounced in and out of range, dropping and climbing and banging into the receptor without latching onto it.

"Shit, shit." Ges was getting worried. The clock was ticking.

Yefgenii couldn't keep silent any longer. "Get the fuck out of there and let me get this fuel."

For the most part, on the ground, Yefgenii played the role he'd been given. He accepted his status, he surrendered to his exile, he mingled with mild manners among lesser men, but not now, not in the air, not on the brink of combat. His voice was the voice of Ivan the Terrible, and every man flying alongside him knew who he was, what he'd done, what he was capable of.

Ges transmitted, "White 3, disengage. White 4 for refuel."

Yefgenii powered into position behind the tanker. The wake turbulence bounced his MiG but it was nothing he couldn't handle and he snagged the fuel line and pretty soon disengaged with full tanks.

Ges ordered, "White 2, try again."

The refueled MiGs flew alongside the tanker as the other two took turns trying to engage the umbilical. They were running low on fuel and, if they didn't get more very soon, they'd not only be unable to climb into combat with Ges and Yefgenii, they'd be unable to make it home at all.

Yefgenii and Ges were watching the clock. Yefgenii transmitted, "Let's get into this."

Ges didn't hesitate. "White 2 and 3, refuel and follow as soon as you're able."

They began the climb to their ceiling. Yefgenii's eyes were trained upward. Nagurskoye Radar had done its best to estimate the contact's position but it was impossible to be precise given that the MiGs were beyond radar and their target could be as much as 6,000 meters above them.

Yefgenii and Ges had their minds fixed on the prospect of battle and they barely heard the first transmission from their comrades. The other two MiGs now lay far behind; not even the tanker was visible, but the first had abandoned his attempt to refuel and was on an emergency recovery to Graham Bell.

"Shit," said Ges. Yefgenii said nothing.

Their comrades' chance of making it back was slim, with only the frozen sea wide and deadly below. A few minutes later the fourth MiG flamed out still struggling to engage the umbilical.

They heard his mayday, quiet and remote, the signal breaking up: a man wouldn't survive long on the ice, if he survived the impact at all.

Ges didn't say anything this time.

Yefgenii kept his gaze upward, searching the patch of sky overhead. "Contact, twelve o'clock high."

"I don't see it."

A minute cross of black metal soared across the high dome, spinning a cotton-thin trail The enormous wingspan, almost double the aircraft's length, made its identity unmistakable.

"I'm visual. Contact is a U-2."

The CIA operated U-2 Spy Planes deep inside Soviet airspace, conducting reconnaissance of military installations from an altitude well above the ceiling of every enemy aircraft and missile system in existence. This one must've been returning to a base somewhere in Greenland or Canada, or even Alaska. The U-2 had the range and was aloof to enemy attack.

Ges said, "Shit, we're never going to catch him."

Yefgenii said, "Either you want to get this fucker or you don't."

Ges searched the sky above. The sunlight was endless, there was nothing else he could see. Nevertheless he transmitted to Nagurskoye, "Nova, White 1, we're visual with contact, repeat we are visual, contact is a U-2, repeat U-2, requesting permission to fire."

Nothing came back. They were out of range.

The MiGs continued over the white wilderness. The U-2 soared a full 10 kilometers above them, but at their own operating height, the MiGs could match it for speed. Yefgenii kept his eyes on the tiny black cross with its gossamer contrail and Ges kept his on the fuel gauge.

Time stretched. They were crossing the white ridge that capped the Pole. Yefgenii's back had seized. His calves tingled, he couldn't feel his feet on the rudders. The two men said nothing to each other the whole way. Deep into evening, the sky shone blue as noon. Yefgenii's eyes strained to keep the enemy in view. A headache tensed in his forehead and probed down into his temples.

Ges didn't even ask him if could still see the U-2. If he lost it, he'd say so; they would turn back. But Yefgenii didn't say a thing. The pain in his back made his eyes water. His focus was so strained even the film of tears made a difference, blinking the aircraft into visibility, blinking it back into a blur.

By now they were only 100 kilometers from the Pole. Their compasses were swinging. Yefgenii let out a gasp of relief. "He's letting down. He thinks he's safe."

Ges felt his mouth go dry.

Yefgenii armed his missiles. His head was pounding, his eyes were sore.

They sat behind the U-2 as it drifted down through 15,000 meters. At last it was under the MiGs' ceiling.

Then, for the first time, Ges saw the target. It was floating down a few kilometers straight ahead. Yeremin had placed them in its six o'clock position the whole time, had kept them invisible every step of the way.

"I'm visual," Ges said. "Engaging."

Yefgenii didn't argue. Ges was the leader. It was his prerogative to take the kill.

The two MiGs bore down on the tail of the U-2. From the belly of Ges's fuselage a missile dropped and lit like a sparkler. It streaked ahead but something went wrong, and it corkscrewed down, trailing a helix of white smoke.

At once the U-2 began to climb again. He knew he was under attack. His ascent wasn't fast but the MiGs were near their ceiling; they were sluggish in the climb, being left behind.

"Shit," said Ges. *"Shit."*

Yefgenii pulled back his stick. His nose struggled up. An approaching stall buffeted the wings. He kept trying to keep the nose up, fighting the buffet, trying to point the aircraft at the diminishing form of the U-2. He held steady till the last second, and then he released a missile. It streaked upward, a second sun that ascended on a plume of white smoke. Fire flashed and they saw the black shape of the enemy distort into a mash of body and wing, trailing soot. The broken plane plummeted toward the ice with Ges calling, "You got him! You got him!" and in Yefgenii's vision the shapes blurred and skipped and his head throbbed.

No parachute bloomed. The broken plane tumbled down in fragments, disappearing long before impact like a shattered lifeboat sinking under the ocean.

At once the MiGs turned back. They headed for Nagurskoye rather than Graham Bell; it was only a matter of kilometers closer, but every second counted, every gram of fuel.

Yefgenii peered at the fuel gauge. He was counting down. "What you got, Ges?"

"Maybe enough, maybe not. You?"

"Same."

They said nothing more. They flew on. The sun blazed, end-less, glinting on their visors and on the buckles of their harnesses. Empty ice lay blank below.

Ges dialed the frequency and started transmitting. "Nova from White Leader, come in. Come in, Nova."

Their engines roared, their fuel burned.

"Nova, do you copy?"

Yefgenii could see shapes far, far ahead, but they were a blur. He wasn't sure if they were reflections, or a mirage.

"Nova, do you copy, White 1?"

"White 1, we copy."

He couldn't contain his excitement. "Nova, we have killed the U-2, 88-30-30 North, 40-30-00 East, White 1."

Cheering came over the channel as Radar Control congratulated them and confirmed the coordinates.

Ges transmitted, "We are low on fuel. Request visual recovery."

"Granted!"

They began the descent. "What you got?" Ges asked.

Yefgenii didn't even need to glance at the gauge. "Not much. You?"

"Vapors," Ges said.

The MiGs were coming down from altitude, throttled back to conserve fuel, half flying and half gliding.

Ges's MiG stuttered. It started to drop back and its descent became steeper. He'd flamed out.

Without power the plane was in a glide, its wings still generating lift as they cut through the air, but without any thrust to hold on the approach slope. He was sinking toward the sea. "I'm not going to make it."

Ges sounded calm but Yefgenii knew what he was facing. He heard the click of Ges keying his transmitter, then an infinitesimal pause, before he heard, "Nova from White 1. Please confirm you're on tape. I want to record a message for my wife."

Ges had gotten married only a year ago. He had only a minute or two to tell her everything that was left to say, before he was gone forever.

Yefgenii peered across at Ges. He was already falling behind and below, on his way down.

"We're recording, White 1. Pass your message."

Yefgenii closed his throttle and eased back in a descending turn.

Ges spotted the maneuver. "Yeremin? What are you doing?"

He lined up on Ges's tail. "I'm going to push you. Hold her straight in the glide."

"You don't have the fuel, Yeremin. Save yourself."

Yefgenii had some fuel, maybe enough, maybe not. The way he flew, he was more precise than the other pilots; he wasted less than they did. He said, "We're too far out. The sea's too cold. You'll be dead in the water before the chopper's halfway here."

Ges said, "You're going to waste what little fuel you've got. Neither of us will make it. Save yourself. That's an order."

"Negative, White Leader. I'm coming in. Just hold her straight."

Yefgenii closed. He was bobbing a little but in the glide the MiG trailed a forgiving vortex. They were pitched down in a shallow dive, passing through 3,000 meters. Ges's tailplane was a sail drifting down to the seabed, the rudder a blade jutting behind. This close, Yefgenii could see the rudder quivering on its hinges. His nose nuzzled under Ges's jet exhaust. One of the aircraft bobbed, it was hard to tell which. Yefgenii's nose struck the rim of Ges's exhaust. A clang reverberated along the fuselage. Chips of paint sprang out into the slipstream and vanished. Yefgenii eased back in again. This time his nose settled into contact with the bottom of Ges's exhaust. One MiG sat upon another. The tailplane loomed over Yefgenii's canopy and his head was only a few meters from the black opening of the jet exhaust.

Nagurskoye cut in, "White 1 from Nova. We're recording. Pass your message."

"Nova, wait, White 1."

Yefgenii warned, "Throttling up."

"I'm ready."

Yefgenii dabbed the throttle forward. His gauges barely flickered. Ges felt a small kick. His wings created a little more lift and he drew back his stick a fraction. He was still pitched below the horizon with his altimeter winding down through 2,500 meters. In slow increments Yefgenii pushed the aircraft sitting on his nose until it was moving fast enough to support more level flight.

The strips of Nagurskoye remained far ahead, possibly they were beyond reach. His fuel gauge was telling him he'd soon flame out himself.

Yefgenii pushed the throttle. Power surged through both aircraft. Ges's tail lifted and then fell back. The collision rang through the planes like a bell and gouged dents out of both. Chips of metal pinged off Yefgenii's wings.

He throttled up harder. Metal groaned in the nose as it reared up into Ges's rudder. The lower hinge ruptured and a small section snapped off the trailing edge.

Ges glanced down into the sea. That's where he'd be now, freezing to death, if his wingman wasn't Yefgenii Yeremin. "I think I can see the airfield." Ges was surprised Yefgenii hadn't seen it first.

Yefgenii flamed out. The jets were silent. Now they were gliding with only the rush of air.

"I see it," Yefgenii said. The strips were blurring into each other. His head throbbed. He thought he was going to vomit, but he could read the geometry now. He was on the glide path behind Ges.

The two MiGs touched down one after the other. Fire trucks were speeding toward them but the pilots were already opening their canopies. Ges stood on his seat, his face red and creased where his mask had been, but showing white teeth in a grin. Yefgenii couldn't get out of his seat. He managed to unhook his oxygen mask and gasp fresh air. At once his head began to clear.

Ground crew helped him out of his straps. They were trying to congratulate him, to shake his hand, but his awareness of them was dim, he was in so much pain all he could say was, "Get me out," which they did, helping him down the ladder like an invalid as Ges looked on in concern, but Ges got distracted by congratulations and handshakes. The next time he looked Yefgenii was stretched flat on the hard snow, his face contorted in suffering.

Ges dropped to one knee and clasped Yefgenii's hand. His eyes glistened. "Thank you. My wife thanks you. Ivan the Terrible."

Yefgenii smiled through the pain. No one had called him that in such a long time.

T HE EYES WERE NO LONGER what they'd been. He told no one, not even the widow. He passed his medical examinations because his sight was no less sharp than any other pilot's, but it was no longer superior. Age had stolen his hair and drawn lines on his face but worst of all it had taken his eyes.

Another winter decked Graham Bell in snow. The wind drove streams of it across the runways and pushed drifts against the sides of hangars and against the walls of the little redbrick house where Yefgenii had lived with the widow and their two children for eight years now. Yefgenii left the house in darkness and took the bus down to the flight lines that pointed like arrows out into the frozen sea; he flew in darkness and returned home in it.

The new year was 1964. Both the United States and the Soviet Union were planning in earnest spaceflights involving multiple crews that would attempt rendezvous, docking, and extravehicular activity, operations essential for a successful lunar landing.

This time one man traveled to Graham Bell. "My name is Doktor Arman Gevorkian. I come from OKB-1. We're looking for pilots who are prepared to test some new military hardware. This matter is of the utmost secrecy."

134

By now the commanding officer was called Pokryshev. Four had come and gone since Kostilev had completed his tour and progressed to a comfortable administrative post somewhere on the mainland. Pokryshev gave a respectful nod. "Of course, Doktor Gevorkian."

"I've come in connection with one pilot in particular—Kapetan Yefgenii Yeremin. Would he agree to fly with me today?"

Pokryshev's cheek muscles twitched. "Someone would have to ask him."

"Is there a problem, polkovnik? I come on the highest authority."

"Of course, Doktor Gevorkian. I meant no offense. Please forgive me."

Yefgenii received orders to report to the flight clothing unit. An official from Moscow wanted to interview him.

When he arrived he thought from behind he recognized the man with Pokryshev. His pace quickened toward the diminutive figure looking ill at ease in a life jacket and immersion suit. The man turned and Yefgenii saw that his complexion was olive, his nose was beaky and his thick black eyebrows met in the middle. Yefgenii felt foolish. How could it have been Gnido? Gnido was long dead, so long dead.

Pokryshev made the introductions and then made an awkward departure. Gevorkian looked up at Yefgenii. He'd never seen a picture of him, had no idea what to expect. He hadn't anticipated someone who looked so sad. That was Yefgenii now, still tall, but gaunt, the white-blond hair all but gone.

The two men stood in the open, in the grayness between an 8 a.m. dawn and 10 a.m. dusk. A freezing wind gusted off the pack ice, carrying showers of hard white flakes. Gevorkian said, "OKB-1 is looking for volunteers."

MiGs were roaring off the runway a kilometer away; the wind was bringing the sound right to them.

"What did you say?"

"I said, 'we're looking for volunteers.' First-class fighter pilots under thirty-five years of age in excellent physical condition."

"To do what?"

"We call them 'cosmonauts.'"

Yefgenii smiled. Gevorkian was surprised to see him smile. He hadn't expected it.

"Who told you I was here?"

"What?"

"Who told you about me?"

"Your victory over the U-2 was not without admirers, even in the highest places."

Yefgenii studied Gevorkian. This was a chance, after all these years, and to question his potential deliverer's motive would be foolish in the extreme.

Gevorkian read the look on Yefgenii's face. "It was Comrade Ges."

Yefgenii nodded. The flying flakes of ice bit into the side of his face.

"He told me about the U-2. Or, rather, he told our Chief Designer. You scored the victory and you saved his life."

"Is that all he said?"

"He said you were the best pilot this country's ever produced and they were keeping you in a glass case, with a sign that says *Break open only in time of national crisis.*"

Yefgenii laughed. "Ges is a cosmonaut now?"

"Yes, Kapetan, he is one of our leading trainees."

"Trainee for what?"

"The Space Committee has finally issued a directive that we must endeavor to send a man to the Moon. We must beat the Americans."

Another MiG accelerated down the runway. The scream of its jet crescendoed and then Yefgenii said, "Sounds like my kind of thing."

Gevorkian saw how excited he looked. He hesitated. "Though, perhaps, with your application, we should be cautious . . ."

Yefgenii felt an ache of hunger. He couldn't disguise it. He'd thought someone in authority had decided he'd served out his exile, at long last. That's what he'd thought.

The wind shook the loose flaps of Yefgenii's clothing. It drove into him, through him. Even after all these years he wasn't used to it.

He said, "I was told you wanted to fly."

"That's right, Kapetan."

"So let's fly."

They climbed to the south, over the bobbing ice floes of the Barents Sea, in a modified MiG trainer equipped with two seats and dual controls. The intercom loop was permanently open and the sounds of Gevorkian in the seat behind disconcerted Yefgenii. He could hear him breathing, he could hear every sniff and slurp.

"Do you believe you'll be successful in sending a man to the Moon?"

"We intend to spread Communism to our closest celestial neighbor. All will go well for the first five years, then there'll be a shortage of moondust." Gevorkian laughed.

Yefgenii opened the throttle all the way and pitched back into the climbing attitude. The white ocean dropped behind them. The stubby white needle of the altimeter began to count up through the thousands. Sheets of cirrus plunged toward them and through and began to sink to earth. The air thinned, the sky darkened, and the world began to curve into a lens. They were topping 15,000 meters, nearing 16,000. A glistening cap of white curved over the top of the planet. The sky was bigger than countries and taller.

The climb shallowed. Even at full throttle the long narrow needle was barely adding on any more height. Yefgenii began a turn. The controls were sluggish. The aircraft was at its ceiling: too much bank and she'd stall and spin all the way down.

Over the ice cap floated a half moon. She was inchoate, she was a blur, a cataract. She seemed to lie just outside the glass of the canopy, hardly beyond their fingertips, but she was already slipping over the top of the world.

Yefgenii eased the aircraft's nose down into a dive. "What's OKB-1?"

The MiG gathered pace. Air roared over the canopy. Gevorkian had to shout. "The rocketry design bureau!" The wings shook till they broke through Mach 1, then they plunged straight down. The needle of the Mach meter continued to creep across the dial. Gevorkian knew they were approaching the MiG's theoretical maximum speed. He clasped his hands hard across his lap. "I like to call my position 'Head of Novel Thinking'!"

Yefgenii throttled back and coaxed the MiG's nose out of the dive. "Why d'you call it that?"

"There's something I discuss with the Chief Designer . . . I'd describe it as my grand enterprise. It involves the attainment of extreme altitude."

"How high?"

"The stars." Gevorkian waited. He could hear the sound of Yefgenii breathing in the seat in front but nothing else. "You're not laughing, Kapetan? Normally they laugh."

"No. I'm not laughing."

Yefgenii leveled off. The pale ocean swung under the nose and then from beneath the fuselage emerged the distant harbor of Murmansk.

"Kapetan Yeremin, I urge you not to despair. The Chief Designer is an admirer of your achievements. He has the ear of those in authority, and they're of a mind to listen."

Yefgenii gazed out across the sea toward land. It was time to turn back for the runways of Franz Josef Land but he held the MiG in its aimless trajectory.

Gevorkian said, "All my life I've loved airplanes. I've loved everything about them. Your name was not unknown to me when mentioned by Comrade Ges. I heard the stories that came back from Korea. What can I say, Kapetan? Your exploits inspired me." Gevorkian felt embarrassed so he continued without a pause. "A faceless apparatchik decided you should wither away in exile; I am not faceless. I can exhort the authorities to reconsider. In the space program, you would not be first in line. That would be a different kind of man, a spotless man, a flawless man—but one day in the future there might be a part for you to play, if you were prepared to wait . . ."

A submarine was surfacing on its return to Murmansk. It churned the waters into a long white wake. The Northern Fleet carried weapons that could destroy the world. The nuclear exchange would be measured in hours. Navies would rust. Air forces would vaporize. Cities would crumble. The ocean swallowed the submarine's wake as it did the wake of every single vessel that passed. Man might obliterate himself from the earth, but the sea would still roll on for a million years or more.

Yefgenii gazed down into the water. Ice floes drifted like tombstones.

"I would wait," he said.

STAR CITY
AND BAIKONUR

1966–1969

)

LIFE WAS GOOD NOW, in comparison. Star City lay on the outskirts of Moscow. There they lived in a smart block of system-built flats with other cosmonaut families. Their home was warm, light and modern. They owned a television set. The widow didn't have to queue for food or clothing; the shops were well stocked. Their larder bulged.

Ges and his wife lived across the hall. The women shopped together. The children attended the local school. They skipped off each morning hand in hand with Yuri Gagarin's children, or Alexei Leonov's.

At last his family had respite from the years of cold and exile, but for Cosmonaut Yefgenii Mikhailovich Yeremin the situation was less comfortable. Though he didn't confess his insecurity, he'd joined an elite group, some of whom had already flown in space and many of whom had been in training for five years or more. His size was a handicap; by some criteria he exceeded the limits laid down for selection, and his eligibility to fly existing and future spacecraft would be evaluated mission by mission. Yet the Chief Designer himself had pressed for his selection, though it was processed in secret; the authorities gave way but had insisted his name could not appear in any official record, so he was obliged to enter under a pseudonym.

He was introduced to the nation's leading pilots, the leading pilots of the culture. Here was Gagarin, here was Komarov, here was Leonov. Almost without exception the Americans chose seasoned test pilots as their astronauts, but in the main the cosmonauts were fighter pilots like him, men who'd made some kind of mark in military aviation; some believed they'd been selected on the strength of a single instance of daring or proficiency. One act could define a man in the eyes of his peers, in the eyes of his nation.

His fellow cosmonauts read the false name on his flight suit. They shook his hand and met his eyes. The use of the pseudonym was a charade—of course they knew who he was. Every man recognized his achievements as a combat pilot, but Korea wasn't just part of the past. For all the lives lost, the war had achieved nothing for the great powers, so it was to be disregarded as a matter of policy. The first war of the nuclear age, the first of the jet age, the unique military confrontation between the new great powers that ruled the planet, had been forgotten in the space of little more than a decade, while Gus Grissom, Wally Schirra, Neil Armstrong and Buzz Aldrin orbited the Earth with Project Gemini. They'd become the giants, not McConnell, not Jabara; they were giants as Ali was a giant, as Pelé, as Laver and Nicklaus were.

Yefgenii underwent intensive preparations at the Cosmonaut Training Center. The physical challenges were tougher than those given to fighter pilots. Now he was a man in his thirties. The stresses hurt him. They stretched his stamina. He needed to adapt to new techniques and learn the engineering of vehicles different from any form of aircraft he'd ever flown.

He adapted. He was a quiet man who listened to instructions. He studied each operation in detail. He analyzed how he could make a technique more efficient or more precise for himself. The technicians noted his improvements. In the simulators, his decisions were quick and accurate. He was always calm, always austere and remote, but this was the hardest work of his life, the steepest hill yet. He dared not show a splinter of strain.

The cramped seats and capsules were designed within payload weight limits. Every gram was crucial. He was nearly a foot taller than Gagarin and his height caused him endless pain, in his knees, in his shoulders and worst of all in his back, but his weight was the greater trouble, because it might exclude him from a mission. He began to refuse the widow's meals, with the excuse that he had to work or that some training exercises were best carried out on an empty stomach. He was becoming like a jockey, light for his height, lean and hard, always hungry.

He made parachute jumps. The pain shot from the base of his spine down his legs but, minutes later, despite a residual ache, he took on the next piece of suffering. He couldn't tell anyone, couldn't ever show, or that would be the end of him.

While the widow put the children to bed, he studied technical manuals. After what supper he might or might not have eaten, he would return to them; hours later, she'd declare she was going to bed, but he'd carry on, into the night, reading fine print till his vision blurred, his stomach aching with hunger.

It reminded him of the orphanage, of the mathematics that had launched his trajectory. That drive he'd found in himself, what he was capable of, this was something he had to find again. The sky above was black, but not with the oppressive clouds of a city in ruins; this was the blank open canvas on which a man could blaze like a comet.

Gevorkian informed Yefgenii they were throwing a New Year's party at OKB-1. Only a handful of cosmonauts were invited, but he was to be one of them, at the personal request of the Chief Designer.

Hundreds of people filled a vast hall decorated with balloons. Outside, fireworks banged and blazed in the night. Ges led him to the buffet table. Champagne bottles stood in rows behind a glinting array of flutes. Ges chatted with fellow trainees while Yefgenii drank straight away to settle his nerves.

He observed the Chief Designer near the band, laughing with Gagarin and Leonov. Then a woman in a ball gown asked him to dance. The Chief Designer obliged and they spun off across the dance floor. The women were elegant and admiring. For the cosmonaut corps, there were always such women.

Komarov joined Gagarin and Leonov. He was a grave older man, a senior test pilot, the command pilot of *Voskhod 1,* which had carried the first three-man crew. These men had missions behind them. They were a breed apart from those who'd trained for space but had never flown. They glowed. They were themselves celestial objects.

Gevorkian approached Yefgenii, poured himself a glass of champagne. He studied the nervousness in Yefgenii's expression. "I'm just a genius," Gevorkian said. "You're a legend."

Gevorkian led Yefgenii across the divide to Gagarin. Gagarin greeted them with a broad handsome grin, this celestial man as great as his nation. He was the most powerful living symbol of Soviet achievement, the most famous pilot in history. His name would live longer than countries.

They toasted the New Year. Gagarin ate canapés. Like the small men, he never worried about his weight; physical exercise would keep him trim. Yefgenii watched the tasty morsels of food passing Gagarin's lips. He declined them, suffering hunger pangs.

The Chief Designer returned. Now a cosmonaut, Yefgenii was permitted to know his name. "S.P. . . ." said Gevorkian.

Sergei Pavlovich Korolev disregarded Yefgenii's pseudonym. "Kapetan Yeremin," he said. "How are you finding our enterprise so far?"

"It's my honor to participate, thank you, Sergei Pavlovich."

"Now you've joined us, I have the team to beat the Americans." He threw an arm round Yefgenii's shoulders. Yefgenii was taken by surprise. He felt awkward at the physical closeness. He worried the Chief Designer was drunk.

Korolev continued, "I've dedicated my intellectual life to achieving firsts. The first satellite, the first probe to the Moon, the first man in space, the first woman, the first three-man crew, the first EVA. You beat the Americans all those times in Korea, Ivan the Terrible. You beat their U-2. Now you'll help us beat them to the Moon."

He beckoned Gagarin, Leonov and Komarov. His gestures were flamboyant. He was a leader, and more, he was a magician. The three cosmonauts joined in. Korolev hugged them as he'd hugged Yefgenii, kissed their foreheads. Yefgenii saw he wasn't drunk. He was brimming with life and ambition. "Come the fiftieth anniversary of the October Revolution," he said, "two of you will be orbiting the Moon."

Korolev raised his glass again, and so did the cosmonauts. The magical Chief Designer had swept away Yefgenii's doubts about the future and his own role in it. Yefgenii grinned and threw his glass in the air, as much a part of the enterprise as any other man.

A few weeks later Korolev was dead. He'd gone into hospital for routine surgery and they'd found a tumor; he bled; his heart and lungs gave out on the operating table; then it was Komarov, piloting the first *Soyuz,* who became the first man to die during spaceflight when the parachutes failed after reentry; and a year later it was Gagarin, killed on a training flight when another aircraft near-collided with his MiG-15. If any man's life had been synecdochic of his nation's, it was his; Yuri Gagarin was the Russian DiMaggio. Even he could be taken, even he, the immortal.

I N A RUSSIA WITHOUT GAGARIN, the air seemed colder, the skies emptier. Something had been lost that was impossible to define. A clock had ticked on the mantelpiece and the occupants of the room had remained oblivious till the second the ticking stopped.

Yefgenii Yeremin rose before dawn. He drank milk to bloat his aching stomach. He ate eggs to feed his muscles. Outside the apartment building the streetlamps of Star City glowed yellow. They were lines pointing to infinity.

He followed the column of trees to the end of the avenue and then increased his pace, beginning a familiar circuit of the city. His breaths blew clouds that hung in the air for an instant before vanishing. He glided past offices and laboratories. Barbed wire bounded the perimeter, beyond it thick woods. Sentries turned as they heard him coming. Their guns swung round then down-pointed. The guards saluted the cosmonaut as he ran past.

Twinges began to prod his chest. His arms felt heavier. His back ached. This was the run home, the push, the pain.

In the apartment he showered. He was quiet, so as not to wake the children. The hot water eased his back. He stretched taut sinewy muscles. He weighed himself. In the mirror his ribs showed, his belly caved in; his iliac crests protruded.

The widow met him in her dressing gown. She insisted on cooking a full breakfast. She was worried about his weight loss; she knew the reason for it, but she feared for his health. He surrendered. He ate the heavy breakfast of sausage and bacon. Later he vomited it up.

That morning the cosmonauts were advised of a restructuring of the training groups. November 7, 1967—the fiftieth anniversary of the Great Socialist Revolution—had passed, Korolev's deadline for a pair of Soviet cosmonauts to orbit the Moon. The program was paralyzed by his death and its vehicles were grounded following the loss of Komarov. But the Americans weren't flying either. At the start of the year, a fire during ground testing of the *Apollo 1* Command Module had killed Gus Grissom and his crew, Ed White and Roger Chaffee, necessitating a lengthy technical review of the Apollo spacecraft.

Korolev's successor as Chief Designer had been his deputy, Vasily Mishin. In the time since his appointment, the corps had learned that he preferred the spacecraft to be automated and a cosmonaut to take control only in the event of a catastrophic systems failure. Engineers had been selected to become cosmonauts. Medical criteria had been relaxed to admit them. Korolev had had his favorites too—Gagarin, of course, and Leonov—and Yefgenii had sensed he might have come to be held in the same regard. While Korolev had placed his trust in the daring of fighter pilots, Mishin was more impressed by technical expertise. Engineers with little training had replaced experienced cosmonauts in mission selection, and then in just as precipitate a fashion this decision had been reversed by the Space Committee. Training groups were formed, restructured and reformed depending on who was favored, pilot or engineer. That morning, it was announced the cosmonauts were required to sit for an examination.

Yefgenii cleared his mind of all distractions and concentrated on pushing himself through the pain. When the test came, he scored highest. He understood the technical particulars of the spacecraft as well as any engineer; his mathematical ability cruised him through orbital mechanics. The corps was divided in two, one group assigned in three-man crews to the Soyuz vehicle and rendezvous-docking operations in Earth orbit, and the other assigned in pairs to fly the two-man Zond spacecraft to the Moon.

Mishin didn't give Yefgenii a slot. He favored an engineer.

Gevorkian called at the new apartment block that had opened the previous summer. Yefgenii swam in the pool whose construction had been overseen by Gagarin himself. In this first summer without him, the summer of 1968, the N-1 booster rocket was behind schedule, the LK lunar lander was still on the drawing board, they were launching unmanned missions in automated Zonds but no men from the USSR were flying to the Moon.

Yefgenii Yeremin felt it in the thickness of the water, how they'd fallen behind for the first time. His thin limbs were heavy, they didn't scissor through. He rolled from front crawl onto his back. A film of water flowed across his face and, when it cleared, the face of Arman Gevorkian was peering at him from the poolside.

"Comrade Mishin's approved the backup assignments at last."

Yefgenii continued to backstroke. His long arms turned in slow arcs, water falling from them in fine curtains.

"The backup lunar pairings have been agreed. I've been selected as a flight engineer."

"An engineer. Of course. Congratulations." Yefgenii reached the end of the pool, turned and switched to front crawl.

"The crews have to be weight balanced, the heavier men paired with the lighter—" Gevorkian scampered along the poolside to keep up, but Yefgenii ducked his head under the water.

When Yefgenii reached the shallow end, Gevorkian was waiting. "Please fuck off."

150

"I asked for you. He said yes. You're the pilot."

Yefgenii stood. Water streamed off his bald head, off his shoulders and chest. His long lean body glistened. A smile burst like the Sun.

They trained in the centrifuge at CTC, the biggest in the world. They practiced carrying out reentry procedures while being subjected to 9, 10, 11 g. They traveled to the planetarium in Moscow and spent hours learning the constellations. To learn the stars of the southern hemisphere, they flew to Somalia. They ventured into the desert where under a clear black sky they pointed sextants into the heavens. The Moon hung overhead. It no longer lay beyond reach.

In September an unmanned Zond traveled to the Moon and back with a pair of tortoises on board. Gevorkian said, "Of course Mishin chose tortoises—he is one," because, despite the success and a subsequent rendezvous of Soyuz capsules in Earth orbit, they were still focusing on reentry problems.

By now the lunar crews were in place. The manned Zond, the L-1, would be flown first by Leonov and Makarov, then Bykofsky and Rukavishnikov, then Popovich and Sevastyanov, all partnerships of command pilots and flight engineers, with Yeremin and Gevorkian as one of the backup crews: three missions would loop round the Moon and return to Earth, and then one crew would be selected to return in the L-3 spacecraft and attempt a landing.

It was Wally Schirra who led America's first Apollo flight, an orbital test of their Command Module. Then came reports the Americans had modified Apollo. Fearing a Soviet circumlunar flight and suffering delays with their Lunar Module, they moved up their first circumlunar attempt and began mounting a manned flight to the Moon using only the Command Module of the Apollo spacecraft. Meanwhile yet another Zond was launched, again unmanned, again it experienced minor reentry problems, again the men who were ready to voyage to the Moon were ordered to stand down.

Frustration and resentment rippled through the cosmonaut

corps. These men wanted to fly. They accepted the risk. Yefgenii as much as any man understood that. When the eyes of the cosmonauts met, they shared the look of men whose days were burning by. Battling the Americans had become introspective and claustrophobic. The open sky had shrunk down to the intense compartments of a capsule simulator or a centrifuge, of aircraft cabins and water tanks.

Yefgenii Yeremin continued to train. His back ached from a wearying day in the simulator. He concentrated on the tiniest movements of his hands, on the position of switches; he shifted in a hard little seat inside a cramped metal box. His limbs were hard rods; his torso was narrow and bony. Every hour he craved a heavy meal. When the pangs of hunger became too intense, he'd binge and vomit.

He knew a way onto the roof of the apartment block. The world expanded around him. City lights swamped the lower portions of the sky but the stars above shone in patterns that for the first time in his life he could recognize and name. A cosmonaut wasn't a true cosmonaut till he flew in space. The single act transformed him from the human to the celestial. Portraits of Gagarin hung everywhere, more than when he'd lived; a new street, a new building was named in his honor almost every week. His life and his act were part of history, they lived in the narrative of the species. Tomorrow would be another day of training, another day in the box.

With Gevorkian he was carrying out a launch-abort drill when Ges came to them with the news they'd expected for weeks, and with each passing day had dreaded more. "*Apollo 8* is on its way to the Moon."

State television ignored the flight. Newspapers reported it in a short column on the inside pages, if at all. The cosmonauts viewed the coverage at the Army's Space Transmissions Corps building on Komsomolsky Avenue. In the dark theater, the men exchanged bitter whispers. *It should've been two of us. If Sergei Pavlovich were still here, it would've been us, we'd've been first.*

Of course, they'd known the Americans were test-flying the

rocket they called the Saturn-5. They'd known they were using it to propel their Apollo Command and Service Module and the three men aboard farther from Earth than any human being had ever traveled; but they'd hoped for some glitch, some technical problem with the Saturn-V, and for the mission to be aborted.

Apollo 8 was sending back pictures from a mere 100 kilometers above the surface. The American astronauts were describing the colors of the terrain. They likened it to a beach.

The next morning, December 25, 1968, Yefgenii returned to Komsomolsky Avenue before dawn. Snow fell on Moscow, dusting the streets and decorating the rooftops like white tinsel. A pale winter Moon hung in its first quarter. In a burst of emotion it struck him: three Americans were up there. They'd sailed across the Far Side, gazed down where no human eye had looked before and seen the earthrise.

He wept. Gevorkian had called him a legend but the old legends were dead. This was a new one, and bigger than any in history: not just Ivan the Terrible, but all of them, the equal of Gagarin: Borman, Lovell and Anders were circling the Moon, reciting verses from the Book of Genesis, and, in America, it was Christmas Eve.

NO WATER RAN HERE, none fell. The Baikonur Cosmodrome stood on a remote desert plain more than 2,000 kilometers from the nearest open sea, and only in winter when the snows came did the land reveal itself to be on Earth and not some other celestial body. When fronts passed through, wind boosted sand off the desert. It got into everything, through the cracks in the windows and doors. Yefgenii felt fine grit rolling across his eyes and round his teeth, felt it scratching his skin.

In February, the cosmonaut corps was summoned to observe the maiden test flight of the N-1 rocket. A bus conveyed them from their accommodation to Pad 110, where they trooped out to gaze up at the gigantic metal candle. Early in the day its nose had pricked the cloudbase. Now the air was clear.

Yefgenii knew nearly every detail of its operation. On a forthcoming flight it would propel the two-man L-3 spacecraft to the Moon and return part of it to the Earth. The L-3 was heavier than the Zond because it comprised a lunar orbiting vehicle and separate lunar lander. The N-1 was the most powerful rocket ever created. At that moment, Yefgenii would've climbed to the top of the great metal pillar and ridden it into the depths of space. He saw the same hungry look in the others' eyes. They were sick of the rehearsal and wanted the performance. They wanted to be first.

The bus scooted them to an observation platform. The cosmonauts stood in rows, with binoculars. When the countdown reached zero, thirty engines lit. First the fires flashed on, then, seconds later, thunder shook the ground. The rocket separated from the Earth with a slow ascent up the gantry, then gained speed, soon streaking in a high arc out over the desert.

Then the fires went out. Yefgenii's eyes strained through his binoculars. The rocket had disappeared. Seconds later an inferno blazed far away in the desert, the Moon above bit by bit masked by a thickening plume of smoke.

The cosmonauts and engineers dispersed into small groups, men who trusted each other. Some were philosophical. It had been a maiden flight. Things go wrong.

Gevorkian's mood was more despondent. He knew more about the engineering of the rockets than any of them. "We don't have the Americans' money, their industry. They're ahead, their vehicles are more advanced."

Yefgenii said, "The Americans spent millions of dollars designing a pen that could work in space. What did *we* do?" Gevorkian's head was down, his eyes were down. *"What did we do?"*

Gevorkian lifted his head. "We used pencils."

"We used pencils."

T HEY TRAINED for the lunar landing in a modified Mi-4. Yefgenii had never flown a helicopter before he entered the cosmonaut program. He soon became adept.

He sat at the top of the craft, under the rotor. The blades levitated storms of sand off the desert floor. The helicopter tipped up into the air, out of the sand, and soared into a blue sky patched by heaped white clouds. It was spring at Baikonur. The desert was dry, the air was hot.

As he climbed, he saw the towering slabs of concrete that housed the N-1 processing plant. They rose out of the center of the Cosmodrome while to either side spread rows of launchpads, and, beyond, barely visible from this part of the desert, the tracking stations and the railway line. Heat haze blurred the railway into a vague gray band.

From ceiling he pitched the helicopter down and guided it toward the training grounds. In principle he was simulating a descent from lunar orbit to a precise initiation point over a potential landing site. The landing would be carried out by the pilot, flying solo in the LK, while the flight engineer orbited the Moon in the stack containing the principal living compartment, the reentry capsule and the main engines of the L-3, all together known as the LOK.

He hovered at just over 100 meters above the training grounds. Markings simulated craters, ridges and boulders. He selected a clear zone and then shut down the engine. The Mi-4 dropped at once, its rotors turning in the rush of air. Yefgenii pitched and yawed the craft, dead-sticking down toward the landing site. He made a soft touchdown on the exact spot he'd nominated.

His performance was scored. He restarted the engine and recovered to the start point to repeat the exercise. He was one of six men training for the lunar landing. His scores ranked number one.

Gevorkian worked on the development of the LK, the lunar lander, but already the American Apollo 9 mission was conducting tests of their own Lunar Module in Earth orbit. Then, in May, *Apollo 10* traveled to the Moon. The Americans undocked their Lunar Module in orbit, descended to within 50,000 feet of the surface to reconnoiter landing sites, ascended for rendezvous with their Command Module, and made a successful return to Earth. Yefgenii knew next time would be the landing attempt: *Apollo 11* was scheduled to launch in July.

Desert preparations continued nonetheless. Sun scorched the sand. Air simmered in the throat. The cosmonauts and technicians suffered during the day and the heat wouldn't let them sleep at night. Scorpions could prevail here, but not men. Yefgenii and the other command pilots of the lunar training group endured the conditions to simulate a descent to the surface of the Moon, but no manned flight was scheduled, only another test of the N-1 sometime that summer.

The fate of these men appeared to be the fate of their nation, to scrabble around in the dust. The mission Yefgenii craved grew no closer.

Gevorkian arrived to address the lunar training group on the subject of the N-1 program. He was one of them now, while still serving as a principal engineer in the project. In the lecture room the blinds hung down. Sunlight daggered through in hot sharp beams that projected a grid on the floor and walls. The windows were open but the air was still, stifling; Gevorkian had to raise his voice to be heard over the whirring fans.

"We've diagnosed the problem with the N-1. As you know, its engines are arranged in two concentric circles. When they thrust, a hypobaric zone is created between the two circles which causes instability in flight."

"Can it be fixed?" Leonov asked.

"We're going to realign the engines. The vehicle will then require another unmanned test."

The cosmonauts knew this would be the procedure, but they shifted in their chairs. Their faces shone with sweat. Their shirts were moist. They sat like schoolchildren in a classroom, their days evaporating like the days of childhood.

"And the LK?" Leonov asked him.

"Once the launch vehicle has been flight-tested, I'm hopeful we will be able to conduct an Earth-orbit test of the LK before the end of the year."

"But is it ready?" Yefgenii asked.

"The computer systems are proving problematic. You must understand, to recognize and interpret the datum marks required for a landing on another planet demands an exceptional piece of kit."

"We've got the kit," Yefgenii said. "There's six of them looking right back at you."

YEFGENII WAITED for his friend on a patch of ground near the engineering outbuildings. The Sun was slipping down behind the launchpad scaffolds that ran in a line west of the enormous rocket-processing plants, but the heat remained, cradled by the desert.

Gevorkian appeared from the building and strode across the sand to him. "You were disrespectful to me as your project manager, as your comrade cosmonaut, and as your friend."

"I'd prefer that you were interested in hearing the idea behind by my comment."

"I understood your remark. The human brain is the most sophisticated computer at our disposal. Men can be trained to navigate by the stars, we can be trained to calculate orbital mechanics—"

"So let's train a crew, and launch them."

"The rocket isn't ready, the lander isn't ready."

"That's not what you said. You said they were."

"We can't kill a crew finding out. The equipment must be tested."

"Then let the Americans win." Yefgenii turned to walk away.

"That's what we're already saying," Gevorkian said.

Yefgenii halted.

"Officially the authorities are claiming there never was a race.

Already Mishin is talking about Salyut. He says a landing on the Moon is a scientific and military non sequitur. Why go there without a plan to establish a Moon base? The next logical step is to establish a space station—to explore the Moon and planets only after that."

"There's a race," Yefgenii said. "I still want us to win it."

"So do I, my friend. I know the cosmonauts are ready, but Mishin doesn't dare lose another man in space after Komarov—"

"That's why they chose us, isn't it? To fly, or die trying?"

Gevorkian sighed. "Every man thinks the same. We all want to lobby the authorities for a circumlunar flight."

"No. The Americans have already done it. Now only the landing matters."

"The N-1, the L-3, the LK—each would have to work perfectly on its maiden flight."

"They have to work sometime."

"Without fully automated systems."

"The crew will fly manually."

Gevorkian measured a pause. "There's something else."

"What?"

"Realigning the engines of the N-1 will affect its thrust. We have to lose weight from the payload."

"How much weight?"

"A lot. Maybe seventy kilos."

Yefgenii said it. "A man," he said.

Gevorkian studied him. His eyes narrowed. "The workload's too intense for one man. He'd have to carry out the lunar-orbit rendezvous alone. He might never make it back."

Yefgenii eyed him but declared nothing.

Gevorkian said, "The objective is to land a man on the Moon and return him safely to the Earth. It wouldn't count."

"It did for Gagarin."

Gevorkian looked around to ensure they couldn't be overhead. One of the most sensitive of state secrets was that Gagarin hadn't landed his capsule. He'd ejected during reentry at around 7,000 meters and parachuted down. By the rules of international aviation records, ejection made the attempt void. Gagarin's flight shouldn't have counted: Shepard was first. But to all the world Yuri Gagarin was the first man in space because he'd been first to get there, and how he'd returned, probably even if he hadn't returned at all, didn't matter.

"And the same went for Laika," Yefgenii said. His eyes were blue fire. "I'm not even here in my own name. If any man's death could be hidden, I'm that man."

IN THE MORNING, he traveled to Star City on three days' leave. By the time he arrived home the children had returned from school. The widow was serving them their tea. She made a sound of joy as she heard the door open; she ran across the apartment to greet him. He held her in his arms and kissed her. The children came down from the table and he hugged them both.

That night in bed the widow said, "You're not flying."

"Why do you say that?" he said.

"They gave you leave. They don't give leave to the men who are going into space."

He said nothing. She held him tighter. She was relieved that he hadn't been selected for the next mission. He was a cosmonaut now. His career was made. The years of exile for him were over, the cold and misery for her and the children, now she was a cosmonaut's wife. Their life would always be good, whether he risked his life in space or not, in the system-built city, in the system.

"It's my job," he said.

Next morning he slipped out for his run. The Sun was up, the air was mild. As he began his circuit of the city it occurred to him to run faster, to run faster and faster, till at the perimeter fence where the

162

sentries saluted him he was in a headlong sprint, his blood rushing, great lungfuls of breath rasping through his throat. It had come to him to run faster because he'd decided not to run home, but to give everything to the outbound leg, and walk or crawl back, whatever his state was. How much faster he flew, not having to save anything for the run home.

When he returned, the children were still dozing. The widow, in her dressing gown, beamed. She cooked breakfast for him. "You will eat, won't you?" she said, but they were interrupted by the older child, the girl, calling for her father.

Yefgenii crept into the children's room. The girl's hair lay across her face. She was curled in a ball, blankets heaped on top of her. He parted the hair from her eyes and kissed her forehead. She gave him a hug and he opened her curtain onto a bright clear summer day. The boy stirred. Yefgenii swept him over his shoulder and carried him, the girl holding his free hand, to the kitchen.

After breakfast Yefgenii vomited in secret and then the family went to the playground built for the children of the cosmonauts and technicians. The girl rode her bicycle, the boy clambered across a climbing frame. Yefgenii watched the boy use his long limbs to swing from rail to rail.

"Are you on holiday, daddy?" said the girl.

She hooked her arms round his midriff and looked up at him. She was tall for her age, her head reaching his chest, and she was bony like he'd become. Her eyes were big, and colored with his blue. He gazed down at her and pulled a joking face. She curled a lip; she was too old for this now. The boy ran across the concrete kicking a football. In the apartment or outdoors, the boy ran everywhere; he carried his father's energy with him. He was getting big. He was getting into fights.

The girl got frustrated when she didn't get her way. She didn't look much like him but she had his drive, his desire to win. The boy was milder. He had blond hair and blue eyes and Yefgenii couldn't stop himself from scuffing his hair. He hugged them both. In his arms snuggled beautiful creatures made of soft pale flesh.

That night Gevorkian called at the apartment. The widow offered him supper but he declined. He had operational matters to discuss with her husband. Yefgenii picked his coat off the hook and the men strolled out to the elevator. He read a look in Gevorkian's face that had been there the moment the widow had opened the door to him. They went out into the dark tree-lined avenue and the look didn't shift.

"You're to report to General Kamanin in the morning," he said. "General Kamanin, the Chief Designer, and the senior members of the Space Committee. General Secretary Brezhnev has been briefed."

The mission was on. Yefgenii Yeremin was the one name unknown to the spies in the West who followed the program. He'd leapfrogged the prime crews of the lunar training group not so much because he was the most able but because he was the most expendable.

"How will it work?" he said.

"Technicians are working round the clock to ready the L-3 for the next N-1 test flight, scheduled for July third. If the flight isn't successful, reports will proclaim the rocket exploded on the launchpad during an unmanned test."

Gevorkian paused. "The proposal will be put to you officially by General Kamanin. You will be given a free choice without fear of reprisals." He kissed Yefgenii on the cheek. "Say no," he said.

Yefgenii lay awake throughout the night. The children would miss him, their mother would miss him. The boy and the girl carried his genes and the few behaviors instilled by his minimal parenting. In this regard they were no different from animals. Man's unique superiority was that his life's legacy could surpass the reproductive, he could create history, exceed his own life and biology, but this applied to very few. No matter how happy and pleasurable their existence, most men were reckoned in terms no better than animals: they consumed, excreted, reproduced, died and decayed. So far, this was the measure of his own life: biology not history. Still the great mission he'd craved had remained elusive, the one that would write his name in the sky and color him celestial.

As dawn came Yefgenii rose in silence. He sat at the edge of the bed, his eyes damp with tears. The widow stirred. She reached out. Her hand brushed his bare back, feeling the ridges of ribs and the hard plates of scapulae that had appeared in recent years not from privation but from single-minded discipline.

"What's the matter?" she said.

He didn't turn. His feet were planted on the floor, his back arched over, his head downturned. A breeze shifted the curtains. A yellow light played across his back and the profile of his head.

"What is it?" she said again.

This time he turned.

"They've got a mission for me," he said, and in his eyes she saw what the mission must be, and she knew here came their destiny; here it came like a train with them on the tracks.

He passed through the rooms of the apartment, past the photographs of their life together, to the sleeping bodies of his children. He touched their heads, first the girl's, then the boy's, these strange and beautiful creatures. His tears fell. Ivan the Terrible was floating over their faces like a cloud passing over the face of the Moon. His form was becoming less solid. He was already becoming a ghost to them.

THE EARTH
AND THE MOON

1969–

)

I VAN THE TERRIBLE sails in a ship named *Voskhodyeniye*. His dark vessel drifts against brilliant colors. Clouds mass in enormous white bands. They glow. He's dazzled by weather the size of continents. In places the sky is empty all the way down. Patches of green dapple brown lands, but most of what curves below shines in great pools of blue. Everything glows. The clouds and seas radiate reflected sunlight. The oceans burn like blue suns. The Sun itself, unfiltered by the atmosphere, is a disc of energy fueling a half sky of unbearable brilliance, bright beyond any glare he's ever endured on Earth, warming one side of the modified Soyuz; then the Sun drifts behind the world, snuffed out by the planet, so that night stretches below and darkness all around, leaving only the flickering lights of the largest cities and the steady points of starlight, and all these sights must cram into stolen glimpses because there's so much work for him to do.

The space inside is cramped. His space suit bulks him out. Only his head and hands are free, since on achieving orbit Mission Control cleared him to remove his bubble helmet and space gloves. He wears a leather communications helmet incorporating earpieces and a microphone. Checklists hang in the air, close-printed paper in plastic sleeves, at first glance motionless but over time sliding in a direction determined by the tiny momentum imparted when he places them. They are task enough for two men, let alone one. Yefgenii carries out the checks step by step. His fingers work the switches and circuit breakers of the SA. His eyes fixate on the switch markings as he checks them off; when a checklist is completed, he plucks the next from the air, seeing it's drifted a few centimeters since the last time he looked.

Once he completes the SA checks, he reports to Mission Control. The SA is the re-entry capsule that will carry him back down to Earth on his return. All its systems are operational. The voice he hears back is Gevorkian's; cosmonauts take turns being the sole member of Mission Control permitted to contact the man in space. Gevorkian clears Yefgenii to proceed into the BO.

He maneuvers through a tunnel out of the SA. His stomach bobs and bounces with every movement. The contents of his abdominal cavity are floating free, something that can be simulated on Earth for only a matter of seconds. He's been weightless for over an hour now, the whole time working and moving, looking for handholds and pitching in every direction. Nausea drags at his stomach.

Emerging from the short access tunnel into the BO, *Voskhodyeniye's* living compartment, he finds more space to work in, and he gets to it straight away. Above the storage locker that contains the Krechet lunar suit, he finds the main instrumentation console, and begins a long work routine of systems tests and checks. By the time he's finished he's circled the Earth and not once glanced out of the portholes to his left and behind him.

Next is scheduled a fifteen-minute break to rest, his first since lift off, and take on water. He drinks from a plastic bottle with a tube and valve from which he sucks in a predetermined load of 500 milliliters of fluid. While he rests, he hovers in the middle of the BO in a fetal position. Without gravity his legs tend to curl up toward his body. Optics obstruct his view out of most of the portholes, but in the gaps he can see segments of Earth and sky. The Earth is huge and brilliant, the sunny part of the sky so bright he must blot it out with metal blinds.

His next assignment is navigation. The rest break allows time to return to darkness, but he's tense and restless, concerned at falling behind in the next critical phase of his work cycle.

The Sun swings behind the world. Night engulfs him. Cabin lights are the only illumination. He dims them and places himself at the portholes, where he secures his position by gripping the handholds. The dull metal craft plunges through space, its portholes pale beacons containing the silhouette of a man, and the only other lights are the stars themselves.

He searches the visible segments of sky for a recognizable pattern of stars. Prior to launch he's learned the specific stars that provide the necessary flight-guidance datum measurements at specific points in the voyage to the Moon. Ground simulations assumed he could visualize the constellation Centaurus. It's his responsibility alone; installing a computer that could carry out the task would have consumed precious months.

His eyes take time to adjust to the darkness. He experiences a few moments of panic, of feeling that this one task is beyond him and therefore so is the entire enterprise. Soon he's confident of what he sees. He presses his face to the eyepiece of a sextant mounted in the porthole, aims at the star Menkent, the first datum star, and then sets about aligning it with the Earth's horizon.

In darkness the arching edge of the planet is invisible. Instead he notes a blank zone of space where the stars disappear: this can only be the Earth. He holds Menkent in the eyepiece and moves the sextant arm in tiny increments until its image becomes superimposed with the edge of the blank zone. His body drifts, losing him the picture. He uses his knees to secure his lower body against the bulkhead; he stiffens his free arm on the handhold.

He tries again. The airglow extinguishes the star but then it relights for a fraction of a second between the airglow and the hard black edge of the world. The tiniest shift in position will invalidate the measurement. The muscles of his arms and legs ache. At last he superimposes the image of the star on the horizon. He shines a dim penlight onto the sextant scale and struggles to read the angle. He manages to accommodate, and he scribbles the result on the pad built into the thigh of his suit. The scratching of his pencil makes the loudest noise in the void.

His orders are to input the angle into the flight-guidance computer before moving on to the second measurement, but he knows he's taken too long recording the first, and is in danger of losing the darkness. Adding another orbit to the flight plan will jeopardize the timing of the launch toward the Moon.

He searches for the constellation Sagittarius. He finds it and identifies the datum star, Nunki. He sets his body rigid again. He feels a small discomfort rising from the base of his back. With a tremulous free hand, he edges the sextant arm along the scale until the datum star drowns in the muddiness of the atmosphere. He sets the arm and shines the penlight. He reads off the angle and notes it on his thigh-pad.

Releasing his grip on the handhold, he pushes off toward the control panel. He raises the cabin lights and then begins to punch the figures into the onboard computer. At the same time he reads them out to Mission Control. Their computers and the spacecraft's onboard computer produce identical calculations. *Voskhodyeniye* is established in an elliptical orbit spanning 200 by 740 kilometers at an inclination to the ecliptic of 50.7 degrees, the exact orbit decreed by the flight plan.

Gevorkian's voice squeaks out of the earpiece cushioned in the soft leather of Yefgenii's communications helmet. "*Voskhodyeniye,* you are go to power up the LK."

A hawser stretches from the LOK to the LK, a short stout umbilical cord containing the electrical cables through which the LOK, the command module of the stack, powers the lander's systems, charges its batteries, and monitors its condition. Yefgenii sets about bringing the LK to life from the remote-command console in the BO. Through the viewport of the docking cupola he watches the lander's lights blink on. They cast a glow across the divide between the two ships. Inside the LK, gauges flash, fans start to turn.

The Sun flows like syrup off the edge of the world, forming a blinding globule of light that pierces the cabin where Yefgenii toils to prepare his craft for the next stage of the journey. The timing is exact. Via Gevorkian he receives Mission Control's clearance to carry out the EVA and LK systems check.

Yefgenii has just over ninety minutes to prepare for the EVA, the duration of one revolution round the Earth. He removes the items he's stored in the locker below the main instrument console, pulling on silk lining gloves and then the Orlan suit's bulky space gloves. He puts a clear bubble helmet over his leather communications cap and locks it into the space suit's metal collar. He checks the suit's environmental control systems. The readings come back nominal. Heating and oxygen supply are in perfect operation. He breathes pure oxygen, purging nitrogen from his blood to prevent the bends.

Next he sets about depressurizing the BO. He seals off the access tunnel to the SA and then operates the spacecraft's environmental control system to vent the atmosphere pressurized within the BO. He hears the rush of the atmosphere being evacuated. The ambient noises of the spacecraft cabin grow quieter. When he is in vacuum, the ship is silent. The sound of his own breathing fills his helmet. He endeavors to disregard it, to not become focused on the process of inspiration and expiration.

The suit's interior is pressurized. Pushing out against vacuum, the suit stiffens like an inflating life vest, becoming inflexible as armor. Every change of posture demands strong muscular effort.

Yefgenii dons the EVA helmet. The protective metal dome covers the inner bubble and locks down onto the metal collar. A visor screens out sunlight. He floats to the hatch in the lower part of the bulkhead to the right of the control panel. He turns the heavy levers that release the hatch from its locks. He swings the hatch open. The procedure has been timed to coincide with the end of the rev. *Voskhodyeniye* has passed from day into night, and now dawn is breaking once again; the next rev begins, the daylit portion measuring a little over three-quarters of an hour as the spacecraft orbits the world.

A safety line tethers him to the ship. He hangs out of the hatch, under the scrutiny of a television camera in the BO. He awaits the order to go. His heart quickens.

"*Voskhodyeniye,* we are visual with you." Gevorkian's voice fills his ears, for a moment replaces the accelerating cycle of his respiration. "You look well, comrade. Proceed with EVA. And good luck!"

Yefgenii passes his head and shoulders through the hatch. His size coupled with the bulk of the space suit creates a tight squeeze. Earth opens out behind his head. He arches his neck and into his upper field of vision drifts the north polar ice cap. Sudden vertigo spins his gaze. He feels nauseated. He grabs at the rail welded onto the outer hull of the BO. In this extraordinary moment he fears he will vomit inside his helmet.

His heart is racing. The electrodes stuck to his chest, for which his chest was shaved the day before launch, are transmitting a continuous ECG to the flight physicians' consoles in Moscow. Gevorkian's voice cuts through the sound of his hyperventilation. For the first time he sounds urgent. "The senior flight physician requests you report your condition."

"I am well, Moscow, thank you."

He eases his head farther back and now he is gazing down at an inverted Europe. He sees the Mediterranean and below it the Alps and below them Scandinavia. The whole continent is framed within his solar visor. His breathing levels, his heart slows.

Gevorkian's voice joins him inside the helmet. "The senior flight physician is satisfied. You may proceed."

Yefgenii works his way along the rail. The tether loops behind him, back into the open hatch of the BO. His muscles strain to bend elbows and knees, flexing against the suit's rigid inflation. His breathing becomes rapid again, sounds coarser within his helmet. He can hear the pounding of his own heart. There are no other sounds. Already the interior capsule of the suit stinks of leather, rubber and his own sweat. He smells the sweat on his upper lip. It's a rank smell, the smell of his bodily fluids.

The world floats beneath him in complete silence. As he maneuvers along the rail, he becomes oriented upward, so his head is now north. He can see the Baltic gliding under his chest, the Black Sea between his feet.

Yefgenii reaches a boom mounted on the outside of the BO. He's transferred himself only a matter of meters from the hatch, but he feels hot and tired already. Every tiny movement in gripping the rail is complicated by an opposite and equal reaction that modifies his position and direction of movement. He struggles to ensure every motion produces the correct effect on his progress.

At last he secures himself to the boom. He activates the boom's motor and the structure telescopes out toward the LK, carrying him with it.

The L-3 spacecraft *Voskhodyeniye* is a stack of modules, a Soyuz 7K-LOK attached to additional propulsion units and the lunar lander, the LK, all housed in a metal payload shroud that curves round the stack like the closed petals of a tulip. The LK is housed on the LOK's nose, the engines sprout from its tail.

Now the stack is passing over Russia. Yefgenii glimpses the Urals floating up from the east, mountains rising in seconds rather than millions of years. He witnesses the illusion of the Earth turning from east to west as the spacecraft girdles the planet once every ninety minutes. The terminator bisects the Soviet Union and curves down into the Indian Ocean. He peers down upon bright blue waters that fade and blur eastward into night. It is night in India, in China, in Japan.

He reaches the hatch of the LK. He depressurizes the module from outside. He receives a green indicator light to proceed and a confirmation from Mission Control. He blows the hatch, unhooks the tether and clips it to the handrail, and then he enters the lunar lander. Outside night falls in an instant.

Inside the lander, the gauges, displays and power lights glow with current. Yefgenii closes the hatch, then repressurizes the cabin. He is breathing hard. His heart is racing. He fights to keep them under control, worried the flight physicians in Moscow will recommend a mission abort.

As the cabin pressure rises, his suit softens. Gevorkian's voice says, "*Voskhodyeniye,* you are advised to rest. Five minutes."

Yefgenii wants to argue but he knows he's completed the daylight-critical transfer as planned. He has more time at his disposal. "Roger, Moscow."

As the atmosphere thickens, sounds return. He hears the hum of current, the whir of fans. When rested, he removes his EVA helmet, his bubble helmet and his space gloves. His gloves and helmets unlock from the metal rings and hover in the lander till he stows them in the storage locker set aside for his Krechet-94 Moonsuit. Fans pump out hot air but it will be many minutes before the cabin warms to room temperature. Vapor balloons from his mouth and nose into perfect evanescent spheres. The chill refreshes him.

He carries out the checks on all the LK's systems. He reports each phase to Mission Control. He does so with a tingle of nerves. One faulty piece of equipment and the flight will be scrubbed.

The flight plan allows for three revs while he works his way through the LK checklists. More than four hours later, in night broken only by the LK's internal lighting, he puts his gloves and helmets back on and depressurizes the cabin. He exits the hatch into dawn. The terminator has tracked five hours west. The line that divides day and night on Earth arches across the Atlantic Ocean from Greenland to Antarctica.

Yefgenii returns to the BO. Once repressurization is complete, he removes the Orlan space suit, getting down to his gray two-piece flight suit. He drifts, with loose limbs. His muscles ache, his back is sore.

From the BO he shuts down the LK's systems. One by one they go to sleep for the voyage to the Moon. Only the lander's batteries hold a charge of their own.

He enjoys a short rest period, with the opportunity to take in food and fluid, while Mission Control evaluates the data he's returned over the past sixteen hours. Sweat drenches his flight suit. Dark patches, fringed with salt, underhang his armpits; damp triangles cover his chest and back. Already the spacecraft reeks of human water in its various forms.

Gevorkian's voice breaks the silence. "*Voskhodyeniye*, congratulations. All your systems are working perfectly. It's been a hard day, but you've performed your duties admirably. You are clear to sleep."

"Thank you."

"Goodnight, *Voskhodyeniye*."

"Goodnight, Moscow." He says it to the TV camera, to the banks of faceless technicians watching in Mission Control, the only people on Earth who are witness to the embarkation of his voyage. In comparison, Apollo astronauts perform live telecasts viewed by millions, by billions—but perhaps something other than the standard operational secrecy of the Soviet system lurks behind the contrast.

When Soviet cosmonauts travel into space, a fear stows away that's harder to shake loose than gravity: a recognition of the fragility of man and his works. Maybe the Americans have been blinded by the photo flashes of ticker-tape parades, but, for the Soviets, it's so much easier to see, particularly since the passing of Gagarin, a man the size of a country who seemed as indestructible. The people he left behind understand that anything valuable can be stolen, anything vital can cease to exist, even those creations possessing the breadth of empires or the length of history.

And so, as Yefgenii Yeremin unfolds the metal frame of his mesh hammock and straps in to sleep, only the officials and technicians of the inner circle are permitted to share the hopes and fears of his perilous voyage; the world is not.

B LINDS COVER THE PORTHOLES of the BO. Through the night sharp daggers of sunlight have stabbed out from their edges. His sleep has been fitful. Too many worries have swooped and dived through his consciousness. The pitch of a fan changes and he wakes. He listens to it, straining in the darkness, till he convinces himself nothing's wrong.

In the end he unstraps himself from the mesh hammock strung across a folding metal frame and floats free. He lifts the blinds an hour early on the start of his second day in space, though at this time his part of the sky remains in darkness. The black Earth turns beneath the portholes. The oceans are blank slabs of slate.

He takes on water from a plastic tube. His mouth feels dirty. He is stubbled and unwashed. He needs to urinate. He pops open his fly and rolls the convene of the waste management system over his penis. He turns the valve and feels a pull that disrupts the normal action of relaxing his urethral sphincter. It takes a few uncomfortable seconds before he passes water. It's deep yellow from his dehydration. He closes the valve and unrolls the convene. A drop of golden liquid escapes. It forms a tiny sphere that drifts away into the cabin. He finds a wipe and folds it over the globule of urine. As he does so, yellow crystals drift past a porthole. His water has been jettisoned to space and turned in an instant to ice, a string of yellow beads. In train the crystals glide Earthward where, on contact with the atmosphere, traveling at orbital velocity, they'll flash to vapor.

An increase in heart rate has alerted the flight physicians that he's awake, but Mission Control has deferred communicating with the spacecraft to preserve an illusion of privacy. Now the flight clock reaches 24:00. "Good morning, *Voskhodyeniye,* come in," says Ges, starting his shift as communicator.

"Good morning, Moscow."

"How is the weather up there, comrade?"

Yefgenii laughs. "Cold outside. Some yellow sleet."

"All systems are continuing to show nominal readings. Please commence countdown sequence for translunar injection."

Yefgenii returns to the pilot's seat for the first time since he's made orbit. He straps in and begins to work through the sequence of checks ordered by Mission Control. His eyes are weary, his back stiff. Smells of rubber and metal fill the ship.

A splinter of sunlight bursts into the darkness. Second by second it streaks into a curving band of orange, white and blue. Cloud, sky and sunlight squeeze through what appears like a crack in the fabric of space. The edge of the dark Earth is rupturing, burning up in a great celestial fire of heat and color as if it has fingers that are struggling to pry open the blackness. He sees the sky opening. It's opening for him.

"*Voskhodyeniye,* you are to initiate TLI burn at mission-elapsed time 25:44:16; burn duration 05:47; do you copy?"

"25:44:16, 05:47, copy that." Yefgenii scratches the numbers onto his thigh-pad.

He punches the numbers into the flight computer. At the end of the sequence his finger hangs over the keyboard for a second or two. He can still choose to de-orbit and splashdown in the Indian Ocean. He presses the key to proceed.

At twenty-five hours, forty-four minutes and sixteen seconds from the moment the N-1 rocket lifted off the pad at Baikonur, the computer initiates ignition of the craft's Block G engine. Yefgenii feels acceleration no more violent than a push. He senses he is veering sideways. The fluid in his inner ear sloshes and he experiences a sudden attack of nausea, but this passes, and he rides the rocket out of orbit. Yefgenii monitors the instruments. He is accelerating from orbital velocity to escape velocity.

A rocket roar travels up through the structure of the ship while the brilliant glow of its tail burns behind him. A creature from Earth is carrying fire to the Moon. The gases freeze in space, becoming a shower of ice particles, and then the crystal shower disperses, drifting back into the Earth's gravity, to burn up in the atmosphere, to vanish in an instant.

Ges's voice cuts through. Yefgenii hears it in his earpiece. "Telemetry shows you are good in the burn, *Voskhodyeniye*."

Now Yefgenii shakes in his seat. The whole vehicle trembles. The rocket engine thrusts toward the culmination of its burn, toward 10,830 meters per second, the speed required in its original orbit to overcome the Earth's gravity.

The lights flicker. Yefgenii feels the brilliance change around him. The light plays across his face and mixes with the yellow glow of the rocket burn that haloes his bald head. His hand grips the throttle. It shakes for the first time he can remember, not since the early days of flight training. The computer clock counts down to the end of the burn but the display flickers. Yefgenii has set the chronometer of his watch; he notes the duration etched on his thigh-pad and starts to perform the countdown himself, off the chronometer. The computer blinks out. The cabin lights blink out. In panic he glances at the control panel behind him, sees circuit breakers tripped and tripping. The burn continues a split second past the auto-shutoff; the computer has failed.

Yefgenii shuts down the engine, but as he does so a bang rattles the entire spacecraft. Storage lockers fly open and their contents spew out into the cabin.

The rocket roar dies in an instant. The afterglow fades. He sees ice crystals glinting in earthlight, a shower of tiny stars, but no light shines within *Voskhodyeniye,* and there are no voices on the radio, not Ges's, nor any other from Earth.

At once he knows something very serious has gone wrong. Objects float round the cabin. A tube of food concentrate bumps his head. An instrument package has ripped open and packing material is swirling out—tiny polystyrene balls. The disarray unsettles him. His hands are still quivering, his stomach flutters. There's no ejector seat or possibility of a glide down to a friendly runway. A paper-thin metal hull is all that protects him from the unsurvivable vacuum of space.

He keys the transmitter on his communications helmet.

"Moscow, come in, *Voskhodyeniye.*"

He waits. He tries again.

"Moscow, come in, *Voskhodyeniye.*"

He waits.

"Moscow, *Voskholdyeniye,* do you copy?"

The spacecraft is rolling slowly to port but none of the thrusters are firing. His mind begins to function again, to diagnose problems and calculate solutions. In a matter of seconds the shaking of his hands has diminished. He releases his straps and hovers. A band of sunlight streams through one of the portholes, illuminating a section of the BO to an unbearable intensity; the remainder lives in an eerie dusk created by the Sun's reflections off glass and metalwork.

With a little push he glides into the sunlight, cutting the beam. Darkness falls across the control panel, and then he clears, and it's lit again, so he can see to reset the communications system circuit breaker. The breaker won't hold. It springs back when he throws it, and the power lights dotted on the radio control board won't blink to life. A bus failure has disarmed nearly all of the ship's electrical systems.

A deep worry grips him. He drags himself hand over hand to the environmental control system. He pulls himself close. He listens. He can hear a flow of oxygen, a hum of motors.

He swings to his left. The fluid in his ear sloshes at the sudden movement, and his stomach churns. He makes a tiny retching sound, but that's all, and the wave of nausea passes.

Out of the portholes, through the constellation of ice crystals, he glimpses the Earth, now a disc that he can visualize from pole to pole in one scan. He pauses to absorb the view, and to ponder his predicament. The burn has accelerated the spacecraft far out of orbit; in the next hour the planet will become nearly 40,000 kilometers more remote. He'll travel a distance roughly equivalent to the circumference of the globe. He forces himself through the moment, back to the task.

Yefgenii hauls himself down the tunnel into the SA. He felt a bang at the end of translunar injection and now he's looking for the cause. Nothing in the SA appears changed from his previous orbital check, apart from the sporadic electrical paralysis. He returns to the BO and peers out of the portholes one by one. A trail of gas is running out from *Voskhodyeniye*. He can't get a view of where it's being vented from, but it's snaking away from the spacecraft, a tiny thread of white cotton he missed the first time he looked out after the bang. The gas is already ice when he sees it.

Without guidance from Mission Control, he must think his way through the steps on his own. He assumes the material being vented from the spacecraft must be related to the bang and the subsequent electrical problems. He holds on to a hope that the fault is confined to the Block G engine. At this point in the flight plan, the engine is all but spent, and should be jettisoned. Yefgenii maneuvers to the control panel. The switch responds. He feels a rush of joy. He still wields some control over the ship and therefore over his fate. He jettisons the Block G.

Yefgenii presses himself against a porthole. Soon the dead rocket drifts into view, in a slow roll, traveling at almost the same velocity as *Voskhodyeniye*. It hangs aft of the stack, spraying crystals, the remnants of its fuel. As it rolls, he gets a sudden glimpse of a V-shaped rupture at the base of its aerocasing. The metal is bent and blackened. He concludes that a small explosion occurred in the Block G engine at the end of the translunar injection burn, possibly due to the sudden ignition of some uncombusted fuel, and that it must have caused collateral damage to the stack.

Loose items continue to drift round the cabin. He collects the larger objects and stows them, then begins the painstaking task of vacuuming up each of the little polystyrene balls. He can grab two or three at a time with the tiny battery-powered vacuum cleaner, then he must place them in a sealed bag or else they'll float free again.

His best hope of contacting Moscow is to make an emergency EVA transfer to the LK to operate its communications system. From the remote command console he attempts to power up the LK but he has limited success, receiving a series of indifferent readings from the lander's control systems. The surge of current has affected the entire *Voskhodyeniye* stack.

He decides to jettison the payload shroud while there's still power to do so, and attempt to dock the LOK to the LK. He positions himself at the docking cupola. Through the viewport he gazes at the hexagonal array of docking receptacles on the leading edge of the lander. With the thrusters he maneuvers the LOK forward, closing the gap between the two ships, till the LOK's docking probe pricks one of the hexagonal holes. He fires the forward thruster and the probe lurches into its home, bonding the two craft together.

Without time for a rest or refreshment break, he clears the flotsam from the cabin, knowing if he doesn't it will all be vented to space when he depressurizes the BO. He is rushing. Sweat damps his brow and back. It takes him over an hour to clear all the objects away and then he hurries to pull on his Orlan space suit. He dons the main body, then the bubble helmet and gloves. He locks his

EVA helmet to the space suit's metal collar. He races to double-check the condition of the suit. Any error made in haste will cost him his life.

He depressurizes the BO. The system works, sparing him having to blow the hatch. He releases the sequence of levered locks on the hatch door. The hatch swings open and he floats on the threshold of deep space. He grips the handhold in sudden trepidation: no man has carried out a spacewalk this far from Earth. He cannot see either the Earth or the Moon, and the Sun blazes on the opposite side of the spacecraft such that the hatch opens into *Voskhodyeniye*'s shadow. Outside stretches vast black void.

Yefgenii pulls himself out of the port. The stiff suit resists his efforts. He is pushing himself harder and faster than on the first EVA. It isn't daylight that'll run out this time. It's electrical power, the very life of his spacecraft, and with it his chance ever to return home.

He squeezes out of the hatch. He glimpses the payload shroud like the leaves of a closed tulip drifting away from the stack in a line of space debris backed by the blackened Block G engine. The giant metal staves of the shroud rotate in a slow dance with the other debris, glinting under incident sunlight.

Yefgenii fixes his position on the handrail to survey the stack. The explosion has damaged the part of *Voskhodyeniye*'s power module adjacent to the Block G. A crack punctures the tank of liquid oxygen feeding the fuel cells that produce electricity for the spacecraft. Gas is escaping into space, sublimating to ice in an instant. A tiny thread of crystals weaves back toward the shroud and the jettisoned Block G. Now he understands how the explosion has caused power fluctuations throughout the stack; in response to a loss of pressure, the fuel-cell safety valves have closed.

He changes direction and maneuvers along the handrails toward the power module. With every grab of a handhold, an equal and opposite force causes him to spin and topple. The tether snakes behind him, transmitting disorienting sinusoidal waves of force up and down the line. He strains to control his motion. His muscles ache. Sweat drips and stinks inside his suit.

The handrails run out before he reaches the power module, since no EVA has been planned to operate in this area of the spacecraft. The trailing edge of the engine curves beyond reach. Aft spreads the coiling filament of ice crystals venting from the lox tank, the payload shroud and the Block G. The Earth burns beyond. The blue disc is diminishing. His chances of returning home are diminishing.

He secures the tethering line in his hand and endeavors to push himself along the hull toward the tank. The first push carries him away from the spacecraft and now he drifts away in a slow backflip. He topples backward and when he is next upright he glimpses the hull more distant and the cord of his tether lengthening. He can gain no purchase to correct the topple so he can only wait till the line pulls taut. In midroll he reaches the end of the tether; he feels a tug as it snaps tight and then he's sprung back toward the hull. Not only is he toppling but he has now been thrown into a slow cartwheel. As he approaches the hull he gathers in loops of tether, so, when he bounces off again, the shorter length wrenches on his hands and prevents him from drifting so far out into space on this oscillation; and so he continues, toppling and cartwheeling as he oscillates along the hull of the spacecraft making slow painful progress toward the leaking lox tank.

When at last he reaches the tank, his helmet strikes the hull and he bounces away again. By controlling the length of the tether he manages to reduce the amplitude of the oscillations, but in doing so he converts the energy into angular momentum. Yefgenii spins and topples faster, he hits the hull harder. He is nauseated and hyperventilating.

On his next bounce he attempts to grab a section of pipework, but his thick gloves glance off and he topples away again. His direction has changed; now when he draws in the tether he moves more or less in parallel to the line of the hull and back toward the hatch.

He has been tumbling in space for almost half an hour and, at the end of it, he is floating back toward the handrails where his EVA commenced. He grabs the first rail but can't close his grip fast enough. The contact twists him into a salchow but on the third rotation he grabs at the next rail and this time clings on.

Yefgenii feels his heart drumming inside his chest. He is hyperventilating. Sweat drips from his brow and stings his eyes. He decides he can't afford to expend more time and effort inspecting the ruptured tank and must press on with his effort to enter the LK.

He attempts to activate the boom but the power supply has died. He moves hand over hand toward the LK. He is overheating inside his suit. The environmental controls can't cope with the amount of sweat and CO_2 he's pumping out, and now his visor starts to fog. In patches the solar screen clouds. At first he can see through the gaps but soon the whole visor is misted. The LK hatch is ahead of him but, after his experience in trying to inspect the lox tank, he dare not risk attempting to float the short distance between the two ships. He pulls himself up toward the LOK's docking probe and then transfers his grip to the hexagonal docking array on the roof of the lander. His gloved fingers just about squeeze into the holes.

Using this position as a base camp, he allows himself a minute's rest to bring down his heart and respiratory rates. He runs a loop of his tethering line over a spacing bar of the docking probe. With the tip of his nose, he wipes an opening in the misted visor.

Now he eases along the lander's hull toward the hatch. The LK is even more fragile than the LOK, so he resists the urge to grab on to any part of it save the handholds circling the hatch. The slightest push sets him in motion and he is no longer traveling parallel to the hull. He is drifting in the direction of the hatch but away from the lander. He reaches out in panic and clips the handrail with his fingertips. He enters a slow rotation. He gathers in his tether and it pulls tight on the docking probe, so that he is sprung back in the direction he has traveled but at a slightly slower rate, slow enough for him this time to grab the handhold and come to rest at the hatch of the LK.

Once again with the tip of his nose he wipes an iris in the mist of his visor. He activates the controls on the outside of the hatch to open the port and he is grateful that they work. The lander's batteries should still retain much of the charge present when he switched the LK into its dormant mode for the transit to the Moon.

He struggles through the oval opening. His suit has swollen and stiffened, or so it seems, but more likely his muscles have weakened. He clambers into the lander and works the levers of the hatch closed. The lights are on, and he's able to pressurize the cabin.

As the atmospheric pressure rises, he feels his spacesuit soften. The material becomes flexible again, but in moving with greater freedom he realizes the inner layers covering his armpits and lower back are soaked and so heavy with sweat they're like wet rags.

With enormous relief he removes his gloves, EVA helmet and bubble helmet. Steam issues from his collar and cuffs. His face is bright red, his hands are swollen. He is gasping for breath but the heating system has yet to warm the LK, or it's failed, so that his teeth and tongue are chilled by mouthfuls of frozen air.

At once he sets to work powering up the LK's communications system. As with the LOK, sporadic electrical failures affect the vehicle's control systems. A power surge has traveled throughout the stack, to the LK possibly from the LOK via the umbilical connection. In any event, he is unable to activate the radio.

Yefgenii toils through a sequence of procedures to open communications. The checklists in the LK offer him a number of alternatives. He tries them all, one by one. He resets switches. He shuts down related systems. He powers up related systems. He repeats the sequence again in its entirety, without success.

He drifts for a time in the cabin. Through the upper viewport he gazes at the arching back of the *Voskhodyeniye* stack. A curve of metal slices the Earth into a glowing crescent of blue and white. He decides to try once again to activate the radio. He turns all the control switches to off and then throws them on one by one. He trips and resets the circuit breaker. The lander's radio is as dead as the LOK's. The crescented Earth hangs in the upper viewport like the down-turned mouth of a sorrowful cartoon.

Following a rapid assessment, Yefgenii concludes that while many of the lander's essential operating systems show promise, in their present condition none of them gives him the option of relaying a message to Earth. The LK possesses no power supply of its own. Apart from the charge in its batteries, it depends on the LOK for electricity.

Yefgenii wipes his visor clean with his silk lining gloves and then relocks the helmets and outer gloves to the suit's metal collar and cuffs. He is anxious and depressed but cannot afford to let himself get diverted. With as much haste as he can muster in his state of fatigue, he shuts down the LK's systems. The lander returns to its dormant state, its batteries spared for another day.

He clambers out of the hatch into unfiltered sunlight. The roll of the spacecraft caused by the Block G explosion has oriented the hatches toward the blinding yellow disc. The space suit's protective lay-ers shield his body from the unattenuated radiation, but, as Yefgenii slides along the tethering line, he begins to feel a scorching pain in his side. He concludes that one or two layers must have torn as he fought to right himself during the earlier violent toppling movements. Now every panel of the spacecraft's hull beams burning UV light at him.

The thread of frozen gas coils from the damaged lox tank back toward the diminishing Earth. This time he is determined to reach the tank in the simplest manner. Gathering in the tether, he floats on past the LOK hatch and aft toward the power module, and now begins to let out the tether with the correct timing to stop it from snapping taut and springing him back or out or whichever wrong way.

Yefgenii manages to ease himself into a small turn, angling his scorched side away from the Sun, and feels a sudden drop in heat and pain. He drifts to the tank and at close quarters inspects the crack in its casing like a crack in an eggshell. One small puncture vents the oxygen. The gas freezes in an instant. The sight is strange. He feels he is watching snowflakes form; he is watching the processes of nature laid bare.

He presses his glove over the puncture. He is able to mend small punctures in his suit with a repair kit and this is the only means at his disposal for attempting to contain the lox leak. He removes his hand to reveal a plaque of ice that pops open with the pressure of gas behind it, the plaque shattering into shards of crystals.

Yefgenii opens the repair kit. In looking down into it, he enters a very slow tumble, which he corrects by throwing his free hand out onto the hull. He bounces off and tumbles in the opposite direction. He feels pain tear at the scorched section of his skin and then, as it turns into the Sun, he feels it light like a fire. He screams in pain but fights not to oppose the rotation. He lets it hurt and then it passes as his body rotates into its own shadow. He brings out the sticky patch from the repair kit and struggles to hold it between fat swollen inflexible fingertips. He is unable to manipulate the patch and unable to uncover the adhesive backing, his fingers are too fat and rigid in the space gloves. He keeps on trying. He is tumbling end over end and he is getting sick, but he keeps struggling to get the patch into a form he can use to stem the leaking lifeblood of his spacecraft, but it's beyond him, it's beyond any man, and the patch slips from between his fingers and he lunges for it, but the gloves are too thick and rigid and he is now turning in the wrong direction, turning to the Sun again; this time, when the sunlight strikes, he can't hold back, he emits a deep primal roar that fills his space suit and reverberates through every layer and joint of it but in the vacuum of space travels no farther.

H E FEELS THE HEAT OF THE SUN on his body, the solid band of light that divides the BO into day and night. Soon the sunward portion of the spacecraft will overheat and the shaded side freeze. He returns to the pilot's seat and straps himself in. He sets and fires a thruster. *Voskhodyeniye* jerks into a slow roll, but, without the computer's assistance, he can manage the maneuver in only an imprecise fashion, so that the spacecraft's rotation is skewed by small amounts of pitch and yaw. He's trying to get the whole stack turning, the LOK and the docked lander, but as a result *Voskhodyeniye* is also wobbling. He feels something in his stomach, the subclinical nausea experienced in an aircraft flying out of rudder trim, but he's done the best he can, and, as the stack rolls, the solar heating is distributed over its shell with an approximate uniformity. He'll have to live with the nausea.

When he pauses to take stock, he becomes conscious of the agony of his sunburn. A scarlet triangle has blistered and tightened on his flank. The spacecraft carries no dressings or ointments; not another gram of weight could've been added to the launch payload. He must take water to avoid dehydration; he must keep the lesion clean to avoid infection. The pain he can only endure.

Out of a porthole, Yefgenii sees that the debris that shook loose when he jettisoned the Block G engine has now drifted clear of the spacecraft. The Block G itself glides about 500 meters behind, no longer shedding small showers of ice, and nearby float the staves of the payload shroud that resemble the leaves of a tulip curling open to the Sun.

He searches for the trail of vented gas. The ship continues its slow roll, and this is how he eventually gets to see it, as the sunlight rolls onto a gentle curving arc of ice crystals threading out from somewhere on the spacecraft and trailing away into space. The tank is still venting. No measure at his disposal can stem the leak. He's losing the raw material from which *Voskhodyeniye*'s fuel cells generate electricity, water and oxygen.

The mission is almost certainly lost. He may never get home. He feels deep, depressing failure. Time is sliding by.

A single act can define the meaning of a man's life. Everything to this point has been a rehearsal. The boy who ascended from the ruins of Stalingrad to the realm of space, the man hardened by cold and exile, this man has longed for the clash of metal against metal in a sky gleaming with beautiful machines, the climactic clash of cymbals of the two greatest powers in history. Like Gagarin, he has become his country. More: a hand drifts in front of the Earth framed in the porthole, and covers it. In space, a man is the size of countries. He must act, he must do what no one else could achieve. Throughout his career, he has craved a mission such as this one. Now he has it.

Major Yefgenii Mikhailovich Yeremin unstows the emergency procedures checklists and begins to follow the protocols, using his penlight when the rotation of the craft transports his section of the BO into darkness, and bringing the metal blinds down when the Sun comes in, leaving just a crack of attenuated sunlight that sprays through the cabin.

He identifies which of the spacecraft's systems are functioning and which are not. The environmental control system, which oxygenates and purifies the cabin atmosphere, is working. The flight-control systems are working when governed manually. The flight computer has crashed and is not recovering when rebooted. The communications system is not functioning.

This task carries him through to the end of his second diurnal cycle in space. Because of his absorption in work, he's missed his food, fluid and rest breaks. He has made himself ill. His sunburn is agonizing. He is hungry, but hunger has become a moral ally in recent years: it reminds him he is disciplined, he will push himself farther than the ordinary man. He is dehydrated, but gulps of warm water renew him. He's tempted to press on, but he is too weary. He opens the plastic pouches and metal tubes and consumes cubes of cheese and borscht in the form of a bland chewy paste. He needs to urinate again. His piss is an even deeper yellow. When he jettisons the waste into space, it doesn't stream toward Earth; instead the crystals glide on the gentle escarpments of gravity, neither toward the planet nor away from it. One day, the ice may be captured by Earth's pull, but till then it'll drift in this cislunar space for countless centuries.

A little of the drinking water he lets out into the air. It forms a perfect sphere that wobbles and drifts in front of his eyes. He captures it in a cloth and lays it on the patch of sunburnt skin that forms a bright red triangle on his right flank. He winces. Every movement hurts. The cloth applies dampness for a mere moment, then, without gravity to hold it in place, it drifts off into the cabin. He snatches it and wrings out a tiny drop that hangs in the air for him to swallow. Then he sets aside the pain and returns to work.

According to the flight plan, now is the period to use any spare time for photography. *Voskhodyeniye*'s rotation is imperceptible apart from the creep of Earth and Moon across the portholes. Yefgenii keys the camera mounted in an optical port and shoots a series of images of the Earth setting and sometime later the Moon rising.

The Moon is waning gibbous. The Sun lights its surface from the west as far as the Sea of Serenity. His eyes rest on the Ocean of Storms, an ancient lava field stretching to the western limb of the lunar disc. Within its bounds lies the landing site selected for the mission, on a basalt plain about 500 kilometers west of the crater Kepler. These features are clearer and larger than he's ever seen. The Moon is growing, though he knows he must be decelerating. The Earth's pull is slowing the ship down but won't ever quite stop it crossing the gravitational ridge into the Moon's influence, and then the Moon will draw him in, ever faster.

Behind *Voskhodyeniye* the Earth is shrinking. Now it's small enough to be banded by the porthole's metal frame.

Yefgenii knows he is presumed lost. On Earth, his colleagues must consider the most likely explanation: that a catastrophic explosion occurred during the burn of the rocket engine. He pictures Gevorkian conveying the news to the widow, or perhaps another cosmonaut that she'd know, like Ges or Leonov. She remained at home with the children as he made final preparations at Baikonur, forbidden to attend Mission Control because it's bad luck to lay eyes on a woman, except of course if she's a technician. The night before liftoff, he went through the rituals, "for luck," of transferring to the small house where Gagarin spent the night before his flight, of taking a sip of champagne with breakfast, of pissing on the wheel of the bus that carried him to the pad. An official telephoned her with the good news: liftoff was successful. He imagines she wept with relief. She hugged the children to her chest. The next call came: successful orbit, but then nothing. So there she is, in the apartment, as Gevorkian or Ges or Leonov, whoever it falls to, informs her they've lost contact with *Voskhodyeniye*. There's another knock at the door. It's Ges's wife, perhaps; another cosmonaut family will take care of the children, just for the time being. The hours crawl by. The telephone rings with a sympathy call from a senior space official, Mishin himself or perhaps even Kamanin, who assures her that everything possible is being undertaken to secure her husband's safe return. She knows that minute by minute the technicians are endeavoring to make contact with the spacecraft; not only are they hearing nothing from the pilot, but also there is no relay of electronic information from the ship's systems. This is explained in gentle terms by Gevorkian or Ges or Leonov, whoever it is. An abrupt termination of telemetry signifies a catastrophic event befalling the spacecraft. The timing, the association with an engine firing, in an undertested propulsion system assembled in haste, all these factors together mean they must fear the worst. Of course, she asks if it might be something else, and of course they say, "yes," but their voices are low and their eyes carry little conviction because a systems failure on the scale that would eliminate total telemetry would in all likelihood also render the spacecraft inoperative. The mission is lost. The craft is lost. Major Yefgenii Mikhailovich Yeremin is lost.

The widow wants to be brave, but she weeps for her dead husband. The space officials too are sorrowful, but now they must address the question of how long to wait before issuing the statement planned in the event of such an outcome, that the N-1 blew up during an unmanned test on July 3.

He knows his name is being expunged from the records. He pictures the documents relating to his false identity being further falsified to show that he was discharged from the cosmonaut corps. They will go back, he imagines, to his flying records and his war records, and they too will vanish. The paper shreds, it burns. The photographs curl and blacken to smoke.

Yefgenii attempts to sleep. He unfolds the narrow metal frame to which he must strap himself, for fear of floating about the BO and causing injury to himself or his craft. He pictures the children asleep in their beds. In the morning their mother will tell them the story. He wonders if they'll shed tears, or be numb, as he is numb now, numb and sleepless, watching a solitary globule of water, his tear, drift and ripple and from time to time glint in the light of the Earth and the Moon.

W HEN HE WAKES, he wonders for a moment where he is. The first thing that comes to mind is that he is a major now. General Kamanin awarded him the rank, at the extraordinary meeting of the Space Committee, in which he volunteered to pilot this mission designated *N1-5L Soyuz-7K-L3-1*. Kamanin asked his reason, and he replied, "To prove the superiority of the Soviet system." He has made such statements so many times in his career that he may even have begun to believe the words, but in one matter there's no question of self-deception. He loves his country, and he aims to see it again.

He feels cold and he's uncertain whether the cabin temperature has dropped or it's because he's just woken from deep sleep. His chronometer shows he's entered the third day of the flight. He can't believe he fell asleep. His worries seemed too great.

Empty space fills the portholes. He searches for the trail of vented gas but either the sunlight isn't striking the crystals or the tank has emptied. The Earth has shrunk again. Soon it won't be much bigger than the face of his wristwatch, yet it remains so bright, much brighter than the most radiant full Moon.

Stubble roughens his face. His mouth is dry. He takes on water then he urinates. He consumes a portion of food concentrate. His bowels move, but the rectal sensation is only of partial fullness, so he prefers to postpone defecation.

Every movement tugs the taut skin of his sunburn; he feels it crack and ooze. He's made a dressing by cutting out a small section of material from his flight suit. Blood and discharge stain the dressing black and yellow. He cannot further damage his flight suit nor risk expending water to wash the wound. The dressing remains in place, held by pieces of tape, melting into the burn, damp and reeking.

Hunger and dehydration accentuate his weakness. No man has traveled so far out by himself, no man has been so alone and apart from mankind. There is no one to speak to, no voice in his ears.

Already a sense of ritual surrounds his approach to the radio. He floats toward it, hoping to see enough of a glimmer in the power lights to put out a signal that he's here, he's alive, he's still trying to hold this mission together. The lights are a row of glassy dots, and blank. He resets the circuit breaker and throws the power. The radio is dead, the ritual concludes. Next he decides to open the communications panel to see if he can identify any burnt-out wiring. He worries he's wasting time on the radio when there's so much else to do, but he longs to call out, and longs for an answering call. All the contacts appear intact. The radio's dead, and he can see no means of reviving it.

To those on Earth he's lived the commonplace tragedy of seeking and preparing for greatness and then being consumed by death while he remains ordinary. His widow and children will remember him as a husband and father. That is what will be passed on. An ordinary life will be recalled in the ordinary way, its events and meanings simplified to mundane accounts of mundane activities, much as our corpses cannot be assimilated whole, so nature breaks them down to simpler commonplace chemicals.

Once again he endeavors to reboot the flight computer. He follows the steps of the emergency checklist protocol. For over an hour he applies and adjusts the circuit settings but, as he expects, he does so without success. Now he decides he must establish his position. Again he follows a protocol established during training. He floats to the pilot's control panel and once more is relieved to discover a response from the craft's attitude control thrusters. This is the only bit of luck in what has befallen him. *Voskhodyeniye* remains his to fly, for the time being at least, and therein lies the chance, however slim, of getting home.

He attempts to arrest the thermal control rotation. Without the computer, his actions are imprecise. He kills most of the roll but the ship's motion has been infected by tiny germs of pitch and yaw that he can't eradicate, and he knows he can't afford to burn kilo after kilo of rocket fuel trying in vain to do so. Like the nagging nausea caused by the wobble, he's just got to live with it.

Yefgenii draws the blinds on the sunward side of the BO and sets himself up at the sextant. One advantage of the extensive power failure is that there is no pollution from the cabin lighting.

He uses his penlight to study the flight plan, which allows for two midcourse corrections. At this point he must carry out a navigation sighting of five stars with respect to Earth's horizon. Because it's so much smaller now, he must add a telescope eyepiece to the sextant in order to identify the substellar point, the nearest part of the horizon to the datum star.

The ship's wobble still sickens him. He struggles to align the sextant as the device's superimposition of star and planet pitches and yaws and rolls in the eyepiece, while he braces himself in a half-kneeling position against the bulkhead. Next he reorients *Voskhodyeniye* so he can carry out the same procedure with respect to the Moon. When it appears in the optics porthole, he draws back. It has swollen into a gray globe whose size is unsettling. The Moon has turned in its orbit round the Earth; the face that always points to the Earth—the Near Side, the Earth side— always does so in synchronous rotation, and this face has become more oblique to the Sun.

Now shadow engulfs the Sea of Serenity, creeping westward over the Caucasus.

When he's completed his observations, he reestablishes *Voskhodyeniye* in the thermal control maneuver that rolls the capsule three times every hour. The new rotation is as contaminated by pitch and yaw as before, but of a new character. He finds the altered sense of jumbled motion difficult to adjust to, having become accustomed to its previous components. He needs to put a vomit bag to his chin. He retches, but nothing comes up. He retches again and this time regurgitates a small clump of food paste and gastric acid, which he spits into the bag. He hovers as still as he can manage. Eventually the motion sickness remits to a tolerable level. He packs the vomit bag into the waste management system, to be jettisoned into space.

Yefgenii compiles his stellar observations and then works with log tables to determine his position. The combined calculations of the onboard computer and those at Mission Control would produce the answer in a matter of minutes, but by hand and mind the process is as difficult as Gevorkian predicted. It consumes three hours.

He takes a break for rest, fluid and food. As he swallows the paste he hears his bowels gurgle. He feels a motion, then more pressure in his rectum. Again he decides to postpone defecation.

His pencil scratches out the final calculations on his thigh-pad. Papers spread in front of him, floating in an array over the flight plan. The flight plan contains sample reference calculations so he can judge with some certainty the accuracy of his own conclusions.

He fears the dysfunctional translunar injection has failed to propel *Voskhodyeniye* into the designated free-return trajectory, or the venting of gas from the ruptured tank is acting like a small rocket and pushing the spacecraft off course, but his own observations show the spacecraft's present translunar coast appears closer to nominal parameters than he dared hope. With no further deviations, he'll slingshot round the Moon and back toward the Earth in a figure eight.

199

Pushing away from the porthole, he drifts to the environmental control system. Air flows, but chills his hand. The heating has gone offline. For a moment he considers what this means. The permutations cross and conflict. He pushes them aside. The spacecraft can work in cold, for the time being at least; a man too.

He must decide whether or not to carry out the first midcourse correction. It's the only way to keep alive the possibility of attempting a Moon landing. However, his own survival is much more likely if he abandons this element of the mission now and concentrates all his efforts on returning safely to Earth.

Yefgenii sets about making the calculations based on how far off the nominal course he's gone since translunar injection. Again, the flight plan offers reference figures to guide him through the intricate process, and he uses the log and trig tables compiled for the purpose.

For a brief interlude his mind revisits the orphanage in Stalingrad. He remembers the lessons in mathematics, where he learned the rules by which the physical universe works, and first set out on the quest to ascend.

When he completes his calculations, hours have elapsed. He judges that the original observations are now out of date, and so he repeats them all, by stabilizing the spacecraft's motion as best he can, remeasuring the positions of the datum stars, and feeding the more current information into his calculations, working as fast as he dares without leaving himself open to error. The reinstatement of the thermal control rotation, crucial now that the cabin heating is nonoperational, nauseates him to the point where he vomits acid and bile from an empty stomach.

Yefgenii drinks water to soothe the burn of vomit in the back of his throat. He drifts in the middle of the BO. He is cold now. The layers of his flight suit are too thin for insulation. He shivers as he considers his situation.

Carrying out the first midcourse correction will establish a greater probability of a successful lunar orbit, but will expend fuel he might want to conserve for a complex reentry into Earth's atmosphere. The chance of a successful landing is even slimmer than it was at liftoff. By all operational rules of spaceflight, his course of action should be to preserve the free-return trajectory and maximize the possibility of getting home alive.

Yefgenii arrests the rotation of the spacecraft to all but a tiny wobble. He must carry out the course correction by firing the lunar lander's Block D engine. He operates the engine from the control panel in the BO. It will fire only if the electrical connections remain functional and the explosion hasn't caused any internal damage to the LK/Block D system.

The Block D engine fires. *Voskhodyeniye* bucks but he holds her steady. His manual control is effective. He times a nine-second burn on his wristwatch before shutdown. The engine cuts out on command.

He tries to sleep, but he can't. He's put the spacecraft into a new thermal control rotation but it makes him feel sick. He decides to repeat his stellar observations to ensure the engine burn has achieved the course correction he calculated.

Voskhodyeniye turns. He views the Earth and the Moon. He's weak, cold, weary and sick, but he's alive, and still flying, and therefore he can still dare to believe that both worlds remain his to conquer.

H E BEGINS THE FOURTH DAY by attempting to purge the fuel cells. Most of them are dead. The lox leak has caused a loss of pressure in the system, and as a fail-safe the valves supplying the fuel cells have shut. He speculates that not all the fuel cells have been starved of oxygen, either because not all the fail-safes have operated as expected or because intermittent pressure fluctuations have been causing the valves to open. In any event, the fuel cells are supplying a dribble of electricity to *Voskhodyeniye,* sufficient only to power the essential flight-control systems.

Something else troubles him even more. The fuel cells combine hydrogen with oxygen to generate electricity, but as a by-product they yield his water supply. Already he's dehydrated. He judges there'll be barely enough water to meet his needs for the remainder of the mission.

The cold has become unbearable. Its fortunate coincident effect is to reduce his need for water, but he must put on the Orlan space suit for insulation. First he accepts that this is the most convenient time to evacuate his rectum. The pressure is intense now.

He removes the lower portion of his flight suit and attaches a fecal collection bag to his buttocks by means of an adhesive strip running round the rim of the bag. On the morning of the launch, a VVS nurse shaved the hair from his buttocks to make this process as comfortable as possible. Once he's ensured the adhesive strip holds fast, he releases the contents of his rectum into the bag. Without gravity, the stools don't fall; he must use his fingers through the plastic of the bag to coax them down. He seals the bag, wipes, seals the wipes in a second bag, and stows them all in the waste disposal unit.

Wearing the Orlan, he feels warmer, but his face and head remain chill. His breath coils in vapors.

The spacecraft plunges toward the Moon. The target floats into the photographic porthole and Yefgenii decides to take a picture. In its mount, the camera studies the object that has swollen from an ivory disc to a giant gray globe. He peers through the viewfinder and keys off a series of images. In its last quarter, the Moon is a perfect hemisphere, divided into a radiant gray-brown west and a black east. It's no longer flat to the eye. Its belly bulges toward him like the prow of a battleship at anchor on a surging tide.

He snaps off half a roll of film and then, on impulse, releases the camera from its mount and turns it on himself. He's hovering, the metal rim of his space-suit collar looping round his chin, his jaw stubbled, his eyes blue and sleepless, his scalp bald. This is the image he captures, not knowing if it will ever be seen, if it'll ever adorn the front page of newspapers or the leaves of history books.

In contrast, the crew of *Apollo 11* was announced at the beginning of the year. They became household names because their flight was slated to be the first attempted Moon landing, and the success of *Apollo 10* confirmed the plan: Armstrong, Aldrin and Collins will fly to the Moon in the second half of July, and, if they secure lunar orbit, Armstrong and Aldrin will attempt a landing in their lunar module, and, if they succeed, Armstrong as commander of the mission will take the first steps out onto the surface.

Yuri Gagarin's identity and his mission weren't announced till he returned. Before him, a cosmonaut called Valentin Bondarenko died in training for the first manned spaceflight. The facts were hidden, documents were locked away, his name remains unknown. And so, by now, the announcement of the failure of the *N1-5L* unmanned test will have been circulated beyond the inner circle. Possibly Western intelligence will acquire the information, or at least some meaningful part of it. Yefgenii Yeremin has gone the way of Valentin Bondarenko: there follows a shuffling away of papers, a closing of vaults, a state secret will be created and eventually forgotten; the world will turn without another nod to his life or his death.

Next comes the effort toward complete erasure. The widow must be sworn to secrecy. She will never be permitted to bear her married name again, nor her children their true family name. She must swear by the official truth, that her husband served with the VVS and his life was lost in training; he never entered the cosmonaut corps, never took on this last greatest mission. And Gevorkian, he must swear too, and Ges, all his colleagues in the cosmonaut corps. The military men will do so without question. They know how to keep a name alive, in whispers late at night in the officers' club, after many vodkas. The secret toasts may survive a generation, that is the best he can hope for.

He anticipates that for a deception so important the authorities must go even further. A senior official will travel to Graham Bell. He'll sequester any logs pertaining to Kapetan Yefgenii Yeremin. He'll trace any man who served with him, and convince him of the national interest to be served by complying, and the reprisals that will result by not. Perhaps it will be the same official or a different one who will confiscate the relevant logs of the 221st IAP, and that same official or a different one who'll find the men who are still alive, the Pilipenkos and the *starshinas*.

To the people of Earth, Ivan the Terrible never existed. Now it might be easier for him to pretend that Earth doesn't exist, that

Voskhodyeniye is the universe, and he the only consciousness in it, a great being sailing through the cosmos.

Yefgenii feels a sudden profound longing to speak to his children. He sees their lives projecting into the future without him. He'll live in their memories for a time, but the authorities will confiscate the photographs, their recollections will fade, they'll be urged never to speak about him. He yearns to tell them where he is and describe these visions to them in detail. Only human beings can transmit a culture to future generations that exists beyond the material written in our genes. It is as if he understands this for the first time, where we live, and what we are.

He carries out the routine tasks that remain. He uses what power there is to charge batteries in the BO. He conducts systems checks. Even inside the lining gloves, his hands are blue with cold. He must rub them together and flex the fingers to keep the blood circulating. His body within the Orlan is tolerating the cold, but his extremities are not. When he can, he huddles in sunlit portions of the BO and lets the harsh brilliant light bathe him with precious warmth. But the temperature within *Voskhodyeniye* keeps falling, and no amount of solar heating will reverse the freeze.

All of a sudden, a drastic change occurs in the world around him. One of the ambient sounds to which he's become accustomed has altered. At first Yefgenii cannot identify the change, then realization comes to him: the fan of the environmental control system has stopped. He floats to it with mounting panic. He holds himself to the metal grill. He feels no flow of oxygen. Frost clings to the grill's tiny bars. He removes his gloves and scratches off some of it with his fingers. He cups the frost in his palm, and when it melts he licks up the precious moisture. He cleans the frost from the duct and then he resets the circuit, but the system doesn't come back to life; it's dead now, as dead as the radio and all the other systems that blinked out one by one, starved of electricity.

He carries out a rapid calculation. Under the tiny probe of his penlight, his pencil scratches out symbols on the pad. He knows the dimensions of the BO and the SA. He knows that at rest a man of his size consumes about 15 liters of oxygen every hour. As he works through the calculation and adds in his estimates of the oxygen reserves contained in his two space-suit backpacks and in the LK tanks, he realizes that sufficient oxygen remains to support a slingshot round the Moon and the return journey to Earth, provided of course that conditions don't alter, with, for example, a fire or a breach of the spacecraft hull.

The flight rules in this instance aren't flexible. As soon as the ship experienced a widespread electrical failure, an attempt at a lunar landing became reckless. Now that oxygen is limited, he must expedite a return to Earth. But *Voskhodyeniye* is already accelerating toward the Moon. The gravity of Earth has lost its influence and now the lesser body is reeling in the tiny metal boat. The great gray sphere looms through every porthole. The Moon has entered its last quarter. The western hemisphere beams back sunlight. At this distance the brilliance is dazzling.

Mission Control's order would be to pitch the spacecraft 180 degrees over on its longitudinal axis in order to swing the LK-Block D assembly aft, then to fire the Block D engine and speed *Voskhodyeniye* along the free-return trajectory, so as to slingshot round the Moon and hurl the spacecraft onto a reciprocal course for Earth.

He shivers. He is drifting in the middle of the BO. His breath forms tiny spherical clouds. Time passes. The Moon grows closer. He is plunging toward the eastern limb, and into lunar shadow. Any further failure of the ship's systems could leave him stranded in the realm of the Moon. *Voskhodyeniye* would orbit till he suffocated and eventually the orbit would decay until the spacecraft crashed somewhere on the airless waterless desolate surface.

Whatever outcome awaits him, Yefgenii must still apply himself to the necessary calculations, to be prepared to burn the engine at a specified time for a specified duration. He works through the numbers, either to accelerate the free-return trajectory or alternatively to decelerate the spacecraft so that it'll be captured by the Moon's gravitation and reeled into orbit.

By the time he completes the calculations, a coat of frost has spread over the coldest surfaces of the capsule, forming from the diminishing quantities of water vapor that he is generating from sweat and respiration. Once again he consults the reference figures in the flight plan. After four days in space, concentration is difficult. He checks and rechecks his working. On a number of occasions he's some way through a calculation, then becomes disoriented and has to start again.

While he floats, while he ponders, the fourth day comes to an end. Decision time arrives, though he can even choose to do nothing and the ship will still travel the free-return trajectory back to Earth.

Ninety-eight hours into the mission, he slows the thermal control roll. He feels sick in the pit of his stomach from motion and hunger. His eyes are tired, and gritty from the dry air. His head aches.

Firing the thrusters causes the ship to stop, but then to begin rolling in the opposite direction. He must apply counterthrust to arrest the motion. He overcompensates and the ship wobbles back. He fires again and steadies her again. He knows he's wasting fuel. Without the onboard computer to carry out maneuvers like this one, his flying is imprecise, it's wasteful; it depletes the spacecraft's fuel but also it depletes him.

The maneuvering is complete. Only six men before him have come this far, the crews of *Apollo 8* and *Apollo 10*. A chance still exists for him to return to Earth, to see home again, to see the cheering crowds in Red Square, but this was not the objective of his ascent. He has not risen so far to emulate the achievements of other men, to choose a glory amortized by repetition; his destiny must be the perfect mission, the unique mission, that which no other man can do, which no other man would do.

Home hangs in a porthole. He raises his hand and just a thumb-nail is enough to cover Earth. This far out, a man is bigger than countries: Yefgenii Yeremin is the size of the planets themselves.

He fires the Block D engine for three minutes and fifty-four seconds, decelerating the spacecraft. The ship no longer possesses the velocity to slingshot round the Moon and be flung home. He has surrendered to gravity and it captures him, like Icarus.

D ARKNESS SURROUNDS THE FRAGILE METAL CRAFT. *Voskhodyeniye* is passing through the shadow of the Moon. Frost speckles the instruments and bulkheads of the cabin. Yefgenii wears his space gloves and communications helmet for warmth, stripping to the lining gloves only for delicate tasks. He huddles a meter above the floor. It doesn't matter which part of the cabin he occupies, there's no sunlight, no source of warmth. He blinks ever slower, falling asleep. Out of the porthole he glimpses a vast black hole in the stars. This is the surface of the Moon, drifting below. He sails across the unlit portion of the Near Side into the unlit portion of the Far Side. Only blackness spans the below.

He wonders if he is dreaming, if he's at sail in a ship of the imagination, on a blank ocean, an ocean of souls. He dreams of Kiriya, and Skomorokhov, and little Gnido, of Bondarenko, Komarov and Gagarin, and of the Americans too, the nameless pilots in Korea whose aircraft shattered and burned before their parachutes could bloom; he dreams of them all, too many and too long ago to picture, and of Grissom, White and Chaffee, burning like Bondarenko burned, in a capsule too rich in oxygen, conquerors of the air being conquered by it.

Then the universe explodes. One star flares, a point of light expanding into a gigantic inferno that spreads across creation in a vast rippling disc of fire that consumes the stars and planets.

He wakes to gaze upon the secret face of the Moon. The Sun has risen across the lunar horizon, and now light is blazing across the craters of the Far Side. Millions of years of meteorite impacts have pitted the surface into a featureless scarred ruin, without mountains, without rilles, without the striking basalt plains of the misnomeric lunar seas. The Moon has passed its last quarter, but this is as viewed from Earth; the Sun lights the Far Side into a waxing gibbous Moon that arches into shadow behind him and curves toward the Near Side ahead.

He drifts toward the Sun, like an etiolated plant struggling toward the light, and bumps against the porthole. The dazzling light scorches through into the cabin. He huddles in it, craving warmth, but frost streaks the panels and gauges and pipework, and even coats his space suit, so that as he moves it crinkles and floats off into the air, where it drifts as glistening confetti.

Perhaps he's still dreaming. His ship of the imagination appears to be traveling backward in time. The lunar shadow recedes from *Voskhodyeniye*. The ship is sinking toward the Sun, then toward the Earth, then he will return to cislunar space, wherein the Moon presents him with yesterday's waning gibbous face hours before last quarter, and he is back in the time of making calculations and planning whether to pitch the spacecraft round and fire the Block D to hurry himself home, or to insert *Voskhodyeniye* into lunar orbit.

Now he remembers. He made the insertion burn. The spacecraft is swinging behind the Moon and heading back toward Earth, not to return but to establish lunar orbit. He's not dreaming. He's here. This is what he's done, and he asks himself if he was right, or if this isn't the supreme folly of a life which, if surveyed backward in the dreamy voyage of his ship of the imagination, falls from the Korean sky glinting with metal and fire where Ivan the Terrible was born, into the soot and ruins of Stalingrad. Babak, that was his name, the boy who raped him: from that nadir Babak is the one who ascends to the flight school at Chkalov, and another VVS ace, Pepelyaev, is the one who wins more jet kills than any pilot in history, and Armstrong and Aldrin will be the first visitors to the surface of the Moon. It may as well be, because Ivan the Terrible never existed, because Earth has assumed him lost and turns with aloof serenity, turns in the sky as if by turning from west to east, from night into day, she is turning her beautiful watery blue back to him.

Yet in gazing down at the secret face below, he feels fulfilled in choosing the Moon over the Earth. For eons the Far Side has been invisible to man, yet it has always been here, and, like his own voyage that is unknown and invisible to those on Earth, it is no less beautiful or dramatic because of it.

So he is here. The one illuminated feature he recognizes drifts below, a plain circular patch of ancient lava, like an ectopic gray eye on a pitted brown face: the Eastern Sea. The curve of the lunar limb bulges ahead. He is sailing from the Far Side onto the Near Side, the Earth Side, and then he glimpses her, rising, the only colored thing in the universe, the brilliant blue-and-white disc of home. She is floating on a black sea, a part submerged buoy that appears to pull against an invisible anchor, straining out of the blackness to mark the solitary known point of water and life.

He weeps. He thinks perhaps it is from tiredness, from the tyrannies of thirst, hunger and cold, but he is a man watching the earthrise, and he is weeping.

His gloved fingers paw his cheeks. He captures the tears on his fingertips and licks the moisture before it freezes. His mouth is dry. His cheeks and lips are numb and cracked. He purges the dying fuel cells. Only one remains working. He gleans its meager production of water, and drinks. He scrapes frost off the cabin's frozen surfaces and cups it in his hand, where it melts, and then he drinks that too.

The Ocean of Storms slides below. The spacecraft has curved round the edge of the visible land and now is traversing the Near Side, which has diminished to a little less than half-lit. The face is a waning crescent, but broad, bulging, and stretching just about as far as the westernmost escarpment of the lunar Appenines.

He identifies the landing site at once, bounded by a triangle of distinctive craters, Kepler, Marius, and Reiner. *Voskhodyeniye* is sailing on, over the Ocean of Storms, over the Bay of Dew and the Bay of Rainbows, over the Sea of Rains and the Sea of Moisture. Now the ancient nomenclature acquires a bitter irony.

Not only is *Voskhodyeniye* crossing the surface, but she should also be rising away from it. The decelerating burn was designed to place the spacecraft in an elliptical orbit spanning 280 kilometers by 100. The closest approach, the pericynthion, should lie over the landing site.

By eye he finds it impossible to judge altitude. The gray-brown beach rolls under the ship, but he has no experience of this perspective, and no instruments to guide him. No precise method of measuring the orbit can operate without the computer and out of contact with Mission Control.

Yefgenii decides he must acquire an approximation of the spacecraft's altitude and velocity. The landing site has been mapped by unmanned probes. The dimensions of its most distinctive features are entered in the flight plan, and they've been used as part of his training, in the hope that he might acquire a sense of visual perspective on the descent to the landing site. Using the sextant he attempts to measure the angles between the craters Kepler and Marius. He works as fast as he can, but the craters speed by before he can take the measurement.

Instead he decides to time an orbit over the crater Copernicus, but he knows he won't be timing a true rev, as the Moon will also rotate on its own axis. He must factor this in for accuracy.

Two hours later he is back over the landing site, and this time set up with the sextant, so that he manages to measure the angle of separation between Kepler and Marius while the spacecraft is directly overhead, and then he watches Copernicus roll under, and marks the time on his chronometer. He also starts the chronometer's second stopwatch.

Without delay he embarks on his calculation. The apparent angular separation of Kepler and Marius will permit him to calculate his altitude above the landing site as the height of an isosceles triangle above the base given by the known distance between the two craters. The duration of one rev will reveal his orbital velocity.

When *Voskhodyeniye* first enters the lunar shadow, the only light in the BO originates from Earth. The clouds and oceans reflect the Sun's light with four times the radiance of the Moon. He braces at a porthole and contorts to bring his notepad into the earthlight. Soon the spacecraft's orbit carries it over the Far Side, and the Earth sets behind the Moon.

Yefgenii slides the penlight out of a pocket of his space suit and continues. After ten minutes, the light flickers and dies. The battery has given out. The mission carried the light for emergency use only, and the engineers deemed a spare battery a luxury, given the flight's strict payload limits. Every item aboard has been weighed and its value calculated. The calculations have been balanced down to whether the mission is better served by an extra roll of film for the camera or by an additional bullet for the crew revolver in the event of a wilderness touchdown and the need to repel wild animals.

His universe is one of cold and almost total darkness. The faint glimmers of stars speckle the black sky, but the light is negligible. The interior of the cabin, even his own body, is invisible to him. The cold oppresses him. He feels it push into his throat and down into his lungs, turning his blood lukewarm. It is chilling his bones.

It seems an age but is in truth only a matter of minutes before the Sun rises over the Far Side. He presses against the porthole to claim every drop of golden syrupy light. The battered surface drifts below. Craters overlap craters, new on top of old. The back of the Moon bears the scars of the outer face of the Earth-Moon system, the shield of an eon's meteorite strikes.

When the second stopwatch indicates he's halfway round this revolution, he identifies the crater Tsiolkovsky directly below, and with the sextant measures its apparent diameter. This measurement he hopes will determine the high point of *Voskhodyeniye*'s orbit, the apocynthion.

An hour of sunlight illuminates Yefgenii's toil, and then lunar night once again engulfs the spacecraft. He must stop, and cannot help contemplating his situation. If his orbital velocity is too slow, *Voskhodyeniye* will soon crash to the surface.

When day breaks again, he continues through his calculations: *Voskhodyeniye* is traveling an acceptable orbit, moving at close to the predicted velocity. His present situation appears stable. He must stop work. He must rest and take sustenance.

He consumes his food allowance. The surviving fuel cell has produced a pittance of water. Little frost is forming on the interior of the cabin now. What water vapor remains in the cabin atmosphere comes from his own breath. He removes his gloves and squeezes out of the spacesuit. The cold stings his flesh. He hurries, he shivers. He seals off and disconnects the filling pipe of his waste collection bag and removes the bag from his suit. A globule of straw-colored fluid floats off the tip of the bag's hose. He puts the hose of the waste collection bag in his mouth and opens the seal. He sucks out the liquid that's a mixture of his urine and sweat. It amounts to only a couple of hundred milliliters. He chases the globule that escaped from the tube. It wobbles and shimmers. Spectra flash off streaks of grease. The surface is already frosting. He closes his mouth over the globule, taking it in one gulp.

After reinstating the waste collection bag, he struggles back into the suit. The material stretches but his muscles and tendons don't. He contorts into it. The sunburn on his flank tears. He screams, tears come to his eyes, and he finds a way to drink those too.

By now the spacecraft is traveling through darkness again. When it emerges, he huddles in the sunlight. The Far Side rolls below. The Moon is small and the ship is close. He gains a sense of speed in contrast to the stately promenade of Earth orbit.

The Eastern Sea slides under the lunar equator. Earth rises again. He sets himself at the porthole with the telescope trained down on the surface. By eye he tracks the appearance of the highlands of the Ocean of Storms' western coastline dominated by the crater Hevelius, 100 kilometers across. Without an atmosphere to burn them up, meteorites have struck the surface intact and gouged out great lumps of rock and dust.

He sees the land flatten. Through the eyepiece of the telescope he surveys the landing site. The lava bed ripples between Reiner and Marius to the northeast. No large craters or cliffs ruin the picture. Eastward streaks of ejecta begin to appear, diverging from their point of origin, Kepler. This closer survey supports the objective of setting down somewhere in a zone measuring about 200 kilometers by 300. No observable feature suggests the landing site is unsuitable.

Voskhodyeniye leaves the Sun behind, and the dazzling yellow disc begins to slide behind the lunar horizon. The shadow is visible ahead, crossing the Sea of Islands east of the crater Copernicus. The illuminated portion of the Near Side is continuing to dwindle. The Ocean of Storms will remain sunlit for a further three days; in six days there'll be a new Moon, when the satellite swings between the Earth and the Sun and the entire Near Side falls into darkness. At present, the Sun angle is optimal for the landing, being oblique to the Ocean of Storms so that craters and hills are thrown into relief, rather than being blasted into a flat panorama that gives an observer no sense of perspective.

Yefgenii is desperate for rest. His head aches with nausea, hunger and dehydration. His body aches from cold. His sunburn is bleeding and sore, he can feel the stinking dressing getting damper. He unfolds the mesh hammock and straps himself in. Darkness swallows *Voskhodyeniye* and, moments later, sleep its occupant.

H E SQUINTS IN THE SUNLIGHT. Ears of corn wave in the breeze. The crop is taller than him. He is running. A narrow path cuts through the cornfield, bordered by the tall stalks that catch on his elbows and spring back as he goes by. He is laughing. Though someone's chasing him, he isn't frightened, because she is laughing too. He feels her gentle hands hook him under the arms and swing him up into the air, so high he is whirling above the ears of corn. Together they are laughing and spinning. He gazes into her face but the sunlight bursts round the curls of her hair, burning out his vision of her. He squints into the glare, searching for her face, the woman laughing and swinging him, and he is laughing too, and so little, but he can't see her because he is dazzled by the Sun.

Voskhodyeniye is blazing with light. He wakes, blinking at the glare bouncing off the metal plates of the BO. He unstraps himself and floats off the mesh hammock. The Ocean of Storms drifts below. He glimpses the triangle of craters, Marius, Reiner, and Kepler, and they appear different to him. He wonders if the orbit has slipped somehow. He glances at his chronometer. He's slept for six hours, making three revs of the Moon since he last surveyed the landing site.

He feels sick and starved. Part of him craves a return to the hammock and straps, so he can huddle in his suit for days as if taking to his bed to break a fever.

The sextant is angled as it was for his previous determination of the orbit's pericynthion. The distinguishing features of the landing site are passing below. He has time enough only for a single measurement, so he chooses the angular separation between Reiner and Kepler: this being the largest angle, it will provide the most accurate comparison. He looks back over his handwritten notes and sees his suspicion confirmed. The angular separation has increased. The orbit is decaying. *Voskhodyeniye* is losing altitude and at some point yet to be determined will plummet down to the surface of the Moon.

He's failed to achieve the orbit demanded by the flight plan. The error is grievous. Most likely his navigation has been imprecise, and he's misjudged the course corrections and the lunar orbit insertion burn. He rues his arrogance, for persisting with the original mission when the more achievable option was always to keep on the free-return trajectory to Earth.

Now he straps himself into the pilot's seat. He intends to fire the Block D engine for an arbitrary period of ten seconds in order to accelerate into a less unstable orbit. That at least will buy sufficient time to plan and execute trans-Earth injection with requisite precision, trans-Earth injection being the burn that will hurl him home.

First he needs to swing the spacecraft round. The engine stands at the leading edge of the stack, in combination with the LK.

The thrusters fail. He is getting no power indications from any of the LOK's systems. He checks the circuit breakers and fuel cells. The LOK is dead. Out of sheer desperation he attempts to fire the thrusters once more, but the propellant doesn't ignite. The electronic connections between the LOK's command power grid and the ship's thrusters have drained.

Maybe from the LK he can still fire the Block D, but he must also turn the ship round, or else the sole effect of ignition will be to decelerate *Voskhodyeniye* and crash it into the Moon. He attempts to power up the LK from the LOK. He throws the switches to open the circuits to the LK but no power lights blink on. Both modules appear lifeless, but the LK may still be in its dormant state; its batteries may yet drive its guidance systems and spark its engines, and its engines are capable of powering the entire stack out of lunar orbit and onto the trajectory home.

His only hope lies with the lander.

The Sun sets. He must wait an hour in pitch blackness, with the orbit decaying by the minute. In darkness he feels his way to the storage locker below the environmental control system. His gloved hands pat the smooth dome of the bubble helmet and the bulky padding of the Krechet-94 Moonsuit. He strips off the Orlan and lets it drift away while he pulls on the Krechet. The freezing atmosphere of the cabin deadens his flesh. He slides into the suit and connects the panels. Any stretching of his frozen skin is excruciating. He fumbles the bubble helmet over his head and onto the metal collar, and locks it in place.

He floats in the darkness, sealed inside his suit, feeling warmth creep back into his body. Blood returns to the muscles and tendons. He twists and stretches, doing what little he can to loosen up. In his enclosed universe he breathes pure oxygen, but he smells his own dank odor, and the blood and goo of his sunburn.

Sunlight explodes across the horizon. The Far Side ignites into gray and brown speckles. The land rolls beneath the ship. For the first time the Sea of Moscow is lit, a dark eye in the upper left quadrant. He wants to take it as an omen. Moscow is watching him.

He dons his Moon helmet. He mounts his backpack and plugs in its cable and hoses, then attaches his tethering line. He belays the line onto a secure handhold and ties it off, leaving only a short loop.

Without power to depressurize the LOK, he must blow the hatch by hand. He turns the first safety lever, then the second. The metal creaks. He hears the locks clicking loose. He grips the handhold to the side of the hatch and releases the final lock. The cabin atmosphere blasts out into space in a single gale that boosts him up into the hatchway. The tether snaps tight but the belay holds firm. The line and his grip strain for a second, perhaps not even that long, and the wind drops. The air has gone. No force propels him outward. All is calm again.

His suit is swollen and rigid; he feels it raking against his sunburn, rupturing blisters that ooze sticky fluid, while outside the spacecraft the expelled air has sublimated in an instant and now a shower of glinting ice crystals shifts in a cloud toward the surface of the Moon.

Silence surrounds him. He sees that the surface has changed motion. It is not only sliding lengthways along the stack, but also rolling toward him. The Eastern Sea is the only feature he can recognize among the crammed overlapping rings of craters, but the Sea is rolling, it is advancing up over the equator toward the lunar north pole.

Then the land drops away from the spacecraft. Empty space begins to roll in, a black void of invisible stars. Venting the BO's atmosphere has set *Voskhodyeniye* into a slow roll; no doubt it has slightly modified its orbit as well.

Yefgenii wiggles his backpack through the gap and squeezes out of the hatch into space. The tether trails behind. He maneuvers onto the handrail and now he is hanging over the northern hemisphere of the Near Side. The Sea of Cold turns under him. He is the first man to conduct an EVA in the realm of the Moon.

He reaches the boom but the motor has no power. He maneuvers by hand along the rails of the LOK fuselage toward the LK. His breath rushes. His heart drums. He must enter the LK before night falls, or else he'll be stranded in darkness on the outside of the revolving stack.

Yefgenii has learned the most efficient method from his previous spacewalk, and secures a first position at the LK's docking array, from which he then floats in parallel to the hull.

The LK hangs silent, cold and airless. Yefgenii secures himself on the handhold outside the hatch and begins to turn the sequence of latches to open the port. The inside of his suit is warmer than the chill air of the LOK, but his limbs remain cold, weak and stiff. No sound travels from the latches; outside the noisy living system of his suit stretches a silent endless vacuum.

When the final lock releases, the hatch remains motionless. He pulls to open it. The heavy door takes an effort to move; it retains all the mass it possessed on Earth. He swings the hatch outward and then attempts to struggle through the elliptical gap into the LK. The Kretchet Moonsuit is even bulkier than the Orlan. He twists onto his side to squeeze through the port. His backpack catches on the frame. Pain sears his sunburn. He snakes and pulls. Suffering bolts through his lower back. For the first time in days of debilitating cold, he sweats.

Inside the LK, he rests. His boots still point out of the hatch. The Sea of Rain floats up into the framed segment of sky, then the Carpathians lift off the soles of his boots, then Copernicus. He is approaching the terminator.

Yefgenii pushes himself away from the hatch. His tether trails out into space, running back to the LOK, holding him back. He maneuvers to the control panel and activates the master switch. The LK draws power from its batteries. The cabin lights blink on. Gauge needles quiver, digital displays glow. He disconnects the tether, shuts the hatch and pressurizes the LK.

His suit softens and he removes his outer helmet, bubble helmet and space gloves. Taking a position at the pilot's station, his priority is to arrest the rolling of the stack caused by blowing the LOK hatch. Flying *Voskhodyeniye* from the LK has never been simulated. The lander's computer is coming online but it isn't configured to the dynamics of the entire stack. He must work by trial and error.

Yefgenii fires the thrusters to oppose the roll. The roll slows but the stack yaws, swinging the LK—the bow of the stack—toward the

Moon, and the stern—the LOK and power module—out into space. In the viewports of the lander the lunar surface sweeps into sight, and then the terminator, and then the spacecraft and the lone cosmonaut are in darkness, tumbling in roll and yaw, divergent on two axes, in a failing orbit less than 100 kilometers above the pitiless surface of the Moon.

FIVE DAYS since Mission Control lost contact with *Voskhodyeniye*, the widow will have accepted his death. She'll be grieving. She'll have sat the children in the living room of the apartment and said she has something very sad to tell them. She explains that their father has gone to a secret place and they will never see him again. The boy stares back at her with big blue eyes. "Where has he gone?"

"I don't know," she says.

"Is he dead?" asks the girl.

The widow nods. "Yes," she says. "He is dead," she says.

Already they are controlling their feelings. The boy is turning tough; he will become a man like his father who erects barriers to emotion. The girl is earnest; she will become more so, more austere. Yefgenii longs to burst into the apartment in their moment of grief and gather them all into his arms and give them the news that he's alive and that he loves them and, in holding them and murmuring to them, reverse the emotional damage wrought by his obsessive pursuit of the perfect mission.

In the flight plan, he would make the landing and then return to orbit for rendezvous with the LOK. But he is losing his battle with the LK's controls. He cannot correct *Voskhodyeniye's* trajectory, so the

LOK will not maintain orbit. It will crash down onto the surface of the Moon. It will not be here when the lander returns from the surface, and the lander itself cannot carry him home. It is too fragile to enter the atmosphere. The flight plan is no longer achievable. It has driven him through the past few days, the plan, always the plan. This thing has been the shape of his life, or his death, and even that has gone. Now it must either be the landing or the return home; it cannot be both.

Major Yefgenii Yeremin undocks the lander. He activates the controls of the Kontakt docking system to effect release of the LOK's male probe from the LK's female grid. He feels a bump as the probe rears away from the grid. Through the upper viewport he gazes at the LOK as it begins a slow drifting recession. The dark vessel turns as it falls behind. The two ships progress into night. Then the LOK— lifeless, powerless, lightless—vanishes.

Deploying its thrusters, he stabilizes the LK. The lander responds; it is nimble, flying under its own control at last, but in the same doomed orbit as the LOK. The computer fails to align the spatial navigation platform. He must assume the system has developed a fault, or has been faulty all along. He shuts it down and carries out a reboot. The computer fails to orient itself once again. He activates the Planeta landing radar. At present the craft's altitude is too great for the system to acquire the surface. That will occur only toward the end of the descent.

The Sun rises. He catches a glint of metal far behind and far below. It's the LOK, now sunk into an even more precarious orbit. The Sea of Moscow stares up at him. He is sailing over the Far Side in the most tiny and fragile craft imaginable. Its fuselage is paper thin. In all it weighs only 5 tonnes.

On impulse he claims an act for himself: he waggles the lander's control sticks. The nimble craft rocks in pure Newtonian motion unmodified by lift or drag, proclaiming there's a man flying this ship, a pilot at the pinnacle of his profession. Yefgenii smiles to himself and presses on.

Next comes the earthrise. He gazes at the blue and white disc gliding from behind the curve of the lunar horizon. No man has come so far away without returning. He crosses onto the Near Side, the Earth Side. The top of the lander points back, the base is leading. He ignites the LK's Block D engine. The craft decelerates and begins the descent toward the surface. He pitches the craft more upright and now he's falling feet first and face down with his back to the direction of the orbit. The lunar terrain scrolls upward through the lower viewport. Through the upper window the Sun plunges toward the edge of the Moon; the Earth glows in the fading light of lunar dusk. The celestial bodies are falling, he is falling.

Without the computer, he cannot judge his altitude. He must keep the radar active. The descent will be gradual over the course of a revolution; he doesn't expect to receive an altitude signal till he's closing in on the Ocean of Storms.

He endures the long lonely night, the cosmonaut in the tiny fragile craft. He stands perched in the straps and braces, a fist round each control stick, his gaze trained on the indifferent quadrangles of black space and black land framed by the upper and lower viewports. The roar of the engine reverberates through the LK's narrow struts and thin metal sheets.

Gray bodies rupture the blackness framed by the lower viewport. They appear like whales rising from the ocean. At first he is uncertain if the forms lie outside the lander or represent reflections created within, and then the shapes gather detail, the clusters of craters, the lines of ridges. They are unrecognizable. The light is too weak and the lander's position beyond determination.

He rolls the craft round and pitches it over so he's plunging facedown and leaning forward into the realm ahead, where a brilliant bomb is detonating at the edge of the Moon. The craters and highlands begin appearing under him in relief in a narrow curving splinter of gray, and then they ripple and burn up in the expanding ball of sunlight, blasting through the tinted glass of the viewports. For a moment the terrible fire burns him up too; he disappears in the flood of rupturing light that blasts into the cabin, and then he is there again, haloed by the brilliance of his final dawn.

Yefgenii drops his gaze to the lower viewport. The collimating lens at its center blots out the scattering rays of sunlight. Looking down past his waist he scans the terrain behind, the craters, the overlapping overwritten rings that mottle the Far Side. The Sea of Moscow slides behind, the eye is averting.

As he crosses the Far Side, the Sun arcs through the sky in an accelerated celestial cycle. Lunar dawn becomes lunar morning in a matter of minutes. The Sun blasts the land in light, destroying the visual relief of rilles and depressions, of craters' rims and their basins, until it has arced over the LK in lunar noon and crept behind. By the time he nears the landing site in the Ocean of Storms, the Sun will hang approximately 10 degrees above the western horizon, the optimum lighting conditions for judging an approach and landing.

Only minutes pass before he hears the first pings of the Planeta. The landing radar has acquired the surface. The digital readout blinks four dashes over and over again until the system's computer interprets the returning signal. The numbers appear. The LK is operating at just over 3,000 meters above the surface, still skittering over the craters of the Far Side. He is far lower than expected, and it terrifies him. He has misjudged the final orbit, has fallen farther still in the lunar night, and now he faces the certainty that he will under-shoot the landing site. In simulations he studied every crater and hummock on the approach to the planned touchdown, but here the surface panorama is beyond recognition. In the lower viewport the craters sweep beneath him, heaped one on top of another, gray and indistinct.

The Planeta rates his speed as over a 100 meters per second. He is too low and too fast. The Ocean of Storms remains on the other side of the world. The landing site lies thousands of kilometers ahead. The Far Side seems a far more desolate and forbidding place because of it.

For the first time he glimpses the LK's shadow. Like some bizarre deformed insect, the angular black shape skitters across the rims and hollows of craters. He is down among the surface features that to this point have been remote and barely imagined. The hills undulate. The peaks and ridges are smooth, not jagged. Shadows gather in crater basins, like the openings of wells.

Next the roar of the engine cuts out. The Block D engine is spent. He jettisons the Block D and ignites the Block E. The LK flies onward, now only a couple of kilometers above the surface. Far ahead appears the foreshortened form of a broad lava plain. It can only be the Eastern Sea. It seems to reside at the very limit of his range, yet even this plain lies many kilometers short of the Near Side.

Out of the corner of his eye he glimpses something, another vehicle, and reacts with shock, then realizes it's the Block D stage, a blackened husk, tumbling toward the surface. It is flying through the vacuum in a long arc and will take nearly a minute to crash.

Moment by moment the LK sheds speed and height. Yefgenii stands perched at the pilot's control, fixed in a meshwork of straps and braces. He rolls to starboard, pointing toward the Eastern Sea, hoping to stretch the descent just far enough to reach its more hospitable terrain.

The Block D stage strikes the surface, throwing up a plume of dust that falls in centrifugal lines of ejecta. A new crater has formed. He gives it the widow's name.

Firing at full thrust, the Block E opposes the LK's descent, but the craft continues its long parabola toward the ground. The Planeta readout counts down: 1,500 meters, 1,400, 1,300 . . . He must slow the descent. He pitches the lander back, standing on its engine.

The lava plain broadens and becomes more foreshortened. It holds its position in the upper viewport. He knows he can make it. The Block E arrests the lander's vertical velocity. The altimeter read-out maintains 500 meters.

Yefgenii slows the craft's forward velocity with thrusters. The forces balance. He throttles back the Block E to 850 kg thrust, balancing the lander's weight in lunar gravity. The LK hangs in a hover some 500 meters above the surface, on the perimeter of the Eastern Sea. A crest of hills arcs to either side of him. Ahead, boulders cover the plain. His fuel gauge estimates he has a minute's worth remaining.

Now he must pitch the LK forward again, and it begins to advance over the terrain ahead. The low rush of the engine whispers through the craft. He glimpses boulders ahead separating into an open field of dark gray basalt scarred by numerous craters. With his right hand he holds one control stick in its forward pitch. The ground scrolls through the lower viewport, that now points almost straight down. He is hanging off the straps and braces, his weight tipped forward, the ground sweeping under him.

A fuel alarm sounds. If the computer was operational, it would call an abort, but he presses on. The fuel restriction stipulated by the flight plan is reserved for the ascent from the surface and orbital rendezvous with the LOK. There can be no rendezvous.

The LK slips into its final descent, the altimeter counting down to 300 meters, 200, 100 . . . A stray thought visits him for an instant, the realization that because he cannot reach the Near Side he'll never see the earthrise, he'll never see the blue Earth again.

The shadow of the LK tracks toward him, slithering over the boulders and into the open ground of his target area. He sees shadows of the spindly legs of the LPU landing gear shortening as he pitches the LK back to the vertical, and then growing like vines over the ground below as he descends.

The engine fires up dust. A cloud swells and swirls around the LPU, blotting out his view of the surface. He flicks his gaze to his instruments, those that are operational, watching that the craft is level and sinking with graceful steadiness toward the surface. A wire sensor dangles below the footpads of the LPU. It brushes the surface and a blue contact light blinks on his control panel, and he shuts down the engine at once.

He falls. The craft drops 3 meters under one-sixth gravity and strikes the surface with a bang that shudders every strut and panel. He hears the vehicle creak as it starts to angle over. For a moment he fears that a footpad hangs over a crater, or that the ground is subsiding, so that the lander will topple over, but then the motion ceases and the craft settles, listing only a few degrees to starboard.

Silence surrounds the LK. The dust settles back to the surface in sheets. No wind tosses it back and forth or carries it into the distance. No rains will wash it away. The footpads of the lander will never rust. The cosmonaut's body will never decompose.

The craft carries an immediate postlanding checklist that, according to the flight plan, must be hurried through in under a minute to determine whether the cosmonaut is safe to stay or must ignite the ascent engine at once. Yefgenii disregards the checklist. There is no option but to stay. The LOK's orbit is decaying so fast it can only be a matter of hours before it crashes into the lunar surface. There is nowhere else in the universe left for him to go.

H E SLEEPS. The stillness cradles him. He cannot even be certain that he remembers his mother's touch. He searches for moments in which her arms cradled him, or her fingers caressed his cheek, but he can't find them. He recalls a night terror, then her soft voice calming him; he begged her not to leave him alone in the dark, so she slept nearby. He sees her there in the gloom, her outline changing shape as she turns, perhaps asleep or just pretending for his benefit. He remembers that her presence gave him the strength to face the darkness, to face terror and loneliness, but his eyes cannot penetrate the gloom, he cannot see her, only her outline changing shape as she turns.

When he wakes, he is tired. He remains as tired as he was when he fell asleep. The fans hum. He lifts his head from the narrow mesh hammock and sees that some of the instrument lights have gone out. The batteries are draining down. The lander is running out of power.

He peers at the blinds covering the viewports. When he moves to them, he senses the strange effect of low gravity, like walking in a dream. He lifts the blinds. It is not a dream.

The eerie terrain of the Eastern Sea stretches to the horizon. In the distance, long escarpments slope up from the plain into blunt hills that curve in gray bands one behind the other. Above them the sky is dense, black and empty. He is in a land of extreme contrast but no color. The surface gleams, the sky is matte black, and the Sun blazes with no mediating atmosphere to diffuse, refract or blur its radiance.

He's slept in his suit and boots. He replaces his bubble helmet and then mounts the outer shell on the metal collar, a Moon helmet bearing three eyeshades and two protective visors to deflect the Sun's unfiltered ultraviolet and infrared radiation. He lifts on the backpack and connects its oxygen and water hoses and plugs in its electricity cables, then dons his gloves and locks.

His movements are slow and final. Stowed in the LK is an eleven-page checklist of items to be accounted for prior to a lunar EVA. He pays it no attention. He takes with him only two items: the flag and the camera.

In depressurizing the cabin, he feels the Krechet Moonsuit swell and stiffen. His weak tired limbs lock into rigid poles. Where the suit presses into his flank, he feels the enduring pain of the sunburn.

He releases the locks one by one and then turns the levers. The hatch moves under a light touch. It swings open and in the oval doorframe appears the flat gray blanket of lunar regolith. He steps forward. He senses his body lift and fall in altered motion. He is light, his downstep is slow, the gravity is one-sixth of Earth's.

The lander casts a long shadow in lunar postmeridian. The surface is unspoiled. The pattern of dust scattered by his landing remains unaltered. Not a single particle has been jogged by wind, not a streak blanked by rain. Here nature does not obliterate the old to prepare a fresh canvas for the new. Any wake left on the lunar seas will never flatten, because no water exists here.

When he remembers Earth, it is its water—the blue and white of oceans, clouds and ice caps—that colors his memory. Water supports life, but rain and snow ablate the signatures of living things. This waterless place will preserve the signature of his landing longer than man will exist, long after nations have toppled and the empires of the Soviet Union and the United States have become as extinct as those of Rome and Greece and their artifacts are buried deep as the Minoans'.

Yefgenii takes the next step, and this one brings him to the top of the ladder. There is the flag to plant, a commemorative photograph to be taken. Afterwards, he can find much to explore in the time that remains. In the lander he can survive for days before the oxygen supply runs out. By days he means Earth days. Daylight in this place won't vanish until the Sun drops below the horizon and the terminator crosses the Eastern Sea; at that phase of the lunar cycle, the Moon will be a waxing crescent as viewed from Earth, and the crew of *Apollo 11* will have begun their voyage to the Sea of Tranquillity. By then he will have perished here on the invisible obverse side of the Moon, alone and unknown for eternity, in a paper-thin metal box the size of a couple of telephone booths.

As an alternative, he considers setting out on foot for the Near Side, but the backpack contains only enough oxygen for 1.5 hours. He won't even cross the Eastern Sea. He'll never see Earth again, though this strikes him in these circumstances as not a good enough reason not to try, if only to be granted one more look at the blue-and-white face of home.

Perhaps over the next hill stands a bar, and the others will be waiting for him there, Gnido, Kiriya and Skomorokhov, Bondarenko and Komarov, Grissom and Gagarin. They will toast one another. Grissom, had he lived, would have been the first American to attempt a landing—so they'll drink together, and talk of what might have been. Or perhaps it will be a quiet place, a farm bathed in golden sunlight, and his mother will chase him as he runs through the cornfield, and this time, as she lifts him into the air, laughing, he'll be granted a vision of her face.

Taking a grip on the handhold, he makes a half turn. Now his back faces the exterior. Yefgenii Yeremin peers down into the ground shimmering between his knees, at the foot of the ladder. He dangles his boot down and feels for the next rung. One more lies below it, then the surface itself.

The print he leaves will remain, it is predicted, for four million years, till a spattering of meteorites obliterates the last stroke of man's signature in the universe. It won't be written in the sky but scratched in the dust of a cold dead satellite.

He pauses. He occupies the zenith of his life, the life of the man known, and unknown, as Ivan the Terrible. When he takes the step, nothing will survive to drive him on. The great moment will have come and gone, and all that will remain will be a thing to be endured. Without goal or purpose, even the one and a half hours will be too much and therefore will be as tragic as the senescent decades of an ordinary life. The footprint he makes will mark the limit of his ascent, as it will of his nation, and of his civilization.

Yefgenii gazes into the cabin. He scans the lights and gauges of the failing instrumentation; they are going out one by one, as if the stars, Sun, Moon and Earth are dimming one by one, as the planet of Shakespeare, da Vinci, Newton and Einstein will one day fade out; and then he blinks, they are all gone, the lights, and he is descending.

ACKNOWLEDGMENTS

Dr. Buzz Aldrin, USAF (retd.)
Mr. Neil A. Armstrong
Dr. Matthew N. Dugas
Dr. James R. Hansen
Flt. Lt. Jad Reece, CFS RAF
Capt. Walter M. Schirra, USN (retd.)

BIBLIOGRAPHY

Cernan, Eugene. *The Last Man on the Moon: Astronaut Eugene Cernan and America's Race in Space.* New York: St. Martin's Press, 1999.

Chaikin, Andrew. *A Man on the Moon: The Voyages of the Apollo Astronauts.* New York: Viking, 1994.

Collins, Michael. *Carrying the Fire: An Astronaut's Journeys.* new ed. New York: Cooper Square Press, 2001.

Davis, Larry. *F-86 Sabre in Action.* Carrollton, TX: Squadron/Signal, 1992.

Dorr, Robert F; Jon Lake; and Warren Thompson. *Korean War Aces.* Botley, England: Osprey, 1995.

Encyclopedia Astronautica at www.astronautix.com.

Hansen, James R. *First Man: The Life of Neil A. Armstrong.* New York: Simon & Schuster, 2005.

Jackson, Robert. *The Red Falcons: The Soviet Air Force in Action, 1919–1969.* Brighton, England: Clifton Books, 1970.

Light, Michael. *Full Moon.* New York: Alfred A. Knopf, 1999; London: Jonathan Cape, 2001.

Lovell, Jim, and Jeffrey Kluger. *Apollo 13.* reissue of *Lost Moon.* New York: Pocket Books, 1995.

Polak, Tomas, with Christopher Shores. *Stalin's Falcons: The Aces of the Red Star.* London: Grub Street, 1998.

Schefter, James. *The Race: The Definitive Story of America's Battle to Beat Russia to the Moon.* London: Arrow, 2000.

Scott, David, and Alexei Leonov. *Two Sides of the Moon: Our Story of the Cold War Space Race.* New York: Simon & Schuster, 2004.

Slayton, Donald K., with Michael Cassutt. *Deke!: U.S. Manned Space, From Mercury to the Shuttle.* New York: Forge, 1994.

Stapfer, Hans-Heiri. *MiG-15 in Action.* Carrollton, TX: Squadron/Signal, 1991.

Umbreit, Andreas. *Spitsbergen, Svalbard, Franz Josef Land, Jan Mayen.* 3rd ed. Chalfont St. Peter, England: Bradt Travel Guides, 2005.

Zhang, Xiaoming. *Red Wings over the Yalu: China, the Soviet Union, and the Air War in Korea.* College Station: Texas A&M University Press, 2002.

AFTERWORD

Although a work of fiction, *Ascent* is partly inspired by actual events, and I have endeavored to be accurate in their descriptions; however, on occasions I have chosen to depart from verifiable historical fact. Some such departures, but not all, are mentioned below.

The 221st IAP *(Istrebitel'nyi Aviatsonnyi Polk)* is a fictional squadron. Following Glasnost, the presence of VVS *(Voenno-Vozdushnye Sily Krasnoi Armii)* units in Korea has been officially confirmed. According to Soviet reports, the two leading aces of the conflict were Yefgenii Pepelyaev (twenty-three kills) and Nikolai Sutyagin (twenty-one kills). However, these figures are disputed. See Dorr and Zhang for details.

Yefgenii Yeremin's Korean War encounters with Neil Armstrong, John Glenn, Gus Grissom and Wally Schirra are fictionalized. Neil Armstrong flew seventy-eight missions in U.S. Navy VF-51. John Glenn flew sixty-three missions with Marine Fighter Squadron 311 and twenty-seven missions as an exchange pilot with the U.S. Air Force. Wally Schirra served with the USAF National Guard, the 154th Fighter Bomber Squadron of the 136th Fighter Bomber Wing. Gus Grissom flew one hundred missions with the 334th Fighter-Interceptor Squadron. Buzz Aldrin flew sixty-six combat missions with the 16th Fighter-Interceptor Squadron.

At the time of the contact with the USS *Essex,* Ensign Armstrong was no longer serving in Korea. See Hansen for details.

The claim that Mikhail Averin shot down George A. Davis is controversial. For more details, see Zhang.

239

The Soviet Air Force operated a base at Nagurskoye. Various other airfields existed on Franz Josef Land during the Cold War. See Umbreit for details.

Soviet Air Defenses shot down a CIA-operated U-2 Spy Plane over Sverdlovsk on May Day 1960, capturing its pilot, Gary Powers. Accounts of the incident are highly contradictory.

The idea that the United States spent millions of dollars developing a space pen while the Soviets used pencils encapsulates the contrast between the two programs; however, the story is considered apocryphal. For more details, visit www.truthorfiction.com.

The engine fault in the N-1 rocket was not detected till later. Hence the N-1 exploded on its launchpad at Baikonur on July 3, 1969, during an unmanned test, ending the Soviet Union's chances of launching a manned lunar mission before the end of the decade.

The stars Menkent and Nunki were used as datum stars by *Apollo 11* in Earth orbit. See Collins for details.

The accident that befalls *Voskhodyeniye* has many similarities to the *Apollo 13* "problem." See Lovell and Chaikin for details.

Yefgenii Yeremin's cislunar EVA is inspired by the *Gemini 9* EVA. See Cernan for details.

Had he not perished in the *Apollo 1* fire, Gus Grissom would have been the first man to walk on the Moon (other events permitting). See Slayton for details.

The secrecy surrounding the Soviet system probably encouraged the myths about undisclosed spaceflights. Since Glasnost, the journals of high-ranking space officials have been revealed, and none of those myths have been supported. For a definitive article on "phantom astronauts," visit *Encyclopedia Astronautica* at www.astronautix.com.

Ascent is a work of fiction, dedicated to the people who did these things for real.

ABOUT THE AUTHOR

Jed Mercurio trained as a doctor and joined the Royal Air Force while at medical school. He received extensive flight training before resigning his commission to practice medicine. While a resident in internal medicine, he wrote a groundbreaking medical drama, *Cardiac Arrest,* for the BBC. His first novel, *Bodies,* published in 2002, was chosen by the *Guardian* as one of the top five debuts of the year. He adapted that novel into an award-winning drama series for the BBC, and he is currently developing an American version for U.S. television. He lives outside London.